Prairie Gold

Contributors:
Arthur Davison Ficke
Hamlin Garland
Emerson Hough

Alpha Editions

This edition published in 2024

ISBN 9789361474057

Design and Setting By

Alpha Editions

www.alphaedis.com

Email - info@alphaedis.com

As per information held with us this book is in Public Domain.
This book is a reproduction of an important historical work.
Alpha Editions uses the best technology to reproduce historical work in
the same manner it was first published to preserve its original nature.
Any marks or number seen are left intentionally to preserve.

Contents

Preface	- 1 -
The Wind in the Corn	- 3 -
The Graven Image	- 4 -
Masterpieces	- 13 -
Bread	- 14 -
That Iowa Town	- 18 -
But Once a Year	- 21 -
The Reminder	- 27 -
"Old Bill"	- 30 -
The Recruit's Story	- 35 -
The Happiest Man in I-O-Way	- 38 -
The Captured Dream	- 40 -
Truth	- 47 -
Work	- 49 -
Some Magic and a Moral	- 50 -
Sonny's Wish	- 57 -
Dog	- 59 -
Tinkling Cymbals	- 65 -
The First Laugh	- 68 -
The Freighter's Dream	- 69 -
A Box From Home	- 72 -
The Spirit of Spring	- 74 -
Work Is a Blessing	- 86 -
September	- 89 -
The Poet of the Future	- 91 -

Putting the Stars with the Bars	- 94 -
The Kings of Saranazett	- 96 -
The Old Cane Mill	- 107 -
The Queer Little Thing	- 110 -
An American Wake	- 120 -
Rochester, Minn.	- 122 -
God's Back Yard	- 123 -
The Wild Crab Apple	- 129 -
A Ballad of the Corn	- 131 -
The Children's Blessing	- 133 -
Kitchener's Mob	- 136 -
The Professor	- 140 -
My Baby's Horse	- 146 -
The Call of the Race	- 147 -
One Wreath of Rue	- 157 -
Woodrow Wilson and Wells, War's Great Authors	- 159 -
A Field	- 162 -
Your Lad, and My Lad	- 165 -
Peace and Then—?	- 166 -
Semper Fidelis	- 170 -
Our Bird Friends	- 171 -
A Load of Hay	- 177 -
Iowa as a Literary Field	- 178 -

Preface

This volume, from the land of the singing corn, is offered to the public by the Iowa Press and Authors' Club as the first bit of co-operative work done by Iowa writers. The anticipated needs of the brave men who have given themselves as a human sacrifice to the establishment of a world-wide democracy, make a strong heart appeal, and the members have come together in spirit to do their bit toward the relief of suffering.

Many members of the club could not be reached during the short time the book was in the making; others doing work every day on schedule time had no opportunity to prepare manuscript for this publication, while still others preferred helping in ways other than with their pens.

The whole is a work of love and representative of the comradeship, the spirit of human sympathy, and the pride of state, existent in the hearts of Iowa authors, artists, playwrights, poets, editors and journalists.

Officers of the club for 1917-18:

- Hamlin Garland, Honorary President.
- Alice C. Weitz, President.
- J. Edward Kirbye, First Vice President.
- Nellie Gregg Tomlinson, Second Vice President.
- Esse V. Hathaway, Secretary.
- Reuben F. Place, Treasurer.
- *Editorial Board:*
- Johnson Brigham.
- Lewis Worthington Smith.
- Helen Cowles LeCron.

The Creed of Iowa

I BELIEVE in Iowa, land of limitless prairies, with rolling hills and fertile valleys, with winding and widening streams, with bounteous crops and fruit-laden trees, yielding to man their wealth and health.

I believe in Iowa, land of golden grains, whose harvests fill the granaries of the nation, making it opulent with the power of earth's fruitfulness.

I believe in Iowa, rich in her men and women of power and might. I believe in her authors and educators, her statesmen and ministers, whose intellectual and moral contribution is one of the mainstays of the republic—true in the hour of danger and steadfast in the hour of triumph.

I believe in Iowa, magnet and meeting place of all nations, fused into a noble unity, Americans all, blended into a free people. I believe in her stalwart sons, her winsome women, in her colleges and churches, in her institutions of philanthropy and mercy, in her press, the voice and instructor of her common mind and will, in her leadership and destiny, in the magnificence of her opportunity and in the fine responsiveness of her citizens to the call of every higher obligation.

I believe in our commonwealth, yet young, and in the process of making, palpitant with energy and faring forth with high hope and swift step; and I covenant with the God of my fathers to give myself in service, mind and money, hand and heart, to explore and develop her physical, intellectual and moral resources, to sing her praises truthfully, to keep her politics pure, her ideals high, and to make better and better her schools and churches, her lands and homes, and to make her in fact what she is by divine right, the queen of all the commonwealths.

—*J. Edward Kirbye.*

The Wind in the Corn

By Alice C. Weitz

THERE stands recorded in the Book of Time a fascinating legend of the Sun, whose golden throne allured but for the day; and when the day was ended in great glee he hurried forth beyond the broad horizon toward a secret trysting place. All his impassioned love, it is said, he poured upon the idol of his heart, the boundless plains. Long years were they alone, the Rolling Prairie and the Golden Sun, until at last they found themselves spied upon by curious Man, who, captivated by the beauty of the two, remained and blessed the tryst thereby.

Here Sun and Soil and Man wrought out a work of art; and here Dame Nature smiled as was her wont, and brought rich gifts and blessings manifold. In sweet content Man's children toiled and wrought until upon the bosom of the sunlit plains there nestled close great fields and prosperous abodes.

And since that time a ceaseless music steals throughout the land in wooing cadences, now crying out in weird and wandering tones, now softly soothing in sweet rhythmic chant.

'Tis the music of the wind within the corn—Iowa's Prairie Gold.

It sang itself into the lonely heart of the pioneer with its promise of golden harvest; it became the cradle song of restless souls that even in their youth longed but to free themselves in verse and song; and down through all the prosperous years it steals like a sweet sustaining accompaniment to the countless activities which have built a great commonwealth.

He who has stood upon the hilltops in his youthful days and listened to the soft, alluring rustle of the wind-swayed leaves retains the music ever in his soul. It draws upon the heart-strings of the absent one, and like the constant singing of the sea insistent calls upon him to return.

Today in spirit come we all to Time's sweet trysting place with story song and jest, to add sweet comfort to the braver ones whose paths lie wide before them, and whose return lies not within our willing. God grant that even in their pains their troubled souls may yet to music be attuned, may know again the solace of that sweetly floating song, the rustle of the wind within the corn.

The Graven Image

By Hamlin Garland

Roger Barnes, son of an elder in the little Iowa Society of Friends and himself "a man of weight," found his faith sorely tried by the death of his young wife, and as the weeks passed without a perceptible lightening of his face, the Meeting came at last to consider his deep grief unseemly and rebellious. He remained deaf to all words of comfort and occupied his Sabbath seat in moody silence, his heart closed to the Spirit, his thought bitter toward life and forgetful of God's grace.

The admonition of the elders at last roused him to defense. "Why should I not ache?" he demanded. "I have been smitten of the rod." And when old Nicholas Asche again reproved him before the assembly, he arose, went out, refusing to return, and several of his friends were greatly troubled, for it was known that for a long time he had been increasingly impatient of the "Discipline" and on terms of undue intimacy with Orrin Bailey, one of "the world's people."

As the spring came on his passionate grief calmed, but a new consideration came, one which troubled him more and more, until at last he opened his heart to his friend.

"Thee knew my wife, friend Bailey. Thee knew her loveliness? Well, now she is gone, and does thee know I am utterly disconsolate, for I have no portrait of her. No image, no shadow of her, exists and I fear I shall lose the memory of her sweet face. Already it is growing dim in my mind. What can I do?"

This was in the days when even daguerreotypes were rare, and Bailey, who had never seen a painted portrait and could not conceive of an artist skillful enough to depict an object he had never known, was not able to advise, and the grieving man's fear remained unassuaged till, some months later, on a trip to Decorah, he came by accident past the gate of a newly established stone-cutter's yard, and there, for the first time in his life, he saw human figures cut enduringly in marble. Cunning cherubs and angels with calm faces and graceful, half-furled wings surrounded granite soldiers standing stiff and straight.

Roger was amazed. The sculptor's magic was an astonishment to him. He had never seen the like, and as he looked upon these figures there came into his sad eyes the light of a startling purpose.

"I will have this workman cut for me an image of my dear Rachel," he resolved and, following this impulse, approached the stone-cutter. "Friend," he said abruptly, "I would have thee chisel for me the form of my dead wife."

Although an aspiring and self-confident artist, Conrad Heffnew was, nevertheless, a little shaken as he drew from his visitor the conditions of this commission. "The lack of even a small drawing or portrait of the subject is discouraging," he said. "If she had a sister, now," he added slowly, "someone about her build, to wear her clothes, I might be able to do the figure."

"She has a sister, Ruth," Roger eagerly answered. "She is slimmer than Rachel was, but her cast of features is much the same. I am sure she will help thee, for she loved Rachel. I will bring her down to see thee."

"Very well," replied Conrad. "If she will sit for me I will see what I can do for you."

Resting upon this arrangement Roger drove away to his prairie home lighter of heart than he had been for many weeks. "Truly an artist is of use in the world after all—one to be honored," he thought.

To Ruth he told the story and expressed his wish, but enjoined secrecy. "Thee knows how some of our elders would pother about this," he added. "Let us conspire together, therefore, so that thee may make the trip to the city without exciting undue comment."

Ruth was quite willing to adventure, for the town far down on the shining river was a lure to her; but the road was long and after a great deal of thought Roger decided to ask the young stone-cutter to come first to Hesper, which he could do without arousing suspicion. "We will contrive to see him afterward in his shop if necessary," he ended decisively, for he could not bring himself to lead Ruth into the society of the world's people to serve as a model, an act which might be mistaken as a wrong-doing.

The sculptor, anticipating a goodly fee (as well as an increase in orders for grave-stones), readily enough consented to visit Hesper, but only to study his problem. He immediately insisted on Ruth's coming to his studio. "I can't do all the work here—I want to make this my best piece," he remarked in explanation. "It is hard to remember the details of face and form. It may require several sittings."

Thereafter, as often as he dared, Roger called at his father-in-law's house for Ruth and drove her down to the sculptor's shop, and although there were many smiling comments on these trips, no one knew their real purpose.

Slowly the figure grew from a harsh marble block into an ever more appealing female figure, and Roger loved to stand beside the artist while he chipped the stone, for Conrad was in very truth a sculptor, a stalwart fist at the chisel, not a weak modeller in clay. He often hummed a tune as he swung his mall; and so, to the lively beat of worldly melodies, the fair form of the Quaker maid emerged from its flinty covering.

One day in early autumn, conditions favoring, Ruth went to town with Roger for the fifth time and ventured timidly into the stone-cutter's yard to gaze with awe upon the nearly-finished snow-white image, and to the artist's skill gave breathless words of praise. "Truly thee is a magician," she said. "Thee has made a beautiful bonnet out of marble and likewise slippers," she added, looking down to where one small foot in its square-toed shoe peeped from the plain skirt. "Thee does right to make it lovely, for my sister was most comely," she ended with a touch of pride.

"My model was also comely," replied Conrad with a glance which made her flush with pleasure.

During all these months Roger had maintained such careful logic in his comings and goings that only Bailey and one or two of his most intimate friends had even a suspicion of what was happening, though many predicted that he and Ruth would wed; for it was known that she had taken his little son to her father's house and was caring for him. Nevertheless Roger well knew that a struggle was preparing for him, and that some of the elders would be shocked by the audacity of his plan, but no fear of man or church could avail against the force of his resolution.

On this final visit, even as they both stood beside him, Conrad threw down his mallet saying: "I can do no more. It is finished," and turning to Ruth, "What do you think of it?" he demanded.

She, gazing upon the finished statue and seeing only her sister in it, said: "I think it beautiful."

And Roger, deeply wrapt in worship of the sculptured face, said: "Thee has done wonders. The sweet smile of my beloved is fixed in marble forever, and my heart is filled with gratitude to thee." All his training was against the graven art, but he gave his hand to the sculptor. "Friend Conrad, I thank thee; thee has made me very happy. Truly thee has caused this cold marble to assume the very image of my Rachel."

As Roger turned again to gaze upon the statue Conrad touched Ruth upon the arm and drew her aside, leaving the bereaved man alone with his memories.

It was all so wonderful, so moving to Roger that he remained before it a long time, absorbed, marveling, exultant. Safe against the years he seemed now, and yet, as he gazed, his pleasure grew into a pain, so vividly did the chiseled stone bring back the grace he had known. Close upon the exultant thought: "Now she can never fade from my memory," came the reflection that his little son would never know how like to his mother this image was. "He will know only the cold marble—his mother will not even be a memory."

One sixth day morning in the eighth month word was brought to Nicholas Asche, leader of the Meeting, that Roger Barnes was about to erect a graven image among the low headstones of the burial grounds, and in amazement and indignation the old man hastened that way.

He found his two sons and several others of the congregation already gathered, gazing with surprise and a touch of awe upon the statue which Conrad and young Bailey had already securely based beneath a graceful young oak in the very centre of his family plot. Gleaming, life-size, it rose above the modest records of the other graves.

As the stern old elder rode up, the throng of onlookers meekly gave way for him. He halted only when he had come so near the offending monument that he could touch it. For a full minute he regarded it with eyes whose anger lit the shadow of his broad-brim, glaring with ever-increasing resentment as he came fully to realize what it meant to have a tall statue thus set up to dwarf the lowly records of its neighbors. It seemed at once impious and rebellious.

Harshly he broke forth: "What has come to thee, Roger Barnes, that thee has broken all the rules of the Discipline relative to burial? Thee well knows our laws. No one could convey a greater insult to the elders, to the dead beneath these other stones, than thee has done by this act. Lay that impious object low or I will fetch thee before the Meeting."

"I will not," replied the young man. "I was even thinking of exalting it still more by putting beneath it another foot of granite block."

"Thee knows full well that by regulation no gravestone can be more than three hands high," Nicholas stormed.

"I know that well, but this is not a gravestone," Roger retorted. "It is a work of art. It is at once a portrait and a thing of beauty."

"That is but paltering. Thee knows well it is at once a forbidden thing and a monument beyond the regulation in height, and therefore doubly offensive to the Meeting. We will not tolerate such folly. I say to thee again, take the unholy thing down. Will thee urge disrespect to the whole

Society? Thee knows it is in opposition to all our teaching. What devil's spirit has seized upon thee?"

"Thee may storm," stoutly answered Roger, "but I am not to be frightened. This plot of ground is mine. This figure is also mine. It is a blessed comfort, a sign of love and not a thing of evil—and I will not take it away from here for thee nor for all the elders."

Nicholas, perceiving that Roger was not to be coerced at the moment, ceased argument, but his wrath did not cool.

"Thee shall come before the Meeting forthwith."

The following day a summons was issued calling a council, and a messenger came to Roger calling him before his elders in judgment.

Thereupon a sharp division was set up among the neighbors and the discussion spread among the Friends. The question of "Free Will in Burial Stones" was hotly debated wherever two or three of the members met, so that the mind of each was firmly made up by the time the Meeting came together to try the question publicly. "I see no wrong in it," said some. "It is disgraceful," others heatedly charged.

Roger's act was denounced by his own family as treason to the Meeting, as well as heretical to the faith, and his father, old Nathan Barnes, rising with solemn and mournful dignity, admitted this.

"I know not what I have done that a son of mine should bring such shame and sorrow to my old age. It is the influence of the world's people whose licentious teachings corrupt even the most steadfast of our youth. We came here—to this lonely place—to get away from the world's people. They thicken about us now, these worldlings; hence I favor another journey into a far wilderness where we can live at peace, shut away from the contamination of these greedy and blasphemous idolators."

All realized that he spoke in anger as well as in sorrow, and the more candid and cool-headed of the Friends deplored his words, for they had long since determined that the world's forces must be met and endured; but Jacob Farnum was quick to declare himself.

"The welfare of our Society demands the punishment of Roger Barnes. I move that a committee be appointed to proceed to the burial ground and throw down and break in pieces this graven image."

Here something unexpectedly hot and fierce filled Roger's heart to the exclusion of his peaceful teaching and his lifelong awe of his elders. Rising to his feet he violently exclaimed: "By what right will thee so act? Is it more wicked to have a marble portrait than an ambrotype? It is true that I learned the secrets of sculpture from one of the world's people; it is true that an outsider has cut the stone, but I believe his trade to be worthy and his work justifiable. I believe in such portraits." He addressed himself to Nicholas Asche: "Had thee permitted Rachel to have had a daguerreotype, it would not have been necessary for me to treat with this carver of stone, who is, notwithstanding, a man of probity. I will not have him traduced by anyone present," he ended with a threat in his eyes; "he is my friend."

Thereupon Nicholas Asche curtly answered: "There also thee is gravely at fault. Thee has brought my daughter Ruth under the baleful influence of this worldling; and she is even now filled with admiration for him. She too needs be admonished of the elders for too much thinking upon light affairs. Thee is a traitor to thy sister-in-law, Roger Barnes, as thee is a traitor to the Meeting. To permit thee to go thy present ways would be to open our gates to vanity and envy and all imaginable folly. If thee does not at once remove this graven image from our burial grounds, we will ourselves proceed against it and break it and throw it into the highway."

Then again young Roger rose in his seat and with his strong hands doubled into weapons cried out: "Thee will do well to take this matter guardedly and my words to heart, for I tell thee that whosoever goes near to lay rude hands on that fair form will himself be thrown down. I will break him like a staff across my knee."

He stood thus for a moment like a proud young athlete, meeting the eye of his opponent, then, as no one spoke, turned and strode out, resolute to be first on the ground, ready to defend with his whole strength the marble embodiment of his vanished wife.

And yet, even as he walked away from the church, hot and blinded with anger, he began to ache with an indefinable, increasing sorrow. He had expected opposition, but not such fury as this. He had noted the downcast eyes of his friends. It seemed as if something very precious had gone out of his life—as though the whole world had suddenly become inimical.

"They were ashamed of me," he said and his heart sank, for notwithstanding his resentment he loved the Meeting and its ways. For the most part the faces of the congregation were dear to him and the pain that sprang from a knowledge that he had cut himself off from those he respected soon softened his indignation. Nevertheless he hurried on to the burying ground.

It was a glorious September day and all through the fields the crickets were softly singing as if in celebration of the gathered ample harvest. They spoke from the green grass above the graves with the same insistent cheer as from the sere stubble, but Roger heard them not, for his ears still rang with the elder's stern voice and his eyes were darkened by the lowering brows of his father's moody face. Only when the statue rose before him white and still and fair in the misty sunlight did his mood lighten.

"How beautiful it is," he exclaimed. "How can they desire to destroy it?"

Nevertheless he was smitten with a kind of dismay as he looked around upon the low, drab headstones and perceived with what singular significance the marble rose above them. "In truth I have dared much in doing this thing." It was as if he had been led by some inner spirit braver than himself.

And then—even as he raised a first glance to the statue—a pang of keen surprise shot through his heart. The face was changed. Something new had come into it. It was not his Rachel! With hand pressed upon his chilling heart he studied it with new understanding. He had known that it somewhat resembled Ruth, for Ruth indeed resembled Rachel—but that it was verily in every line and shadow a portrait of the living and not of the dead he now realized for the first time.

"The sculptor has deceived me!" he cried. "He loves Ruth and with the craft of a lover has wrought out his design deliberately and with cunning. He has carved the cold stone to the form of his own desire. How blind I have been."

In complete comprehension he addressed the statue: "Thee is but a symbol of this artist's love for another after all. Nicholas Asche was right. This sculptor under cover of my love—in pretending to work out my ideal—has betrayed me and bewitched Ruth."

Ruth, his constant sunny companion, the keeper, the almost second mother of his child, had been snared by the fowler! He no longer doubted it. He recalled the gladness with which she always accompanied him to the sculptor's studio and her silence and preoccupation on the homeward drive. She loved the artist. She was about to be taken away.

Something fierce and wild clutched at his throat and with a groan he fell upon the ground beneath the figure: "Oh, Ruth, Ruth! Am I to lose thee too?"

At this moment he forgot all else but the sweet girl who had become so necessary to his life. Truly, to lose all hope of her was to be doubly bereaved. "I am now most surely solitary," he mourned. "What will become of me hereafter? Who will care for my little son?"

While still he lay there, dark with despair and lax with weakness, Ruth and the sculptor came up the walk to the gate and saw his prostrate form. Ruth checked the sculptor's advance. "Let me go up to him alone," she said, and approached where Roger lay. She did not know the true cause of his grief, but she pitied him: "Do not grieve, Roger; they will not dare to touch the figure."

He looked up at her with a glance which was at once old and strange, but uttered no word of reply, only steadfastly regarded her; then his head dropped upon his arm and his body shook only with sobbing.

She spoke again: "Thee must not despair. There are quite as many for thee as there are against thee. All the young people are on thy side. No one will dare to harm the statue."

As they stood thus Conrad approached and said: "What does it matter? Come out from among these narrow folk. Ruth is to come out and be my wife. Why do you stay to be worried by the elders who——"

He spoke no further, for Roger waved his hand in dismissal of them and cried out in most lamentable voice: "Leave me. Leave me," and again hid his face in his hands.

In troubled wonder the young people moved away slowly, Ruth with tear-filled eyes, Conrad very grave. Together they took their stand at the gate to guard against the approach of others less sympathetic. "His grief is profound," said Ruth, "but the statue will comfort him."

Roger, overwhelmed now by another emotion—a sense of shame, of deep contrition—was face to face with a clear conception of his disloyalty to the dead. Aye, the statue was Ruth. Its youth, its tender, timid smile, its arch brow, all were hers, and as he remembered how Conrad had taken the small unresisting hand in his, he knew himself to be baser than Nicholas Asche had dared imagine. "I loved thee," he confessed; "not as I loved Rachel—but in a most human way. My life has closed round thee. I have unconsciously thought of thee as the guardian of my child. Thy shining figure I have placed in the glow of my fire."

This was true. Ruth had not displaced the love he still bore for his sweet wife—but she had made it an echo of passion, a dim song, a tender and haunting memory of his youth.

The sun sank and dusk came on while still he lay at the statue's feet in remorseful agony of soul, and those who came near enough to speak with him respected his wish and left him undisturbed.

Softly the darkness rose and a warm and mellow night covered the mourner, clothing the marble maid with mystery.

The crickets singing innumerably all about him came at last to express in some subtle way the futility of his own purpose, the smallness of his own affairs, and as he listened he lost the sharpness of his grief. His despair lightened. He ceased to accuse; his desire of battle died. "How could Conrad know that I had grown disloyal? And how was Ruth to perceive my change of heart? The treachery is mine, all mine, dear angel, but I will atone. I will atone. Forgive me. Come to me and forgive me! Comfort me."

Within his heart the spirit of resentment gave way to one of humbleness, of submission. The contest for a place among these gray old monuments no longer seemed worthy—or rather he felt himself no longer worthy to wage it. His disloyalty to his dead disqualified him as a base act disqualified the knights of old. "My cause is lost because my heart was false!" he said.

So during the long hours of the night he kept remorseful vigil. The moon set, the darkness deepened, cool, odorous, musical with lulling songs of insects; and still he lingered, imploring solace, seeking relief from self-reproach. At last, just before dawn, the spirit of his dead Rachel stepped from the shadow. She approached him and bending above him softly said:

"Dear heart, it is true I am not within the graven image. You have no need of it. Go home. There I am, always near thee and the child. I am not for others; I am thine. Return. Make thy peace with the elders. Thee must not live solitary and sad. Our son waits for thee, and when thee sits beside his bed, I will be there."

He woke chilled and wet with the midnight damp, but in his heart a new-found sense of peace had come. His interest in the statue was at an end. He now knew that it was neither the monument he had desired nor the image of his love. "How gross I have been," he said, addressing himself to the unseen presence, "to think that the beauty of my dead could be embodied in stone! Ruth shall go her ways to happiness with my blessing."

In this mood he rose and went to his home, deeply resolved to put aside his idolatry of Ruth even as he had put behind him the gleaming, beautiful figure beneath the shadow of the oak.

Masterpieces

By Ethel Hueston

Give me my pen,
For I would write fine thoughts, pure thoughts,
To touch men's hearts with tenderness,
To fire with zeal for service grim,
To cheer with mirth when skies are dull;
Give me my pen,
For I would write a masterpiece.

Yet stay a while,
For I must put away these toys,
And wash this chubby, grimy face,
And kiss this little hurting bruise,
And hum a bedtime lullaby—
Take back the pen:
This is a woman's masterpiece.

Bread

By *Ellis Parker Butler*

They came to Iowa in a prairie schooner with a rounded canvas top and where the canvas was brought together at the rear of the wagon it left a little window above the tailboard. On the floor of the wagon was a heap of hay and an old quilt out of which the matted cotton protruded, and on this Martha and Eben used to sit, looking out of the window. Martha was a little over two years old and Eben was four.

They crossed the Mississippi at Muscatine on the ferry. It was about noon and old Hodges, the crew of the ferry, who was as crooked as the branches of an English oak because the huge branch of an English oak had fallen on him when he was young, took his dinner from his tin pail. He looked up and saw the two eager little faces.

"Want a bite to eat?" he asked, and he peeled apart two thick slices of bread, thickly buttered, and handed them up to the two youngsters. This, a slice of Mrs. Hodges' good wheat bread, was Martha's welcome to Iowa. The butter was as fragrant as a flower and the bread was moist and succulent, delicious to the touch and the taste. Martha ate it all, even to the last crumb of crust, and, although she did not know it, the gift, the acceptance and the eating was a sacrament—the welcome of bountiful Iowa.

As the prairie schooner rolled its slow way inward into the state there were more slices of bread. The father stopped the weary horses at many houses, shacks and dugouts; and always there was a woman to come to the wagon with a slice of bread for Martha, and one for Eben, for that was the Iowa way. Sometimes the bread was buttered, sometimes it was spread with jelly, sometimes it was bread alone. It was all good bread.

There were days at a time, after they reached the new home, when there was nothing to eat but bread, but there was always that. The neighbors did not wait to be asked to lend; they brought flour unasked and Martha's mother kneaded it and set it to rise and baked it. Then the harvests began to come in uninterrupted succession of wealth, and the dugout became a house, and barns arose, and a school was built, and Martha and Eben went along the dusty, unfenced road, barefooted, happy, well fed, or in winter leaped through the snowdrifts. In their well-filled lunch pail there was always plenty and always bread.

In time Martha taught school, now in one district and now in another; and everywhere, wherever she boarded, there was good wheat bread and plenty of it. She remembered the boarding places by their bread. Some had bread as good as her mother's; some had bread not as good. During her first vacation her mother taught her to make bread. Her very first baking was a success. John Cartwright, coming to the kitchen door just as she was drawing the black bread-pan from the oven on that hot July day, saw her eyes sparkle with triumph as she saw the rich brown loaves.

"Isn't it beautiful? It is my first bread, John," she said, as she stood, flushed and triumphant.

"It smells like mother's," he said, "but she don't seem to get her'n so nice and brown."

"I guess Martha is a natural bread-maker," said her mother proudly. "Some is and some ain't."

Always good bread and plenty of it! That was Iowa. And it was of Martha's bread they partook around the kitchen table the next year—Eben and John, Martha and her father and mother—just before the two young men drove to the county seat to enlist.

"I guess we won't get bread like this in the army," John said, and he was right.

"When I'm chawing this sow-belly and hard tack," Eben wrote, "I wish I had some of that bread of yours, Marth. I guess this war won't last long and the minute it is over you'll see me skedaddling home for some of your bread. Tell ma I'm well and——"

They brought his body home because he was not killed outright but lived almost two weeks in the hospital at St. Louis after he was wounded. Martha scraped the dough from her fingers to go to the door when her father drove up with the precious, lifeless form. That day her bread was not as good as usual.

Martha and John were married the month he came back from the war, and the bread that was eaten at the wedding dinner was Martha's own baking. The bread that was eaten by those who came to prepare her mother for the grave and by those who came, a year later, to lay away her father, was Martha's. Once, twice, three times, four times Martha did a double baking, to "last over," so that there might be bread in the house while the babies were being born. Every week, except those four weeks, she baked bread.

In succession the small boys and girls of her own began coming to the kitchen door pleading, "Ma, may I have a piece of bread an' butter?" Always they might. There was always plenty of bread; it was Iowa.

In time Martha became something of a fanatic about flour. One kind was the best flour in the world; she would have no other. Once, when John brought back another brand, she sent him back to town with it. Her bread was so well known that the flour dealer in town was wont to say, "This is the kind Mis' Cartwright uses; I guess I can't say no more'n that." Eight times in twenty years she won the blue ribbon at the county fair for her loaves; the twelve other times John swore the judges were prejudiced. "It ain't the flour; that I do know!" Martha would answer.

Presently there were children of her children coming on Sunday to spend the day with the "old folks," and there was always enough bread for all. Sometime in the afternoon the big loaf would be taken out of the discarded tin boiler that served as a bread-box and the children would have a "piece"—huge slices of bread, limber in the hand, spread with brown sugar, or jelly, or honey, or dripping with jam. Then, one Sunday, young John's wife brought a loaf of her own bread to show Martha. They battled pleasantly for two hours over the merits of two brands of flour, comparing the bread, but Martha would no more have given up her own brand than she would have deserted the Methodist Church to become a Mahometan!

Then came a time when John had difficulty in holding his pipe in his mouth because his "pipe tooth" was gone. He no longer ate the crusts of Martha's bread except when he dipped them in his coffee. There was a strong, young girl to do the housework but Martha still made the bread, just such beautiful, richly browned, fragrant bread as she had made in her younger days. There had never been a week without the good bread, for this was Iowa.

One day, as she was kneading the dough, she stopped suddenly and put her hand to her side, under her heart. She had to wait several minutes before she could go on with the kneading. Then she shaped the bread into loaves and put it in the pan and put the pan in the oven. She went out on the porch, where John was sitting, and talked about the weather, and then of a grandson, Horace, who was the first to enlist for the great war that was wracking the world. She mentioned the poor Belgians.

"And us so comfortable here, and all!" she said. "When I think of them not having bread enough to eat——"

"I warrant they never did have bread like yours to eat, ma," said John.

She rocked slowly, happy and proud that her man thought that, and then she went in to take the fresh loaves from the oven. They were crisp and golden brown as always, great, plump, nourishing loaves of good wheat bread. She carried the pan to the table.

"Bertha," she said, "I'll let you put the bread away. I guess I'll go up and lie down awhile; I don't feel right well."

She stopped at the foot of the stairs to tell John she was going up; that she did not feel very well.

"If I don't come down to supper," she said, "you can have Bertha cut a loaf of the fresh bread, but you'd better not eat too much of it, John; it don't always agree with you. There's plenty of the other loaf left."

She did not come down again, not Martha herself. She did not mourn because she could not come down again. She had lived her life and it had been a good life, happy, well-nourished, satisfying as her own bread had been. And so, when they came back from leaving Martha beside the brother who had died so many years before, the last loaf of her last baking was cut and eaten around the kitchen table—the youngsters biting eagerly into the thick slices, the elders tasting with thoughts not on the bread at all, and old John crumbling the bread in his fingers and thinking of long past years.

At Kamakura: 1917

By Arthur Davison Ficke

The world shakes with the terrible tramp of war

And the foe's menace swirls through every sea.

But here the Buddha still broods ceaselessly

In hush more real than our strange tumults are.

Here where the fighting hosts of long ago

Once clashed and fell, here where the armored hordes

Razed the great city with their flashing swords,

Now only waves flash, only breezes blow.

That Iowa Town

By Oney Fred Sweet

According to the popular songs, we are apt to get the impression that the only section of the country where there is moonlight and a waiting sweetheart and a home worth longing for is down in Dixie. Judging from the movies, a plot to appeal must have a mountain or a desert setting of the West. Fictionists, so many of them, seem to think they must locate their heroines on Fifth Avenue and their heroes at sea. But could I write songs or direct cinema dramas or pen novels I'd get my inspiration from that Iowa town.

Did you ever drive in from an Iowa farm to a Fourth of July celebration? A few years back the land wasn't worth quite so much an acre; the sloughs hadn't been tiled yet and the country hadn't discovered what a limited section of real good corn land there was after all. But she was Iowa then! Remember how the hot sun dawned early to shimmer across the knee-high fields and blaze against the side of the big red barn, how the shadows of the willow windbreak shortened and the fan on top of the tall windmill faintly creaked? The hired man had decorated his buggy-whip with a tiny ribbon of red, white and blue. Buggy-whip—sound queer now? Well, there were only three automobiles in the county then and they were the feature of the morning parade. Remember how the two blocks of Main Street were draped with bunting and flags, and the courthouse lawn was dotted with white dresses? Well, anyhow you remember the girls with parasols who represented the states, and the float bearing the Goddess of Liberty. And then the storm came in the middle of the afternoon. The lightning and the thunder, and the bunting with the red, white and blue somewhat streaked together but still fluttering. And just before sunset, you remember, it brightened up again, and out past the low-roofed depot and the tall grain elevator you could see the streak of blue and the play of the departing sun against the spent clouds. Nowhere else, above no other town, could clouds pile just like that.

You remember that morning, once a year, when the lilacs had just turned purple out by the front gate, and the dew was still wet on the green grass, the faint strains of band-music drifting out above the maples of the town, and flags hanging out on the porches—Decoration Day! How we used to hunt through the freshly awakened woods north of town for the rarest wildflowers! Tender petaled bloodroots there were in plenty, and cowslips down by the spring, and honeysuckles on the creek bank those late May days, but the lady's slippers and the jack in the pulpits—one had to know the hidden recesses where they grew. Withered they became before the hot sun sank, sending rays from the west that made the tombstones gleam like gold. Somehow, on those days, the sky seemed a bluer blue when the words of the speaker at the "Monument of the Unknown Dead" were carried off by the faint breeze that muffled, too, the song of the quartet and the music of the band. But close in your ears were the chirps of the insects in the bluegrass and the robins that hopped about in the branches of the evergreens.

We had our quota of civil war veterans in that Iowa town. We had our company that went down to Chickamauga in '98. And now—well, you know what to expect from the youth of that sort of a community. Prosperity can't rob a place like that of its pioneer virtues. That Iowa town is an American town and it simply wouldn't fit into the German system at all. There's nothing old world about it. The present generation may have it easier than their fathers did; they may ride in automobiles instead of lumber wagons; they may wear pinch back coats and long beak caps instead of overalls and straw hats, but they've inherited something beside material wealth. We who owned none of its surrounding acres when they were cheap and find them now so out of reach, are yet rich, fabulously rich in inheritance. The last I heard from that Iowa town its youth was donning khaki for the purpose of helping to keep the Kaiser on the other side of the sea.

But it was of the town we used to know that I was speaking. Changed? We must realize that. It was the sort that improves rather than grows. But we remember the place as it was before the blacksmith shop was turned into a garage and before the harness shop was given an electric lighted front and transformed into a movie. I guess the new generation has long since passed up the old opera house above the drug store for the rejuvenated harness shop and the actors that come by express in canned celluloid. But at county fair time, you remember, the Cora Warner Comedy Company used to come for a week's engagement, Cora Warner, noticeably wrinkled as she walked through the park from the hotel, donning a blonde wig that enabled her to play soubrette parts of the old school. And then there were the Beach and Bowers minstrels with their band that swung breezily up Main Street to form a circle on the bank corner and lift the whole center of the town out of the commonplace by the blare of trombones and the tenderness of clarinets. You remember how we Boy Scouts, who didn't know we were Boy Scouts, used to clamor for the front row of kitchen chairs after peddling bills for "The Octoroon" or "Nevada, and the Lost Mine"?

Oh, well, we're uninteresting old-timers now. And it used to be that I knew everyone in town—even the transient baker whose family had no garden and chickens but lived up over the furniture store, and the temporary telephone man who sat out in front of the hotel evenings with the pale-faced traveling man. That hotel—haunted with an atmosphere that was brought in from the outside world! Remember how you used to walk past it with awe, the hot sun on the plank sidewalk burning your bare feet, and your eyes wistful as you heard the bus man on the steps call a train? And the time came when we took the train ourselves. And when we came back—

When we came back, the town was still there, but the wondrous age when all life is roseate belonged to us no longer.

And yet that town, to me, will always be as it was in those days when the world was giving me its first pink-tinted impressions. And when my tussle with the world as it really is comes to a close, I want to go back there and take my last long sleep beneath one of those evergreens on the hillside where I know the robins hop along the branches. I know how each season's change comes there—the white drifts, the dew on the bluegrass, the rustling of crimsoned leaves. I'll know that off on the prairies beyond, the cornfields will still wave green in summer, and that from back across the creek, over in the school yard, there will float the old hushed echo of youth at play.

But Once a Year

By R. O'Grady

A shabby little woman detached herself from the steadily marching throng on the avenue and paused before a shop window, from which solid rows of electric bulbs flashed brilliantly into the December twilight. The ever-increasing current of Christmas shoppers flowed on. Now and then it rolled up, like the waters of the Jordan, while a lady with rich warm furs about her shoulders made safe passage from her car to the tropic atmosphere of the great department store.

Warmth, and the savory smells from a bakery kitchen wafted up through the grating of a near-by pavement, modifying the nipping air. The shabby little woman, only half conscious of such gratuitous comfort, adjusted her blinking gaze to the brightness and looked hungrily at the costumes shimmering under the lights. Wax figures draped with rainbow-tinted, filmy evening gowns caught her passing admiration, but she lingered over the street costumes, the silk-lined coats and soft, warm furs. Elbowed by others who like herself were eager to look, even though they could not buy, she held her ground until she had made her choice.

With her wistful gaze still fixed upon her favorite, she had begun to edge her way through the crowd at the window, when she felt, rather than saw, someone different from the rest, close at her side. At the same instant, she caught the scent of fresh-cut flowers and looked up into the eyes of a tall young girl in a white-plumed velvet hat, with a bunch of English violets in her brown mink fur.

As their glances met, the shabby little woman checked a start, and half-defensively dropped her lids. The smile that shone evanescently from the girl's cordial eyes had aroused in her a feeling of something unwonted, and strangely intimate. There had flashed over the mobile face beneath the velvet hat a look of personal interest—an unmistakable impulse to speak.

The thrill of response that set the woman's pulses throbbing died suddenly. The red that mottled her grayish cheeks was the red of shame. Through the window, in a mirrored panel cruelly ablaze with light, she saw herself: her made-over turban, her short, pigeon-tailed jacket of a style long past, and her old otter cape with its queer caudal decorations and its yellowed cracks grinning through the plucked and ragged fur.

One glance at her own image was enough. The little woman pushed determinedly into the slow-moving crush, and headed toward the nearest elevated station, to be carried on irresistibly by the army of pedestrians.

She caught a last glimpse of the tall young girl, coming in her direction, still watching her with that same eager look. But what of that? She knew why women stared curiously at her. By the time her station was reached, the occurrence had assumed in her mind a painful significance which emphasized the sordidness of her evening's routine. She made her way along a narrow, dimly lighted street, walking with the aimless gait of one who neither expects nor is expected.

But, loiter as she might, she soon reached a neighborhood where rows of narrow brick tenements brooded over dingy, cluttered basement shops. Here she found it necessary to accelerate her pace to make way for romping children and bareheaded women hurrying from the shops with their suppers in paper bags.

In spite of the wintry chill, the section had an air of activity all its own. Neither did it lack occasional evidences of Christmas cheer. In the window of a little news and fruit shop, against the smeared and partly frosted glass, a holly wreath was hanging, and within stood a rack of gaudy, tinseled Christmas cards. The woman hesitated, as if about to enter the shop, then abruptly passed on. She ascended one of the stoops that were all alike. Standing in a blur of reddish light that filtered through the broken glass above the door, she looked back the way she had come.

For an instant her pulses quickened again as they had done on the avenue down-town. At the corner, a tall girl with a white-plumed velvet hat was smilingly picking her way through the swarming element so foreign, apparently, to one of her class. As the white plume came nearer and nearer, the tremulous little woman regained her self-control. It was but one of the coincidences of the city, she told herself, turning resolutely away. The door slammed shut behind her.

Odd, she thought, as she groped her way through the dimly lighted lower hall, and the complete darkness of the upper, that such a girl should be living in such a neighborhood. Then, with an effort, she dismissed the matter from her mind.

To find a match and light the sputtering gas required but very few steps in her tiny box of a room. When that was accomplished, she could think of nothing more to do. Her little taste of excitement had spoiled her zest for any of the homy rites which at other times formed the biggest events of her day. As she sank down upon the cot without removing her wraps, she was greeted by the usual creaking of rusty springs; her table with its meager array of dishes, its coffee pot and little alcohol burner, sat as ever in its corner, inviting the preparation of her evening meal. But to-night she did not want to eat. She had not visited the bake-shop on her way home. She had not even bought her daily paper at the corner stand where the postcards were—those gay Christmas cards that bring you greetings from friends.

As she slowly removed her turban, her jacket and fur cape and, without getting up, tossed them across a chair against the opposite wall, the dull ache of dissatisfaction in her heart grew slowly to a sharp pain of desire. She wanted to do something, to have something happen that might break the sordid routine of her existence.

Still, habit and environment would continue to force at least a part of this routine upon her. She glanced at her fingers, stained to an oily, bluish grime by the cheap dye of the garments that furnished her daily work. Mechanically she rose to wash.

While her hands were immersed in the lather of rankly perfumed toilet soap, there came a gentle knock at the door.

"Come in," invited the woman, expecting some famine-pressed neighbor for a spoonful of coffee or a drawing of tea.

The door opened slowly, a tentative aperture.

"May I come in?" asked a voice that was sweeter than the breath of violets that preceded the caller into the room.

With the towel clutched in her dripping hands, the woman flung wide open the door, then hastened to unload the chair which held her wraps—her only chair.

"Thank you; don't bother," urged the visitor. "I shall like sitting on the couch."

There was a melody of enthusiasm in this remark, which the complaining of the cot, as the girl dropped easily upon it, could not wholly drown.

The woman, having absently hung her towel on the doorknob, stared dazedly at the visitant. She could hardly credit her eyes. It was—it was indeed the girl with the white ostrich plume and the bouquet of violets in her brown mink fur.

"I feel like an intruder," began the girl, "and, do you know—" her appraising glance directed to the old fur collar on the chair, was guiltily withdrawn as she spoke—"do you know, I've such a silly excuse for coming." She laughed, and the laugh brought added music to her voice.

The woman, now at last recalled from her abstraction, smiled, and the weariness passed from her face. She seated herself at the extreme end of the humpy, complaining cot.

"I'm sure you'll understand," resumed the girl. "At least, I hope you'll not be offended.... I heard ... that is, I noticed you had a rare fur-piece—" her vivid glance returned to the pile of wraps on the chair—"and I want to ask a very great favor of you. I—now *please* don't be shocked—I've been ransacking the city for something like it, and—" with a determined air of taking the plunge—"I should like to buy it of you!"

"Buy it!" scorned the woman, with a sudden dull red staining her sallow cheeks. "I can't see why anyone would want to pay money for such a thing as that."

"It—it's a rare pattern, you know," groped the girl, her sweet tones assuming an eloquent, persuasive quiver, "and—and you don't know how glad I'd be to have it."

The indignant color faded out of the woman's face. "If you really want the thing—" abruptly she put her bizarre possession into her strange visitor's lap—"If you really want it—but I don't see—" yearning crept into her work-dimmed eyes, a yearning that seemed to struggle with disillusionment. "Tell me," she broke off, "is that all you came here for?"

Apparently oblivious to the question, the young woman rose to her feet. "You'll sell it to me then!" she triumphed, opening her gold-bound purse.

"But, see here," demurred the woman, "I can't—it ain't worth——"

The girl's gloved hands went fumbling into her purse, while the old fur cape hung limply across one velvet arm.

"You leave it to me," she commanded, and smiled, a radiant, winning smile.

Impulsively the woman drew close to her guest. "Excuse me," she faltered, "but, do you know—you look ever-so-much like a little niece of mine back—home?"

"Do I? That's nice." The visitor looked at her watch. A note of abstraction had crept into her beautiful voice, but it still held the caress that invited the woman's confidence.

"Yes, my little niece—excuse me—I haven't seen her for twelve years—most fifteen years, I guess. She'd be growed up, but I thought—when I saw you down-town——"

"Oh, you remember me, then! Forgive me for following—" The girl seized the woman's soap-reddened hands in a sudden fervent clasp. "I understand," she breathed. "You must be lonely.... I'll try to see you again—I surely will.... Good-bye...."

The girl was gone and all at once the room seemed colder and dingier than it ever had before. But the woman was not cold. As she sat huddled on the cot, warmth and vitality glowed within her, kindled by the memory of a recent kindly human touch.

The following evening, after working hours, the shabby woman, wearing a faded scarf about her neck to replace the old fur collar, diffidently accosted a saleslady at the Sixth Avenue department store. She wanted to buy a brown mink collar, just like one worn by a figure in green in the window.

It was unusual to sell expensive furs to such a customer. But people might send what freaks of servants they pleased to do their Christmas shopping, provided they sent the money, too. In this case, the shabby little woman was prepared. She produced three crisp ten-dollar bills—the fabulous sum which the girl had left in her hand at parting—and two dollars more from the savings in her worn little purse. Then, hugging the big flat box against the tight-fitting bosom of her jacket, she triumphantly left the store.

In a sort of tender ecstasy she dallied along until she came to a florist's window. As she paused to gaze at great bunches of carnations and roses, tied with broad and streaming ribbons, the anxious look that attends the doubtful shopper returned to her face. Would it be of any use to go in? Since she must either keep moving or be carried along by the crowd, she edged through the revolving door.

"English violets?—Fifty cents for the small bunches," clipped off the red-cheeked salesgirl, in reply to the woman's groping inquiry.

The perturbed shopper turned reluctantly away, hesitated, and then asked:

"But the roses? A single, half-blown rose—?"

"Twenty-five apiece," replied the girl in the same mechanical tones, while she busied herself in rearranging a basket of flowers.

"I—I'll take the rose."

At the express office, where scores were waiting before her, the woman had ample time to untie her box and slip the rosebud beneath the tissue paper of the inner wrapping. Then, having retied it securely and stuck a "Do-not-open-until-Christmas" tag in a conspicuous place, she took her stand in line. When it finally came her turn at the desk, a stout clerk, who worked like an automaton and breathed like an ox, tore the package from her lingering grasp and dashed across the wrapper the address she gave.

She paid the charges, wadded the receipt into her purse and turned briskly away.

Fresh crullers she took to her room from the bake-shop, having bought them from a dark, greasy woman, whom she wished a "Merry Christmas" in a voice that almost sang. At dusk she had coffee in her room. It was Christmas Eve and she must begin early to get her full share of the season's peculiar indulgences. After she had read her paper for an hour or so by the recklessly flaming gas jet, she bustled about to brew another cup of coffee, and feasted upon crullers for the second time. At last she filled a water-bottle with tepid water from a faucet in the hall, and prepared for bed.

The chill of the bedclothes, upon which the tepid water-bottle had little effect, could not touch the cozy warmth about the woman's heart. Neither were the happy memories of her strange and lovely visitor disturbed by knowledge of an incident that was taking place at that very hour. As she bounced into her cot, humming a little tune, she did not know that at a down-town theater a popular young actress was just responding to an insistent curtain call. Nor could she have recognized the graceful young girl, issuing from the wings in a new character part—an extreme type of eccentric maidenhood—except for the plucked and ragged fur-piece which formed the keynote of the performer's quaint attire.

No knowledge of this episode disturbed the half-drowsy, half-blissful state which supplanted the woman's sleep that night. The incident cast no cloud upon her eager awakening, nor retarded her active leap from bed when the voice of her landlady aroused her with a start on Christmas morning.

"*Eggs*-press, *eggs*-press ... a package for Miss Law-lor-r-r!"

Full-chested and lingering, the call reverberated up three flights of naked stairs, and by the time the woman had donned her skirt and sweater and had emerged into the twilight of the upper hall, frowsy, curious heads protruded from every door.

She carried the bulky Christmas package to her own room, moving deliberately, in shy, half-guilty triumph, and placed it on the cot. Behind her closed door she untied it, removed the cover and smilingly bent down to draw an eager inhalation from the tissue paper folds. Then, with careful fingers, she parted the crisp inner wrappings and unearthed a wilting, half-blown rose from its nest in the brown mink fur.

The Reminder

By Allan Updegraff

A little Belgian and an old violin—
A short, dumpy, melancholy little Belgian
And a very fine old violin....

An inconsequential small Belgian
Wearing a discouraged bit of mustache,
American "store" clothes that didn't fit,
Cheap American shoes, shined but shapeless....
(And yet he had often played in high honor
Before great audiences in Belgium;
But that was before Hell's lid was lifted
Somewhere in the North of Germany—
May it be clamped down, hard, before long!)

So this shabby, fat, discouraged oldish Belgian
(Too old and fat for military service),
And his very old beautiful violin,
(Borrowed—he'd lost his better one to his conquerors),
Appeared before a dubious tag-end of an audience
In a music hall built in the woods
Near an American summer resort,
And played a dozen selections for forty-five dollars.

Then we learned why he had often played in high honor
Before great audiences in Belgium;
And why his king and his country
Had given him the honors he still wore,

The riches recently taken away
By his conquerors.

Then we saw what manner of man he was,
How that his soul was finely clad, upright,
Nobly statured, crowned with Apollo's bays.
Then we knew, when he played Tartini's sonata for violin,
That Belgium would own once more
Its little place in the sun.

For the old Italian master might have written that sonata
With the devastated Belgium of these days in mind.
First, streaming from beneath the Belgian's sentient bow,
The music told of peace and common things,
With some bickering, some trivialities,
But much melody and deep harmony underneath.
The third movement, *affetuoso*, awoke to ruin—
To ruin too sudden and complete.

Too bloody and bestial and cruel
And thorough and filthy and Prussian
To be more than wailed over softly.

There was a stabbed child
Lying in the mud beneath a half-burned house,
Beside the naked corpse of its mother,
The mutilated bodies of its old grandfather,
And young sister;
And the child cried faintly, and moaned,
And cried again....
And then was silent.

A while after, from far away,

Rose dull outcries, trampling feet,

Voices indomitable—

Retreating, returning, joined by others, dying, reviving,

Always indomitable.

And still others joined those beaten but unconquered ones,

And the end came in one long, high,

Indomitable cry.

Then we knew, and bowed our heads,

And were ashamed of our poor part,

And prayed God we might bear a nobler part,

In the reply to that most cold-planned,

Murderously carried out,

Unexpurgable horror over there.

"Old Bill"

By Henry C. Wallace

We buried Old Bill to-day. As we came back to the house it seemed almost as if we had laid away a member of the family. All afternoon I have been thinking of him, and this evening I want to tell you the story.

Old Bill was a horse, and he was owned by four generations of our family. He was forty-one years old when he died, so you will understand that for many years he was what some might call a "dead-beat boarder." But long ago he had paid in advance for his board as long as he might stay with us. In winter a warm corner of the stable was his as a matter of right, and not a day went by but a lump of sugar, an apple, or some other tidbit found its way to him from the hands of those who loved him. Old Bill was never in the slightest danger of meeting the sad fate of many a faithful old horse in the hands of the huckster or trader.

My grandfather liked a good horse. He loved to draw the lines over a team that trotted up into the bits as if they enjoyed it. He had such a team in a span of eleven-hundred pound mares, full sisters, and well matched both as to appearance and disposition. The old gentleman said they were Morgan bred. Whether they were or not, they had a lot of warm blood in them. He raised several colts from these mares by light horses, but none of them had either the spirit or the quality of their dams. One year a neighbor brought in a Percheron horse, a rangy fellow weighing about seventeen hundred and fifty pounds, clean of limb, and with plenty of life, as were most of the earlier horses of that breed, and grandfather bred these mares to him. The colts foaled the next spring, developed into a fine span, weighing about twelve hundred and fifty each, sound as nuts, willing workers and free movers. Grandfather gave this team to my father the spring he started to farm for himself. They were then three years old, and one of them was Old Bill.

In those days the young farmer's capital was not very large: a team of horses, a cow, two or three pigs, and a few farm implements, the horses being by far the most important part of it. I shall not try to tell of the part these horses played in helping father win out. They were never sick; they were always ready for work. And well do I remember father's grief when Bill's mate slipped on the ice in the barnyard one cold winter day and had to be shot. It was that evening that my father talked of the important part a good horse plays in the life of a farmer, and gave us a little lecture on the treatment of horses and other animals. I was but a lad of ten at that time, but something father said, or the way he said it, made a deep impression on me, and from that time forward I looked upon horses as my friends and treated them as such. What a fine thing it would be if all parents would teach the youngsters at an early age the right way to treat our dumb animals.

Bill was already "Old Bill" when he became mine. He was four years older than I when we started courting together, and my success must have been due in large part to his age and experience. We had but a mile and a half to go, and of a summer evening Bill would trot this off at a pace equal to a much younger horse. When the girl of my affection was snugly seated in the buggy, he would move off briskly for half a mile, after which he dropped to a dignified walk, understanding full well the importance of the business in hand. He knew where it was safe to leave the beaten track and walk quietly along the turf at the side, and he had a positive genius for finding nice shady places where he could browse the overhanging branches, looking back once in a while to see that everything was going along as it should be. I suppose I am old-fashioned, but I don't see how a really first-class job of courting can be done without such a horse as Old Bill. He seemed to take just about as much interest in the matter as I did. One night Jennie brought out a couple of lumps of sugar for him (a hopeful sign to me, by the way), and after that there was no time lost in getting to her house, where Bill very promptly announced our arrival by two or three nickers.

One time I jokingly said to my wife that evidently she married Bill as much as she did me. That remark was a mistake. She admitted it more cheerfully than seemed necessary, and on sundry occasions afterward made free to remind me of it. Sometimes she drew comparisons to my discredit, and if Old Bill could have understood them, he would have enjoyed a real horse laugh. Jennie always said Bill knew more than some real folks.

After the wedding, Old Bill took us on our honeymoon trip—not a very long one, you may be sure—and the three of us settled down to the steady grind of farm life. We asked nothing hard of Old Bill, but he helped chore around, and took Jennie safely where she wanted to go. I felt perfectly at ease when she was driving him. I wish I had a picture of the three of them when she brought out the boy to show to Old Bill. I can close my eyes and see her standing in front of the old horse, with the boy cuddled up in a blanket in her arms. I can see the proud light in her eyes, and I can see Old Bill's sensitive upper lip nuzzling at the blanket. He evidently understood Jennie perfectly, and seemed just as proud as she was.

The youngster learned to ride Old Bill at the age most children are riding broomsticks. Jennie used to put him on Old Bill's back and lead him around, but Old Bill seemed so careful that before a great while she would trust him alone with the boy in the front yard, she sitting on the porch. I remember a scare I had one summer evening. Old Bill did not have much hair left on his withers, but he had a long mane lock just in front of the collar mark, and the youngster held onto this. I was walking up toward the house, where Bill was marching the youngster around in front, Jennie sitting on the porch. Evidently a botfly was bothering Bill's front legs, for he threw his head down quickly, whereupon the youngster, holding tightly to this mane lock, slid down his neck and flopped to the ground. You may be sure I got there in a hurry, almost as quickly as Jennie, who was but a few steps away, calling as I ran: "Did he step on him?" You should have seen the look of scorn Jennie gave me. Such an insult to Old Bill deserved no answer. The old horse seemed as much concerned as we were and Jennie promptly replaced the boy on his back and the ride was resumed, with me relegated to the corner of the porch in disgrace. As if Old Bill would hurt her boy!

Old Bill's later years were full of contentment and happiness, if I know what constitutes horse happiness. In the winter he had the best corner in the stable. In the summer he was the autocrat of the small pasture where we kept the colts. He taught the boy to ride properly and with due respect for his steed. He would give him a gallop now and then, but as a rule he insisted upon a dignified walk, and if the youngster armed himself with a switch and tried to have his way about it, the old fellow would quickly show who was boss by nipping his little legs just hard enough to serve as a warning of what he could do.

Bill had a lot of fun with the mares and colts. We never allowed the colts to follow the mares in the fields, but kept them in the five-acre pasture with Bill for company. At noon, we would lead the mares in after they had cooled off, and let the colts suck, and at night we turned the mares into the pasture with them. Bill had a keen sense of humor. He would fool around until the colts had finished, and then gallop off with all the colts in full tilt after him. Naturally the mares resented this. They followed around in great indignation, but it did them no good. We used to walk over to the pasture fence and watch this little byplay, and I think Bill enjoyed having us there, for he kept up the fun as long as we would watch. He surely was not popular with the mares. They regarded him about as the proud mother regards grandfather when he entices away her darling boy and teaches him tricks of which she does not approve.

Although Bill took delight in teaching the colts mean little tricks during their days of irresponsibility, when they reached the proper age he enjoyed the part he had to play in their training with a grim satisfaction. For more than twenty-five years he was our main reliance in breaking the colts to work. It was amusing to watch a colt the first time he was harnessed and hooked up to the wagon alongside Bill, his halter strap being tied back to the hames on Bill's collar.

Our colts were always handled more or less from infancy, and we had little trouble in harnessing them. When led out to the wagon with Bill, the colt invariably assumed he was out for a good time. But the Bill he found now was not the Bill he had known in the pasture, and he very quickly learned that he was in for real business.

Bill was a very strict disciplinarian; he tolerated no familiarities; with his teeth he promptly suppressed any undue exuberance of spirit; he was kind but firm. As he grew older, he would lose patience now and then with the colts that persisted in their unruly ways. When they lunged forward, he settled back against their plunges with a bored air, as much as to say: "Take it easy, my young friend; you surely don't think you can run away with Old Bill!" When they sulked, he pulled them along for a bit. But if they continued obstreperous he turned upon them with his teeth in an almost savage manner, and the way he would bring them out of the sulky spell was a joy to see.

Finally, when the tired and bewildered colt had settled down to an orderly walk, and had learned to respond to the guiding reins, Bill would reward him with a caress on the neck and other evidences of his esteem.

Old Bill knew the game thoroughly, and was invaluable in this work of training the young ones. But after the first round at the wagon with him, the colts always seemed to feel as if they had lost a boon companion; they kept their friendship for him, but they maintained a very respectful attitude, and never after took liberties unless assured by his manner that they would be tolerated.

I got a collie dog for the youngster when he was about three years old. When he was riding Old Bill, Jack would rush back and forth, in front and behind, barking joyously. Old Bill disliked such frivolity. To him it was a serious occasion. I think he never forgot the time the boy fell off, for nothing could tempt him out of a steady walk until the youngster got to an age when his seat was reasonably secure. When the ride was over, Old Bill would lay back his ears and go after Jack so viciously that the collie would seek refuge under the porch. Except when the boy was about, however, Old Bill and Jack were good friends, and in very cold weather Jack would beg a place in Bill's stall, curling up between his legs, to the apparent satisfaction of both. There was a very real friendship between them, but just as real jealousy for the favors of the little fellow. They were much like human beings in this respect.

Until the last year of his life Bill was a most useful member of the family. Jennie liked a good garden and used to say before we were married that when we had our own home, she would have a garden that was a garden, and that she did not propose to wear herself out with a hoe as her mother had done. She laid out her garden in a long, narrow strip of ground between the pasture and the windbreak, just back of the house, and with Bill's help she had the garden she talked about. Bill plowed the ground and cultivated it, and the care with which he walked the long narrow rows was astonishing. This was another place where he did not want to be bothered with Jack. He was willing Jack should sit at one end and watch the proceedings, but he must keep out of the way.

During the school season Bill's regular job was to take the children to school, a mile away. They rode him, turning him loose to come home alone. He learned to go back for them in the afternoon, and he delivered them at the porch with an air as much as to say: "There are your little folks, safe and sound, thanks to Old Bill." Jennie always met him with an apple or a lump of sugar. She and Old Bill seemed to be in partnership in about everything he could have a part in. They understood each other perfectly, and I don't mind confessing now that once in a great while I felt rather jealous of Old Bill.

Well, as I said in the beginning, we buried Old Bill to-day. He died peacefully, and, as we say of some esteemed citizen, "full of honors." He was buried on the farm he helped pay for; and, foolish as it may seem to some folks, before long a modest stone will mark his last resting place. And sometimes, of a summer afternoon, if I find Jennie sitting with her needlework in the shade of the big oak tree under which Old Bill rests, I will know that tender memories of a faithful servant are being woven into her neat stitches.

The Recruit's Story

By Frank Luther Mott

Last Sunday afternoon I wandered into Smith Park and sat down on a bench near the fountain. It was a fine day. The sun shone warmly and I was one of many men who lounged on those benches and luxuriated in the grateful warmth of the early spring sunshine.

Men of many kinds were there. There were a few old men, but many were young, or middle-aged. Unless I am a very poor observer, not a few of them were drifters.

As I sat there I watched the play of the water falling in the fountain. I observed the bronze figures of women sitting in the center, musing over who knows what great world problem; and I saw, surmounting all, the towering figure of a soldier of the Civil War. There he stood in his quiet power—apotheosis of the common soldier in the war for the Union. He wore the great-coat and military cape of the old uniform. He stood at ease, his left foot advanced, and the butt of his gun resting on the ground in front of him, while he held the gun-barrel with his left hand and rested his forearm on the muzzle. He gazed a little past me, steadfastly, toward a corner of the park. On his face was the look of the man who is ready—the man undaunted by any emergency—the man unafraid in the quiet strength of soul and body.

"He it was," I reflected, "who leaped to the colors when Father Abraham called, and by the might of his loyalty and sacrifice saved his country in the hour of her greatest need."

Glancing across the park, I saw a poster glaring from the great window of a salesroom. I could make out three words, printed in giant type:

MEN WANTED NOW!

Again I looked about me at the men lounging, as I was lounging, there on the benches in the sunlight, some of them asleep. I too felt the soporific influence of the May sun, and might soon have lapsed into unconsciousness myself had it not been for a strange thing that happened just then.

I saw the Union soldier turn his head a little and look directly at me.

I am not given to illusions, being generally considered a matter-of-fact young man. But, as I live, I saw that Union soldier turn his head! And more than that, I knew just why he did it.

I had read the papers, and knew my country's need. I had read the flaming posters calling for men to enlist in her armies. I had read President Wilson's classic-to-be concerning America's purpose in our greatest war for liberty. I had not meant to be a slacker; but, some way, I had not been strongly moved. I was letting the other fellow fill up the ranks, intending hazily to rally to the colors myself when the need seemed greater. Even now, I was inclined to argue the matter.

I leaned back in my seat and said, in a conversational tone:

"Now look here, Mr. Union Soldier, the need was greater when you joined the colors. The Union was threatened; the very existence of the nation was at hazard. I too will answer the call if worse comes to worst in this war."

"Young man," replied the soldier, his eyes fixed on mine and his voice deep and calm, "young man, your country's call is your country's call. This time it is no question of union; thank God, the states stand indivisible forever. But this time the crisis is even greater, the need of vision and sacrifice even more vital. This time the liberty, not of the black man alone, but of the world, is in the balance. Are you deaf to the call?"

"But listen," I answered. "This is not our war. Nobody has crossed the sea to strike us."

"Have they not?" he countered. "By spies, by intrigue, by a treacherous diplomacy, by an unscrupulous policy of world subjugation, the enemy has invaded our shores. Yet it is not that alone. As I have stood here, I have heard the cries of the people of ravished Belgium; I have heard the despairing screams of men and women sinking in watery graves; the wails of perishing Armenia assail my ears. Do you say it is not our war? It is! Just as the fate of the black man touched the hearts of us Northerners, just as the misfortune of the traveler to Jericho touched the heart of the Samaritan, just as the suffering Christ on the cross has touched the heart of the world—just so must the woeful cry of a world perishing to-day touch the heart of America.... And yet I look about me here! These men drowsing in the sunshine! Are these Americans? From the field I rushed when Lincoln called, scarcely pausing to bid my mother good-bye; and I braved cold, and heat, and sickness, and privation, and terrors by day and night, and rain of shot and shell, and wounds and suffering and death—all because my country called!"

As he spoke his voice rose to a commanding resonance. He raised his right arm from the muzzle of the gun where it had rested—raised it high in impassioned appeal. At last I was moved; tears ran down my cheeks.

I started—awoke. I had been asleep, and the water from the fountain was blowing in my face. But was it the spray from the fountain alone that made my cheeks wet?

I looked up at the bronze figure surmounting the fountain. There the soldier stood at rest, left foot advanced, arm resting on his gun. His eyes looked steadfastly toward the corner of the park. But did I not see a glow of passion on that bronze face—a passion for the Liberty of the World?

I turned to my neighbor on the bench at my left. His eyes were half shut, drowsily.

"Pardon me, brother," I said. "Can you tell me where the nearest recruiting station is located?"

The Happiest Man in I-O-Way

By Rupert Hughes

Jes' down the road a piece, 'ith the dust so deep
It teched the bay mare's fetlocks; an' the sun
So b'ilin' hot, the pewees dassn't peep;
Seemed like midsummer 'fore the spring's begun!
An' me plumb beat an' good-fer-nothin'-like
An' awful lonedsome fer a sight o' you …
I come to that big locus' by the pike,
An' she was all in bloom, an' trembly, too,
With breezes like drug-store perfumery.
I stood up in my stirrups, with my head
So deep in flowers they almost smothered me.
I kind o' liked to think that I was dead …
An' if I hed 'a' died like that to-day,
I'd 'a' be'n the happiest man in I-o-way.

For whut's the us't o' goin' on like this?
Your pa not 'lowin me around the place …
Well, fust I knowed, I'd give them blooms a kiss;
They tasted like Good-Night on your white face.
I reached my arms out wide, an' hugged 'em—say,
I dreamp' your little heart was hammerin' me!

I broke this branch off for a love-bo'quet;
'F I'd be'n a giant, I'd 'a' plucked the tree!
The blooms is kind o' dusty from the road,
But you won't mind. And, as the feller said,

"When this you see remember me"—I knowed
Another poem; but I've lost my head
From seein' you! 'Bout all that I kin say
Is—"I'm the happiest man in I-o-way."

Well, comin' 'long the road I seen your ma
Drive by to town—she didn't speak to me!
An' in the farthest field I seen your pa
At his spring-plowin', like I'd ought to be.
But, knowin' you'd be here all by yourself,
I hed to come—for now's our livin' chance.
Take off yer apern, leave things on the shelf—
Our preacher needs what th' feller calls "romance."
Ain't got no red-wheeled buggy; but the mare
Will carry double, like we've trained her to.
Jes' put a locus'-blossom in your hair
An' let's ride straight to heaven—me an' you!
I'll build y' a little house, an' folks'll say:
"There lives the happiest pair in I-o-way."

The Captured Dream

By Octave Thanet

Somers rode slowly over the low Iowa hills, fitting an air in his mind to Andrew Lang's dainty verses. Presently, being quite alone on the country road, he began to sing:

"In dreams doth he behold her,

Still fair and kind and young."

The gentle strain of melancholy and baffled desire faded into silence, but the young man's thoughts pursued it. A memory of his own that sometimes stung him, sometimes plaintively caressed him, stirred in his heart. "I am afraid you hit it, Andy," he muttered, "and I should have found it only a dream had I won."

At thirty Somers imagined himself mighty cynical. He consorted with daring critics, and believed the worst both of art and letters. He was making campaign cartoons for a daily journal instead of painting the picture of the future; the panic of '93 had stripped him of his little fortune, and his sweetheart had refused to marry him. Therefore he said incessantly in the language of Job, "I do well to be angry."

The rubber tires revolved more slowly as his eyes turned from the wayside to the smiling hills. The corn ears were sheathed in silvery yellow, but the afternoon sun jewelled the green pastures, fresh as in May, for rain had fallen in the morning, and maples, oaks and elms blended exquisite gradations of color and shade here and there among the open fields. Long rows of poplars recalled France to Somers and he sighed. "These houses are all comfortable and all ugly," thought the artist. "I never saw anything less picturesque. The life hasn't even the dismal interest of poverty and revolt, for they are all beastly prosperous; and one of the farmers has offered me a hundred dollars and my expenses to come here and make a pastel of his wife. And I have taken the offer because I want to pay my board bill and buy a second-hand bicycle. The chances are he is after something like a colored photograph, something slick and smooth, and every hair painted—Oh, Lord! But I have to have the money; and I won't sign the cursed thing. What does he want it for though? I wonder, did he ever know love's dream? Dream? It's all a dream—a mirage of the senses or the fancy. Confound it, why need I be harking back to it? I must be near his house. House near the corner, they said, where the roads cross. Ugh! How it jumps at the eyes."

The house before him was yellow with pea-green blinds; the great barns were Indian red; the yard a riot of color from blooming flowers.

Somers wheeled up to the gate and asked of the old man who was leaning upon the fence where Mr. Gates lived.

"Here," said the old man, not removing his elbows from the fence bar.

"And, may I ask, are you Mr. Gates?" said Somers.

"Yes, sir. But if you're the young man was round selling 'Mother, Home and Heaven,' and going to call again to see if we liked it, we don't want it. My wife can't read and we're taking a Chicago paper now, and ain't got any time."

Somers smiled. "I'm not selling anything but pictures," said he, "and I believe you want me to make one for you."

"Are you Mr. Somers, F. J. S.?" cried the farmer, his face lighting in a surprising manner. "Well, I'm glad to see you, sir. My wife said you'd come this afternoon and I wouldn't believe her. I'm always caught when I don't believe my wife. Come right in. Oh, did you bring your tools with you?"

He guided Somers into the house and into a room so dark that he stumbled.

"There's the sofy; set down," said Gates, who seemed full of hospitable cheer. "I'll get a blind open. Girl's gone to the fair and Mother's setting out on the back piazza, listening to the noises on the road. She's all ready. Make yourself to home. Pastel like them pictures on the wall's what I want. My daughter done them." His tone changed on the last sentence, but Somers did not notice it; he was drinking in the details of the room to describe them afterwards to his sympathizing friends in Chicago.

"What a chamber of horrors," he thought, "and one can see he is proud of it." The carpet was soft to the foot, covered with a jungle of flowers and green leaves—the pattern of carpet which fashion leaves behind for disappointed salesmen to mark lower and lower until it shall be pushed into the ranks of shopworn bargains. The cheap paper on the wall was delicately tinted, but this boon came plainly from the designers, and not the taste of the buyer, since there was a simply terrible chair that swung by machinery, and had four brilliant hues of plush to vex the eye, besides a paroxysm of embroidery and lace to which was still attached the red ticket of the county fair. More embroidery figured on the cabinet organ and two tables, and another red ticket peeped coyly from under the ornate frame of a pastel landscape displaying every natural beauty—forest, mountain, sunlit lake, and meadow—at their bluest and greenest. There were three other pictures in the room, two very large colored photographs of a lad of twelve and of a pretty girl who might be sixteen, in a white gown with a roll of parchment in her hand tied with a blue ribbon; and the photograph of a cross of flowers.

The girl's dark, wistful, timid eyes seemed to follow the young artist as he walked about the room. They appealed to him. "Poor little girl," he thought, "to have to live here." Then he heard a dragging footfall, and there entered the mistress of the house. She was a tall woman who stooped. Her hair was gray and scanty, and so ill-arranged on the top of her head that the mournful tonsure of age showed under the false gray braid. She was thin with the gaunt thinness of years and toil, not the poetic, appealing slenderness of youth. She had attired herself for the picture in a black silken gown, sparkling with jet that tinkled as she moved; the harsh, black, bristling line at the neck defined her withered throat brutally. Yet Somer's sneer was transient. He was struck by two things—the woman was blind, and she had once worn a face like that of the pretty girl. With a sensation of pity he recalled Andrew Lang's verses; inaudibly, while she greeted him he was repeating:

"Who watches day by day

The dust of time that stains her,

The griefs that leave her gray,

The flesh that still enchains her,

Whose grace has passed away."

Her eyes were closed but she came straight toward him, holding out her hand. It was her left hand that was extended; her right closed over the top of a cane, and this added to the impression of decrepitude conveyed by her whole presence. She spoke in a gentle, monotonous, pleasant voice. "I guess this is Mr. Somers, the artist. I feel—we feel very glad to have the honor of meeting you, sir."

No one had ever felt honored to meet Somers before. He thought how much refinement and sadness were in a blind woman's face. In his most deferential manner he proffered her a chair. "I presume I am to paint you, madam?" he said.

She blushed faintly. "Ain't it rediculous?" she apologized. "But Mr. Gates will have it. He has been at me to have somebody paint a picture of me ever since I had my photograph taken. It was a big picture and most folks said it was real good, though not flattering; but he wouldn't hang it. He took it off and I don't know what he did do to it. 'I want a real artist to paint you, Mother,' he said. I guess if Kitty had lived she'd have suited him, though she was all for landscape; never did much figures. You noticed her work in this room, ain't you—on the table and chair and organ—art needlework? Kitty could do anything. She took six prizes at the county fair; two of 'em come in after she was in her last sickness. She was so pleased that she had the picture—that's the picture right above the sofy; it's a pastel—and the tidy, I mean the art needle work—put on her bed, and she looked at them the longest while. Her paw would never let the tickets be took off." She reached forth her hand to the chair near her and felt the ticket, stroking it absently, her chin quivering a little, while her lips smiled. "Mr. Gates was thinking," she said, "that maybe you'd paint a head of me—pastel like that landscape—that's why he likes pastel so. And he was thinking if—if maybe—my eyes was jest like Kitty's when we were married—if you would put in eyes, he would be awful much obliged and be willing to pay extra if necessary. Would it be hard?"

Somers dissembled a great dismay. "Certainly not," said he, rather dryly; and he was ashamed of himself at the sensitive flutter in the old features.

"Of course I know," she said, in a different tone than she had used before, "I understand how comical it must seem to a young man to have to draw an old woman's picture; but it ain't comical to my husband. He wants it very much. He's the kindest man that ever lived, to me, caring for me all the time. He's got me that organ—me that can't play a note, and never could—just because I love to hear music, and sometimes if we have an instrument, the neighbors will come in, especially Hattie Knight, who used to know Kittie, and is a splendid performer; she comes and plays and sings. It is a comfort to me. And though I guess you young folks can't understand it, it will be a comfort to him to have a picture of me. I mistrusted you'd be thinking it comical, and I hurried to come in and speak to you, lest, not meaning anything, you might, just by chance, let fall something might hurt his feelings—like you thought it queer or some sech thing. And he thinks so much of you, and having you here, that I couldn't bear there'd be any mistake."

"Surely it is the most natural thing in the world that he should want a portrait of you," Somers hastily interrupted.

"Yes, it is," she answered in her mild, even tones, "but it mightn't seem so to young folks. Young folks think they know all there is about loving. And it is very sweet and nice to enjoy things together; and you don't hardly seem to be in the world at all when you're courting, your feet and your head and your heart feel so light. But they don't know what it is to need each other? It's when folks suffer together that they find out what loving is. I never knew what I felt towards my husband till I lost my first baby; and I'd wake up in the night and there'd be no cradle there—and he'd comfort me. Do you see that picture under the photograph of the cross?"

"He's a pretty boy," said Somers.

"Yes, sir. He was drownded in the river. A lot of boys in playing, and one got too far, and Eddy, he swum out to help him. And he clumb up on Eddy and the man on shore didn't get there in time. He was a real good boy and liked to play home with me 'most as well as with the boys. Father was proud as he could be of him, though he wouldn't let on. That cross was what his schoolmates sent; and teacher she cried when she told me how hard Eddy was trying to win the prize to please his pa. Father and I went through that together. And we had to change all the things we used to talk of together, because Eddy was always in them; and we had to try not to let each other see how our hearts were breaking, and not shadder Kitty's life by letting her see how we missed him. Only once father broke down; it was when he give Kitty Eddy's colt." She stopped, for she could not go on.

"Don't—don't distress yourself," Somers begged lamely. His cheeks were very hot.

"It don't distress me," she answered, "only for the minnit; I'm always thinking of Eddy and Kitty too. Sometimes I think it was harder for father when his girl went than anything else. And then my blindness and my rheumatism come; and it seemed he was trying to make up to me for the daughter and the son I'd lost, and be all to once to me. He has been, too. And do you think that two old people that have grown old together, like us, and have been through losses like that—do you think they ain't drawed closer and kinder and tenderer to each other, like the Lord to his church? Why, I'm plain, and old and blind and crooked—but he don't know it. Now, do you understand?"

"Yes," said Somers, "I understand."

"And you'll please excuse me for speaking so free; it was only so father's feelings shouldn't get hurt by noticing maybe a look like you wanted to laugh."

"God knows I don't want to laugh," Somers burst in. "But I'm glad you spoke. It—it will be a better picture. Now may I ask you something? I want you to let me dress you—I mean put something about your neck, soft and white; and then I want to make two sketches of you—one, as Mr.

Gates wishes, the head alone; the other of you sitting in the rustic chair outside."

"But—" she looked troubled—"it will be so expensive; and I know it will be foolish. If you'd just the same———"

"But I shouldn't; I want to do it. And it will not cost you anything. A hundred dollars will repay me well enough. I wish—I truly wish I could afford to do it all for nothing."

She gasped. "A hundred dollars! Oh, it ain't right. That was why he wouldn't buy the new buggy. And jest for a picture of me." But suddenly she flushed like a girl and smiled.

At this instant the old man, immaculate in his heavy black suit and glossy white shirt, appeared in the doorway bearing a tray.

"Father," said the old wife, "do you mean to tell me you are going to pay a hundred dollars jest for a picture of me?"

"Well, Mother, you know there's no fool like an old fool," he replied, jocosely; but when the old wife turned her sightless face toward the old husband's voice and he looked at her, Somers bowed his head.

He spent the afternoon over his sketches. Riding away in the twilight, he knew he had done better work than he had ever done before in his life, slight as its form might be; nevertheless he was not thinking of himself at all. He was trying to shape his own vague perception that the show of dainty thinking and the pomp of refinement are in truth amiable and lovely things, yet are they no more than the husks of life; not only under them, but under ungracious and sordid conditions, may be the human semblance of that "beauty most ancient, beauty most new," that the old saint found too late. He felt the elusive presence of something in love higher than his youthful dream; stronger than passion, fairer than delight. To this commonplace man and woman had come the deepest gift of life.

"A dream?" he murmured. "Yes, perhaps he has captured it."

"Ding" by Wing

Truth

By Carrie Moss Hawley

The archives of history contain wonderful revelations of the growth and physical development of man. Going back to the beginning of time, when creation donned its immortal robe of life and nature gave utterance to the thought that nothing perishes, we follow down the aisle of centuries until we find ourselves to-day where we realize that thought has become the most powerful factor in advancement. Gradations are everywhere, yet mental processes and volitions take control of the wheel of progress and guide everything with majestic power.

The mind, as we commonly think of it, is not a safe guide unless directed by wisdom. So we appeal for light to give direction to the ideas or conceptions that filter through the brain from the all-holding universal thought. How to distinguish true from false conceptions is the labor of philosophy.

Truth may be tested by one infallible rule: its power to construct. You may see it forming what may terminate in evil, and doing unmistakable harm. Then you say: How can this be truth if it creates disaster? But all that is created does not act one way. There is the gross and the refined, the blemished and the perfect. All is good in the sense that it comes from a perfect law. It is the direction creation takes that determines the outcome.

The next step is how to direct truth that it may produce only the end desired. There are millions of beings on this sphere, each of whom has the same access to truth. Many of these do not even know of their power in production, and, with sensualized vision which has not been renovated, they keep on bringing forth that which another class, further advanced, is endeavoring to exterminate. This will continue indefinitely, for there will always be growing souls that have to learn. Since what appears as evil must exist, when it has become abhorrent to you in all its forms, your privilege and power is to convert all that comes within your radius into what you desire it to be. Minimize your fear of all effects in the negative, and take firm hold of the actual forces and mold them into whatever *you desire*.

Were you a sculptor and had a piece of marble before you, you would not feel obliged to chisel out of it a cat, because a cat chanced to be rubbing her head against your leg in a friendly way. While you would be conscious of the cat she would be something outside the realm of your perceptions when you struck your first blow upon the marble. You would build from your perceptions that have been brought to the foreground by your conceptions of the valuable.

Man must reach a certain plane in his development before he realizes there are things worthless and things of worth, and that he may possess which he will. But when the moral milestone is passed he sees the dawn of a new day that will bring him his hopes realized.

Thus, the way to attain truth is first to see it from the vantage-point that comes through illumination; then realize that the cosmic world possesses all the material you need for its development. What surrounds you that does not appeal to you, merely touches and draws attention to its existence, need come into your creation no more than the cat came into the artist's production.

Work

By Irving N. Brant

Let me once more in Druid forest wander,
To gain its legacy of ancient lore;
Make me its prophet, as I dreamed of yore,
A priest, on holy mysteries to ponder.
Lead me to realms of quiet, or the fonder
Scenes of the rising sea's unruly roar.
Or turn my gaze upon the vistaed floor
Of quiet valleys, and the blue haze yonder
On the opposing hills. Let me traverse
The shadows of man's immemorial mind,
The haunt of fear, joy, sorrow and despair,
God-given wonder and the primal curse.
Within the throbbing heart of humankind
Give me my work, or let me perish there.

Some Magic and a Moral

By Virginia H. Reichard

Along in the early nineties as I was traveling in the West, selling shoes, I left the train at the little junction of Skywaw and surveyed the town. I found that the proverbial hotel, blacksmith shop, general store and a handful of houses, beside the depot, comprised the town.

After supper at the hotel, where I was waited upon by the landlord's pretty daughter, I asked about the storekeeper across the way and found to my surprise that he carried about a ten or twelve thousand dollar general stock which included everything from a sheepskin to a paper of needles. The farming country being so good, it was no wonder that this man did almost as big a business as many others in much larger towns, so the daughter told me, while the landlord himself chipped in with a question: "Why, don't you know this is just the richest spot in Wahoo County? In fact the ground is too rich. Just think of it—too rich to grow pumpkins."

"Why," I asked, "can't you grow pumpkins?"

With a smile of confidence that his joke was entirely new he replied: "The vines grow so fast it drags them over the ground and wears them out. Go up and see the storekeeper and if you sell him you get your money for the goods sure thing, for he sells for cash only."

I picked up my grips and started to see my man at once; found him standing in the door chewing a quid and spitting out into the street at any stray chicken or dog that chanced to wander by. As he stood there indifferent, expressionless, he looked the typical Westerner, with an air of "do as you darn please" about him; pants tucked into a pair of boots that were run over and worn off at the toe in a peculiar way that would indicate to a shoeologist that he was a sharp, keen trader, very suspicious of strangers, hard to strike a trade with unless he could see a hundred per cent in it for himself. In early days he had been a horse trader and a dealer in buffalo hides, and had never seen the time when he couldn't tell what o'clock it was better by the sun than by a watch; a hard man to approach on the shoe subject as his mind didn't seem to hover around shoes.

There must have been a depression in his skull where his bump of order was supposed to be, as from the general appearance it looked as if the devil had held an auction there the day before. I began my little "spiel" by telling my business—who I was, where I was from—and asked if my conversation would interest him at all if I talked about shoes for awhile, remarking incidentally: "You'll have some business now sure. Trade will get good right away, as I never opened up my samples in a man's store in my life but what customers came dropping in."

"Well, then, for God's sake open them up. I need the business all right enough," quoth he.

Then strange to say, as if to cinch what I had said, up rode six country boys on horseback, and in a minute the big strapping fellows came tramping in. You know the kind that work on a farm all day, ride to town to buy one pound of sugar for family use and ten pounds of chewing tobacco for their own use, and other articles in like proportion while they are having a good time.

Taking seats on the counter opposite, they began a lot of loud talking.

One picked up a turnip and began peeling it, poising it on the tip of his knife-blade, taking large bites, and never for a minute losing sight of what we were doing in the shoe line.

It took a lot of persuading to get the proprietor to look at my samples, but I soon noticed the shrewd gleam of his eyes that told that he had had hold of good leather before and was a much better judge of my line than I expected to find in such a place. But talk about exhorting! How I worked with that fellow. And after keeping it up for two whole hours—from seven until nine, I finally landed him, selling him a little over five hundred dollars' worth of shoes. As I was getting a straight eight per cent commission at that time, the sale made me a little over forty dollars for two hours' work, and I was feeling mighty good. Even my cold-blooded customer had warmed up some from the effects of the deal on which he saw he was bound to make a good thing.

While I was packing up my samples he said, sort of edging around: "Say, can't you sing us a song or dance us a jig or do something to entertain us all? You travelin' fellers allus know somethin' new, and are up to whatever is goin' on over the country, ain't ye?"

I replied: "I can't sing; I am out of voice; but if you can furnish the music I can dance a jig or clog. Oh, by the way, did you ever see any sleight of hand or legerdemain tricks?"

None of them ever had; didn't even know what they were, and solemnly assured me they were something new in that burg.

As I had been practicing coin tricks and other feats of sleight of hand for the last ten years and could do many of the former, making the coins appear and disappear at will in a mysterious manner, I decided to try this form of amusement, thinking I had an easy bunch to work on. So I showed them a silver dollar, giving it to one of them to examine, passing it on to each one of them in succession, just to show them that it was a genuine, everyday piece. Then taking it in my hand, I proceeded to manipulate the coin by picking it out from underneath one fellow's foot as he sat on the counter dangling his long legs; taking it from another fellow's chin; picking it out from the pocket of the jumper one of them had on; finding it in the next man's ear; and finally, coming to the proprietor, I told him to hold his thumb and finger together, pointing up; then took the coin from between his own thumb and finger without his realizing how it got there or how it got away. I caught his startled look—the fellows jumped down off the counter and crowded close together—wonder and amazement written all over them. This was the first time in their lives they had ever seen a sleight of hand trick, where the motion of the hand is so quick the sight cannot follow it.

But presto, chango, begono, magico, came near being too much for them. They were absolutely horror stricken. Some of them were unable to speak; some were afraid to; others couldn't speak above a whisper; and one of these desired to know when I would be back in that country again. He wanted Brother Bill to see it; in fact he would like to bring the whole family in.

The proprietor's face was a study. Doubt, surprise and suspicion passed over his face in succession, but gave way to fresh curiosity when I asked him to bring me two hats and I would do Hermann's parlor trick with two hats and four balls. The method of doing this is to place the four balls in a square about three feet apart on a counter or a table, then place the hats over two of the balls; the object being to find all four balls under one hat, without, of course, anybody seeing how they got there. This I accomplished successfully, and this performance seemed to bring them close to the limit. They had been craning their necks to see, but when it was over they all straightened up, took a step backward in line and looked at one another. Then one of them said solemnly:

"Folks is gettin' geniuser and geniuser every day, boys. Ain't it so?" And Pete nudged Jim to make sure it was no dream, then spat excitedly on the rusty stove.

The proprietor had been eyeing me with suspicion for a good while. I noticed whenever I would pass in front of him he would step back and plant his hands tight on his pockets where he kept his money, as if he thought I might somehow coax it to jump out unless he held it in by main force. Legerdemain had scared him some and made him both suspicious and wary.

Pretty soon I began to realize I had done a little too much; in fact, I had given them a little more than they had been able to digest. But like many another fool who has overstepped, I tried to make up by giving them something in another line.

The proprietor looked up with a distrustful glance. "Is that all you can do?"

"That's all in the trick line, gentlemen. But I have something that I can do that is out of the line of tricks. It's a gift—mind-reading. Only about one in six millions has it. I do the same as Brown, Johnson or Bishop—those big guns you have heard about—in finding any given object. And if you, sir (to the proprietor), will place your mind on any one of the ten thousand articles in this store, concentrating your mind on it, I will get the object you are thinking about and hand it to you."

"You can't do that; it ain't possible," he said.

One of the boys spoke up: "Aw, let him try, Dan. Gosh! Let him try."

After looking around the store and meditating a little he said: "Durn it all, then, go ahead. I've picked out the thing I want you to get and by jigger I'll keep my mind on it all right."

Taking his hand, placing it upon my forehead, and holding it there with one of mine, I started down the store, the other six rubbering after us with all their might. After going about thirty feet with an occasional kick or bump at a basket or barrel that happened to be in the way, I turned to the left; stopping at the show-case, and sliding back the doors, I reached in, picked up a razor—his own razor—that lay in the case and handed it to him.

"Great Scott," he yelled. "The very razor I shave myself with—when I shave; and that's the very thing I had my mind on too, by thunder." The sweat stood out in great drops on his forehead and for a few minutes his emotion seemed to be too much for him. So I said:

"Well, boys, this concludes the evening's performance; meeting's out, boys."

Dazed with wonder, the six riders looked blankly at each other, turned to me grinning foolishly, then filed out, jumped on their horses and galloped away, whooping like Comanche Indians.

Bidding the proprietor good night I started for the door.

"Hold on a minute!" he cried. "I want to see you, young feller." He strode up to within about two feet of me, hands thrust deep in his pockets, looking as if he would like to fight. Then he burst out with:

"Say, you're about the slickest thing I ever saw in my life, ain't you? You're durned slick. You're smooth—a little too smooth; and you hear me, you needn't send them goods I bought to-night. I won't take 'em."

"What!" I cried.

"You hear me; you needn't send 'em. I won't take the goods," he said in a tone there was no mistaking.

I commenced to argue. But no. "You've done killed yourself with me," was all I could get out of him, and nothing I could say or do would make any difference. But I was bound not to lose the forty dollars without a struggle and brought all the arts, arguments and persuasions to bear that I could think of; but without avail. He seemed to be convinced that if I wasn't the devil himself, at least I was a near relation, and he would have none of me.

Then I did what I never had done before: took the dollar and carefully showed him just how I had done the trick, explaining that sight was really slower than motion sometimes and that the whole thing was intended to be harmless and amusing.

"If that's the way you did with the money, how about the four-ball trick?" he asked gruffly.

Still bent upon making the proposition stick, I explained the ball trick too, by going over it and explaining how the eye could be deceived. You see, I was growing more and more anxious all the time to cinch my commission, and felt that my efforts were worth while. When suddenly, dubious and still unconvinced, he turned to me and asked:

"Well, how in time did you find the razor?"

"I was very particular to tell you," I said, "before I went after that razor that it wasn't a trick. It's a gift I can't explain; nobody can; nobody ever did. I can't do it; I don't know how or why. Some call it mind-reading and some people have been kept guessing to give it a name. I am one of the few who can do it, that's all. When I went after the article you had in mind, I didn't know it was a razor; I didn't know what it was; but when I came in contact with what you had in mind I picked it up and handed it to you. This is my explanation—the only one I can give. I call it 'mind-reading,' that's all."

After some more talk I left him mystified and distrustful, in spite of all I had said and done, still refusing to reinstate the order. I left my grips in the store as it was near the station, and went to the hotel to spend a restless night, kicking myself for a fool meanwhile, since my attempts to amuse had lost me the neat little sum of forty dollars.

I slept a couple of hours when I was awakened by the most horrible noise it was ever my fortune to hear: Two car-loads of calves, just a day away from their mothers, were being shipped and their bawling was intolerable. Talk about your quiet country towns for rest and sleep! No more for me that night, I thought. So I dressed, took a smoke, and decided to tackle my man again in the morning and to try to change his mind.

A little after daylight I saw him sweeping the sidewalk in front of the door, handling the broom as a man does a flail on the barn floor. I went over and said: "Good morning." As he looked up I saw that his glance was as surly and suspicious as it had been the night before, but thought I would make a good start by approaching him upon some of his hobbies the landlord had told me about. In his capacity as horse trader he prided himself on his ability to judge a good horse. So I opened up by telling him about a horse I owned, and asked if he had anything to trade for him. This seemed to bring the right twinkle into his eye, and he began to brace up and take notice a little. So I talked on until I saw the smoke of the approaching train away down the valley seven or eight miles along the old Kantopey trail. Then I made a last attempt.

"Now see here, Mister," I said, "I came into your store last night and showed you my samples, showed you the names of some of the best merchants who have bought big bills of me and I sold you a bill of goods in good faith. Then you proposed that I entertain you as you had very little amusement in a place like this. I told you I couldn't sing but would do what I could with such sleight of hand tricks as I knew, and I did exactly what I said I would. It seemed to meet with plenty of approval all around until the mind-reading came up, when you turned me down for no reason whatever. Now, I ask you a question: Is that a square deal to a man on a business proposition?"

He looked at the floor and was silent, though apparently a little uneasy. He shook his head doubtfully, which made me feel that he was perhaps not so unfriendly after all, and might possibly do the right thing yet. Hearing the distant whistle, I said:

"Train's coming; have to go. Wish you good luck, just the same as if you'd treated me square. Wish you good crops and plenty of water for your stock. As long as you live don't turn another fellow down like you have me, just because he's done his best to give you a good time." And I made a rush for the depot to check my baggage.

The train came in; there was the usual hurry and noise. The old fellow stood there, leaning against the weather-boarding of the depot like a picture of Uncle Sam—a queer, awkward figure with his hay-colored whiskers, pipe in the corner of his mouth, and hands still planted firmly in his pockets, his eyes riveted on every move I made.

I boarded the train, said "Howdy" to a friend, and looking back saw old Dan standing where I had left him as if glued to the spot. The engine puffed and snorted; the wheels began to go around. "Good-bye," I shouted from the platform as if answering his steady gaze.

All of a sudden the long, gaunt figure limbered up, like a corpse that had been touched by a galvanic battery. He came chasing down the track after the train, waving his arms like a windmill and yelling like Bedlam let loose: "Hey! Say there, you young feller; hey there! I'll take them goods; send 'em along. I'll take them goods. D'ye hear?"

And I called back to him with great gusto: "All right," as the train rounded a curve.

Moral: When you have sold your goods make your get-away.

Sonny's Wish

By Bertha M. H. Shambaugh

Sometimes before I go to bed
I 'member things that Grandpa said
When I sat close beside his knee
And Grandpa laid his hand on me.

I 'member how he'd smile and say,
"Well, what did Sonny do to-day?"
'Cause Grandpa always liked to know
(I s'pose that's why I miss him so).

I never had to coax and plead
For things I really didn't need:
I'd 'splain it in an off-hand way
And Grandpa brought it home next day.

When I grow up I'd like to be
A grandpa with a boy like me
To live with and to bring things to:
That's what I'd like the *most* to do.

I'd rummage 'round and hunt about
For things the boy could do without,
Because you see of course I'd know
That's why the boy would like them so.

And when I'd bring some brand new toy
And someone said, "You'll spoil that boy!"
I'd only shake my head and say,

"A *good boy* isn't spoiled that way."

When Sonny said he'd like to get
A nice wee doggie for a pet,
And when the grown-ups one and all
Said, "Oh, no, Son! You're much too small,"

I'd whisper, "Come, don't look so blue
'Cause Grandpa bought a dog for you,
A birthday present! Schh! Don't cry!
He's black and just about *so* high."

Oh, yes! I'm sure I'd like to be
A grandpa with a boy like me
To live with and to bring things to:
That's what I'd like the *most* to do.

Dog

By Edwin L. Sabin

The dog we have always with us; if not active in the garden or passive on the best bed, then gracing or disgracing himself in other domestic capacities. For the dog is a curious combination, wherein heredity constantly opposes culture; and therefore though your dog be a woolly dog or a smooth dog, a large dog or a small dog, a house-dog, yard-dog, hunting-dog or farm-dog, he will be ever a delight and a scandal according as he reveals the complexities of his character. Just as soon as you have decided that he is almost human, he will straightway unmistakably indicate that he is still very much dog.

As example, select, if you please, the most pampered and carefully nurtured dog in dog tribe: some lady's dog—beribboned King Charles, bejeweled poodle, befatted pug—and give him the luxury of a half-hour in the nearest genuine alley. Do you think that he turns up his delicate nose at the luscious smells there encountered? Do you think that because of his repeated scented baths he sedulously keeps to the middle of the narrow way? Do you venture to assert that he whose jaded palate has recently declined the breast of chicken is now nauseated by the prodigal waste encountered amidst the garbage cans?

Fie on him, the ingrate! Why, the little rascal fairly revels in the riot of débris, and ten to one he will even proudly return lugging the most unsavoury of bones filched from a particularly odorous repository! His lapse into atavism has been prompt and certain. I agree with Robert Louis Stevenson that every dog is a vagabond at heart; in adapting himself to the companionship of man and woman, and the comforts of board and lodging, he leads a double life.

In this respect the dog is far more servile than the cat, his contemporary. Generations of attempted coercion have little influenced the cat. She (it seems a proper distinction to speak of the cat as "she") steadfastly maintains the distance that shall divide cat life from man life. Without duress, and in spite of duress, she accepts the material favors of civilization and domesticity only to an extent that will not inconvenience her; she has no notion of responsibilities or indebtedness. Having achieved her demands for a warm nap or a full stomach, she then makes no false motions in following her own inclinations entirely. But the dog, occupying a limbo between his natural instincts and his acquired conscience, must always be a master of duplicity.

The dog (as again points out the admirable Stevenson) has become an accomplished actor. Observe his ceremonious approach to other dogs. Mark the mutual dignity, the stiff-leggedness, the self-conscious strut, the rivalrous emulation, all of which plainly says: "I am *Mister* So-and-So; who in the deuce are you?" No dog so small, and only a few faint-hearts so squalid, that they do not carry a chip on their shoulder. Compare with their progenitors, the wolves in a city park. Here encounters are quick and decisive. The one wolf stands, the other cringes. Rank and character are recognized at once. The pretences of human society have not perverted wolf ethics.

Take a dog at his tricks: not the game of seeking and fetching, which he enjoys when in good humor, but parlor tricks. He has learned through fear of punishment and hope of reward. Having performed, either sheepishly or promptly, with what wrigglings and prancings and waggings, or else with what proud self-appreciation does he court approval. He knows very well that he is assuming not to be a dog, and trusts that you will admit he is smarter than mere dog. On the contrary, the cat tribe, jumping through a hoop, does it with a negligent, spontaneous grace that makes the act a condescension. The cat does not aspire to be human; she is fully content with being cat.

Elevate a dog to a seat in an automobile (any automobile), or even to the box of a rattle-trap farm-wagon. How it affects him, this promotion from walking to riding! It metamorphoses the meekest, humblest of so-called curs into a grandee aristocrat, who by supercilious look and offensive words insults every other dog that he passes. He calls upon the world about to witness that he is of man-kind, not of dog-kind. A dog riding abroad is to me the epitome of satisfied assumption.

It would be interesting to know how much, if any, the dog's brain has been increased by constant efforts to be humanized. The Boston bull is, I should judge, (and of course!) faster in his intellectual activities than is the ordinary English bull. And then I might refer to the truly marvelous feats of the sheep-dog, who will, when told, cut out any one sheep in a thousand; and I might refer to the finely bred setter, or pointer, and his almost human field work; and I can refer to my own dog, whose smartness, both natural and acquired, generally is extraordinary—although at times woefully askew, as when he buries pancakes in the fall expecting, if we may believe that he expects, to dig them up during the winter.

And there are dogs with great souls and dogs with small souls. We are told of dogs noble enough to sit by and let a needy dog gobble the meal from the platter—but I suspect that such dogs are complacent because comfortably fixed. We hear of dogs making valiant defenses of life and property—which perhaps is the development of the animal instinct to guard anything which the animal considers its own. And dogs sometimes effect heroic rescues, by orders or voluntarily—although one may query whether they consider all the consequences.

The dog's brain must be an oddly struggling mass of fact and fancy. We have done our best for him, and as a rule he creditably responds. I love my dog; he appears to love me; and by efforts of me and mine he has been humanized into a very adaptable personage. But I am certain that first principles remain the same with him as when he was a wolf-dog of cave age. He might grab me by the collar and swim ashore with me, but if on the desert island there was only one piece of meat between us and starvation, and he had it, I'd hate to have to risk getting my share without fighting for it.

The Unredeemed

THE BALLAD OF THE LUSITANIA BABES

By Emerson Hough

THE HOLY THREE BEHOLD

God the Father leaned out from Heaven,

His white beard swept His knee;

His eye was sad as He looked far out,

Full on the face of the sea.

Saith God the Father, "In My Kingdom

Never was thing like this;

For yonder are sinless unredeemed,

And they may not enter Our bliss."

And Mary the Mother, She stood near by,

Her eyes full sad and grieved.

Saith Mary the Mother, "Alas! Alas!

That they may not be received.

Now never since Heaven began," saith She,

"Hath sight like this meseemed,

That there be sinless dead below
Who may not be redeemed!"

And Jesu, the Saviour, He stood also,
And aye! His eyes were wet.
Saith Jesu the Saviour, "Since Time began,
Never was this thing yet!
For these be the Children, the Little Ones,
Afloat on the icy sea.
They are doomed, they are dead, they are perished,
And they may not come unto Me!"

THE CHILDREN CRY OUT

They float, forever unburied,
Their faces turned to the sky;
With their little hands uplifted,
And their lips forever cry:

"Oh, we are the helpless murdered ones,
Blown far on the icy tide!
No sin was ours, but through all the days,
On the northern seas we ride.
No cerements ever enshroud us,
We know no roof of the sod;
We float forever unburied,
With our faces turned to God.

"So foul the deed that undid us,
So damned in its dull disgrace,
That even the sea refused us,
And would not give us place.

Nor ever a place in the sky—
We are lost, we are dead, we are perished,
Ah, Jesu, tell us why!"

*   *   *   *   *

Now the Three who heard They wept as one,
But Their tears they might not cease.
Saith God the Father, "While unavenged
These may not know Our peace!
When the sons of men are men again,
And have smitten full with the sword,
At last these sinless but unredeemed
Shall enter unto their Lord.

"But deed like this is a common debt;
It lies on the earth-race whole.
Till these be avenged they be unredeemed—
Each piteous infant soul.
We must weep, We must weep, till the debt be paid,
Te debt of the sons of men—
But well avenged, they are aye redeemed;
Ah, how shall We welcome them then!"

THE SONS OF MEN HEARKEN

Are ye worth the kiss of a woman?
Were ye worth the roof of a womb?
Are ye worth the price of your grave-clothes?
Are ye worth the name on a tomb?

Nay! None of these is your earning,
And none of these be your meed,

If the deathless wail of their yearning
Shall add to your pulse no speed.

Never by hand of a warrior,
Never by act of a man,
Have the Little Ones thus perished,
Since ever that Heaven began.
Such deed and the beings who wrought it—
Ah! deep must the cutting go
To cure the world of the memory
Of the Little Ones in woe.

The Three watch high in Their Heaven,
And aye! the Three be grieved;
The sword is the key of Their Heaven,
If the babes shall be received.

Rise then, men of our banner—
Speak in our ancient tone—
Each of you for his mother,
Each of you for his own!
Smite full and fell and fearless,
Till that these be set free—
These, slain of the foulest slaying
That ever made red the sea.

The sword of the Great Avenger
Is now for the sons of men;
It must redden in errand holy
Till the babes be cradled again.

Copyrighted, 1917, by Emerson Hough

Tinkling Cymbals

By Helen Sherman Griffith

It was in the spring of 1915 that Margaret Durant came back to her home in Greenfield, Iowa, from a visit to friends in the East, and brought with her a clear, shining flame of patriotism, with which she proceeded to fire the town. Margaret had always been a leader, the foremost in civic betterment, in government reform, and in the activities of her church and woman's club. She was a born orator, and loved nothing better than haranguing—and swaying—a crowd.

A fund was started for the purchase of an ambulance, which, Margaret insisted, must be driven by a Greenfield man. And she expressed sorrow on every occasion—particularly in the hearing of the mothers of young men—that she had no son to offer. The Red Cross rooms became the centre of Greenfield social activity, and the young people never dreamed of giving an entertainment for any purpose save to benefit the Red Cross, the British Relief or the Lafayette Fund. This last became presently the object of Margaret's special activities, since her husband, Paul, some four generations previously, had come of French blood. "So that it is almost like working for my own country," Margaret said proudly. And she glowed with gratification whenever the French were praised.

So complete and self-sacrificing was her enthusiasm that she announced, as the spring advanced, her intention of taking no summer vacation, but to dedicate the money thus saved to the Lafayette Fund, and to work for that organization during the entire summer.

Her friends were thrilled with admiration at Margaret's attitude, and some of them emulated her heroic example. To be sure, staying at home that summer was a popular form of self-denial, since a good many families, even in Greenfield, Iowa, were beginning to feel the pinch of war.

One summer afternoon, Margaret strolled home from an animated meeting of the Lafayette Fund, exalted and tingling with emotion. She had addressed the meeting, and her speech had been declared the epitome of all that was splendid and noble. She had moved even herself to tears by her appeal for patriotism. She entered the house, still mentally enshrouded by intoxicating murmurs of "Isn't she wonderful!" "Doesn't she make you wish you were a man, to go yourself!" and so forth.

Softly humming the Marseillaise, she mounted the steps to her own room, to remove her hat. She stopped short on the threshhold with a sudden startled cry. Her husband was there, walking up and down the room, and also humming the Marseillaise. It was half an hour before his usual homecoming time, but that was not why Margaret cried out.

Paul was dressed in khaki! He was walking up and down in front of the cheval glass, taking in the effect from different angles. He looked around foolishly when he heard his wife.

"Just trying it on," he said lightly. "How do you like me?"

"But Paul—what—what does it *mean?*"

"Just what you have guessed. I've signed up. I'm to drive the Greenfield ambulance," he added with justifiable pride.

Margaret stared, gasped, tottered. She would have fallen if she had not sat down suddenly. Paul stared, too, astonished.

"Why, old girl, I thought it was what you wanted! I—you said——"

"Paul, Paul! You! It can't be! Why—why, you are all I have!"

"That is one reason the more for my going—we have no son to send."

"But Paul—it—I—the war is so far away! It isn't as if—as if we were at war."

"Almost—'France is the land of my ancestors'—your very words, Margaret."

"I know, but——"

"'And the cause is so just.'"

"But, Paul, I did not mean——"

"Did not mean what!" Paul turned and faced her sternly. "Margaret, your eloquence has sent a good many young men to the front. I wonder—" He paused, and a new expression dawned in his eyes; an expression that Margaret could not bear: an accusation, a suspicion.

Margaret cowered in her chair and hid her face.

"Oh, Paul, not that, not that! Leave me a moment, please. I—I want time to—to grasp it."

When she was alone she sat upright and faced the look she had seen in Paul's eyes.

"I am a canting hypocrite. I see it now, plainly. I read it in Paul's eyes. But I will show him he's mistaken. God! is hypocrisy always so cruelly punished? Merciful God, have pity upon me!"

Rising to her feet, Margaret staggered to the door and called. The enthusiasm, the exaltation, had faded from her face, leaving it pinched and gray. But in her eyes a new expression had been born, which lent a soft radiance to her features, the light of complete self-denial. Paul entered, gave one look, then knelt at his wife's feet.

"Forgive me, my love, for misunderstanding you. The fault was mine. You've been afraid I would not make good, and were testing me. Ah, my love."

For one terrible moment Margaret hesitated. Then she whispered:

"No, Paul, you were right at first; but love has conquered. Not *our* love, but a greater, nobler sentiment: love of Right and Justice. Do you remember the verse: 'Though I speak with the tongues of men and of angels, and have not love, I am become as sounding brass or a tinkling cymbal.' I—I am *not* a tinkling cymbal, Paul. I—Oh, Paul, take me with you! I can be of some use over there. We will go together."

Paul rose and embraced her.

"My precious one! How Greenfield will honor you!"

Margaret winced and hid her face in his breast.

"No, Paul, no, no. Don't let them know! Let us go away quietly, in the night. Please, please, Paul. I—I could not bear any other way!"

Durant kissed her and said no more. And if he understood, he never let her know that he did.

The First Laugh

By Reuben F. Place

In the life of every baby there is a continuous succession of first impressions and adventures. The first tooth, the first crawl, the first step, the first word, each mark a milestone in the child's career. But more interesting than any of these is the first laugh—the first genuine, sustained, prolonged, whole-hearted laugh. If it is a tinkling, bubbling, echoing laugh, it sends its merry waves in all directions—the kind that brings smiles to sober faces.

What hope springs up in the parents' breasts at the sound of that first laugh! How thoroughly it denotes the future!

A hearty laugh or no laugh in later years may mean the difference between fame and obscurity, fortune and poverty, friends and enemies.

"How much lies in laughter: the cipher key, wherewith we decipher the whole man!" wrote Carlyle.

A good laugh is a charming, invaluable attribute. It saves the day, maintains the health, makes friends, soothes injured feelings, and saves big situations.

Laughter is a distinguishing mark between man and beast. It is the sign of character and the mirror in which is reflected disposition.

To laugh is to live.

The babe's first laugh is a precious family memory. A load of responsibility goes with it. It should be guarded and guided and cultivated until it becomes "Laughter that opens the lips and heart, that shows at the same time pearls and the soul."

The Freighter's Dream

By Ida M. Huntington

"Squeak! Squ-e-a-k! Scr-e-e-ch!" The shrill, monotonous sound rent the hot noontide air like a wail of complaint.

"Thar she goes ag'in, a-cussin' of her driver!" grumbled old Hi, as he walked at the head of his lead oxen, Poly and Bony, with Buck and Berry panting behind them. "Jest listen at her! An' 'twas only day afore yistiddy that I put in a hull half hour a-greasin of her. Wal, she'll hev to fuss till mornin'. We ain't got no time to stop a minute in this hot place. If we make the springs afore the beasteses gin out 'twill be more'n I look fer!"

Old Hi anxiously gazed ahead, trying to see through the shimmering haze of the desert the far-distant little spot of ground where bubbled up the precious spring by which they might halt for rest and refreshment. "G'lang, Poly! That's right, Bony! Keep it up, ol' fellers!" Hi strove to encourage the patient oxen as they plodded wearily along through the fearful heat and the suffocating clouds of fine alkali dust.

For weeks the long train of covered wagons had moved steadily westward over the dim trails. Starting away back in Ohio, loaded with necessities for the prospectors in the far West, they had crossed the fertile prairies, stuck in the muddy sloughs, forded the swollen rivers, rumbled over the plains and wound in and out the mountain passes. Now they were crawling over the desert, man and beast almost exhausted, even the seasoned wagons seeming to protest against the strain put upon them.

All that afternoon Hi walked with his oxen, talking and whistling, as much to keep up his own courage as to quicken their pace. For a few moments at a time they would rest, and then onward again towards the springs indicated on the map by which they traveled.

Half blind and dizzy from the dust and heat, sometimes Hi stumbled and staggered and nearly fell. He dared not turn to see how it fared with the men and teams behind him. Wrecks of wagons and bones of oxen by the side of the trail told an all-too-plain story. Some there were in every train who dropped by the way; men who raved in fever and died calling for water; faithful oxen who were shot to put them out of misery. Wagons were abandoned with their valuable freight when the teams could no longer pull them.

All afternoon they crept forward; the reiterating "Squeak! Squ-e-a-k! Scr-e-e-ch!" of the wagon sounded like a maddened human voice to poor Hi, fevered and half delirious.

At last the sun sank like a ball of fire in the haze. A cool breath of air sighed across the plain. The prairie dogs barked from their burrows. The coyotes yapped in the distance. But not yet could the long train stop, for rest without water meant death.

Far into the night the white-topped wagons crept on like specters. No sound was heard except that of the plodding feet of the oxen, the rumble of the heavy wagons and the "Squeak! Squ-e-a-k! Scr-e-e-ch!" that had troubled Hi since noon. Suddenly the oxen lifted their heads, sniffed the air eagerly, and without urging quickened their pace.

"What is it, ol' fellers?" asked Hi, as hope revived. "Is it the water ye are smellin'? Stiddy, thar! Stiddy!"

A few moments more, and Hi gave a shout of joy that was taken up and sounded down the line. "The spring! The spring!"

A halt was made. Every drop of the precious water was carefully portioned out so that each might have his share. Preparations were made for the night. The wagons were pulled up in a circle. The oxen were carefully secured that they might not wander away. Here and there a flickering little fire was seen as the scanty "grub" was cooked. After Hi had bolted his share he wrapped himself in his blanket and lay down near his wagon. The large white top loomed dimly before him in the darkness.

A little while he stretched and twisted and turned uneasily until his tired muscles relaxed. In his ears yet seemed to sound the "Squeak! Squ-e-a-k! Scr-e-e-ch!" of the complaining wagon as it had bothered him all afternoon. "Darn ye! Won't ye ever shet up?" he muttered as he drifted off to sleep.

"Won't I ever shet up? I won't till I git good and ready!" The sharp, shrill voice made Hi open his eyes with a start. Above him leaned the huge form of an old woman in a white cap drawn close about her wrinkled, seamed face, only partly distinguishable in the darkness. As he lay blinking, trying to see her more plainly, the high falsetto voice continued its plaint.

"Won't I ever shet up? A nice way thet is to talk to me, Hi Smith! Do I iver grumble and snarl when ye treat me right? Hain't I been faithful to ye through thick an' thin? Hain't I made a home fer ye all this hull endurin' trip? Hain't I looked after yer grub and yer blankets and done ever'thin' I could to make ye comfortable? Hain't I kep' the rain offen ye at night? An' thet time the Injuns was after ye, didn't I stand atween ye an' the redskins and pertect ye? Didn't I keep ye from gittin' drownded when ye crossed thet river whar the current swep' the beasteses offen their feet? Didn't I watch over ye and shield ye from the sun when ye lay sick of the fever and hadn't nary wife to look after ye? Hain't I follered after them dumb beasteses through mud and water and over gravel and through clouds of alkali dust thick enough to choke a person, and niver said a word? An' now, jest bekase I'm fair swizzled up with the heat and ye fergit to give me some grease to rub on my achin' j'ints, ye cuss me! Yis, I heerd ye! Ye needn't deny it! A-cussin' of me who has taken the place of home an' mother to ye fer years! I heerd ye! I he-e-rd ye! What d'ye mean, I say!" And the tirade ended in a perfect screech of anger.

Thoroughly aroused, Hi rolled over and jumped hastily to his feet. He looked all around. The old woman had mysteriously vanished. A coyotte sneaked past him. Day was breaking in the east. The first gleam of light fell on the white-topped wagon drawn up beside him.

He rubbed his eyes. "Wal, I swan!" he muttered, as he gazed bewilderedly at the close-drawn white top looming above him. "Glad I woke up airly! I'll hev time ter grease that thar wagon afore we start!"

A Box From Home

By Helen Cowles LeCron

I'll send to you in France, my dear,
A box with treasures in it:
The patch of sky that meets our hill
And changes every minute,
The grape-vine that you taught to grow—
My pansies young with dew,
The plum-tree by the kitchen door—
These things I'll send to you.

I'll pack with care our fragile dawn—
The dawn we laughed to greet;
I'll send the comfort of the grass
That once caressed your feet.
No yearning love of mine I'll send
To tear your heart in two—
Just earth-peace—home-peace—still and strong—
These things I'll send to you.

For you must tire of flags, and guns,
And courage high, and pain,
And long to rest your heart upon
The common things again,
And so I'll send no prayers, no tears,
No longings—only dew
And garden-rows, and goldenrod
And country roads to you!

Since life has given you to know
The gentle tenderness
Of growing things, I cannot think
That death would give you less!
Hold fast, hold fast within your heart
The earth-sweet hours we knew,
And keep, my dear, where'er you are
These things I send to you.

The Spirit of Spring

By Laura L. Hinkley

Margaret Hazeltine sat on her porch with the spring wind blowing over her elusive wafts of fragrance—plum-blossom, apple-blossom, young grass, budding wood scents, pure, growing earth-smells.

"It is like breathing poetry," Margaret thought.

She was sewing, but now and then her hands fell in her lap while she lifted her head, catching in some wandering sweetness with a sharp breath, like a sigh.

It was four o'clock in the afternoon. Sunshine mellowed the new greenness of short, tender grass on the lawns. It shone upon all the bare, budded branches up and down the street, seeking, caressing, stimulating. It lay kindly, genially, on the mid-road dust.

Margaret's father was pottering about the garden. He was a very old man, with stooping shoulders, but tall and slender like his daughter. He came up to the porch and stood leaning on his hoe. The wind fluttered his shabby garden-coat and thin, white beard. He rested his wrinkled old hands on the top of his hoe handle, and cast up his faded, sunken eyes to the intense young blue of the sky with its fleecy clouds floating.

Mr. Hazeltine addressed his daughter in the strain of conversational piety habitual with him, and in a voice which age and earnestness made tremulous:

"Seems like every spring I get more certain of my eternal home up yonder!"

Margaret smiled acquiescently. Long since she had silently drifted outside the zone of her father's simple, rigid creed; but to-day its bald egoism did not repel her. It seemed at one with the sweet will to live all about them.

Mr. Hazeltine went back to the garden. A girl appeared on the porch of the house opposite. The Hazeltine house was small and old and not lately painted. The house opposite was large, fresh, trim, and commodious in every visible detail. White cement walks enclosed and divided its neatly kept lawns and parking. Its fruit-trees breathed out of the unfolding whiteness of their bosoms the sweetest of those perfumes that drifted across to Margaret. The girl on the porch pushed the wicker chairs about for a moment, then, disdaining them all, sat down on the cement steps and rested her chin in her palm.

After a quick look and smile Margaret sewed busily, affecting not to see the other. She felt a little sympathetic flutter of pleasure and suspense. "Jean is waiting for Frank," she said to herself.

A piano began to play in a house up the street. Through the open windows rang joyous, vibrant music. White moths fluttered across the street and the lawn and parking opposite, veering vaguely over scattered yellow dandelion heads. Around the house opposite on the cement walk strutted a very young kitten on soft paws, its short tail sticking straight up, its gray coat still rough from its mother's tongue.

"Me-ow!" said the kitten plaintively, appalled at its own daring.

Jean sprang up, laughing, snatched up the kitten and carried it back to her seat, cuddling it under her chin.

Down the street came a young girl wheeling a baby's cab. The girl was but just past childhood, and she had been a homely child. But of late she had bloomed as mysteriously and almost as quickly as the plum-trees. She wore a light summer dress with a leaf-brown design upon it, in which her girlish form still half-confessed the child. Her complexion was clear and bright, the cheeks flushed; and the strongly-marked features seemed ready to melt and fuse to a softer mould. Her brown eyes had grown wistful and winning.

As they advanced, Margaret ran down the rickety wooden walk.

"Oh, is that the new baby?" she cried delightedly. "May I look?"

The girl smiled assent.

Softly Margaret drew back the woolly carriage robe and gazed adoringly. The baby was about six weeks old. Its tiny face was translucent, pinky white, the closed eyelids with their fringe of fine lashes inconceivably delicate. Its wee hands cuddled about its head; the curled, pink fingers, each tipped with its infinitesimal, dainty nail, were perfection in miniature. The formless mouth, pinker than the rest of the face, moved in sleep, betraying the one dream the baby knew.

Margaret drew a long, still breath of rapture, hanging over the little pink pearl of humanity.

"Will he wake if I kiss him?" she pleaded.

The girl smiled doubtfully. "Maybe," she said.

She was equally indifferent to the baby and to Margaret. Her wistful eyes wandered eagerly down the street, watching each sidewalk, and the glow in her cheeks and eyes seemed to kindle and waver momently.

Margaret did not kiss the baby. She only bent her head close over his, close enough to feel his warm, quick breathing, to catch the rhythm of his palpitating little life.

When she came back to her porch, after the girl had gone on, Margaret saw that Jean's caller had come.

The young man sat beside Jean. His head was bare, his black hair brushed stiffly up from his forehead pompadour-fashion, his new spring suit palpably in its original creases. He and Jean talked eagerly, sometimes with shouts of young laughter, at which Margaret smiled sympathetically; sometimes with swift, earnest interchange; sometimes with lazy, contented intervals of silence. Occasionally he put out his hand to pat or tease the kitten which lay in Jean's lap. She defended it. Whenever their fingers chanced to touch they started consciously apart—covertly to tempt the chance again.

Two little girls came skipping down the street, their white dresses tossed about their knees. Their loose hair, of the dusky fairness of brunette children, tossed about their shoulders and an immense white ribbon bow quivered on the top of each little bare head. Their dress and their dancing run gave them the look and the wavering allure of butterflies.

They were on Jean's side of the street. They fluttered past the house unnoticed by the two on the porch, who were in the midst of an especially interesting quarrel about the kitten. The little girls passed over the crossing with traces of conscientious care for their white slippers, and came up on Margaret's side. Opposite her they paused in consultation.

"Won't you come in," she called to them, "and talk to me a minute?"

The two advanced hesitatingly and stood before her at a little distance on the young grass in attitudes clearly tentative. They were shy little misses, and had not lived long on that street.

"Someone told me," said Margaret, "that your names were Enid and Elaine. Which is which?"

The taller one pointed first to her embroidered bosom, then to her sister.

"I'm Enid; she's Elaine."

"I've read about you in a book of poetry," observed Margaret—"it must have been you! I suppose if you had a little sister her name would be Guinevere?"

The large dark eyes of the two exchanged glances of denial. The small Elaine shook her head decidedly.

"We *got* a little sister!" announced Enid, "but her name ain't that; it's Katherine."

They were both pretty with the adorable prettiness of small girls, half baby's beauty, and half woman's. But Enid's good looks would always depend more or less upon happy accident—her time of life, her flow of spirits, her fortune in costume. Her face was rather long, with chin and forehead a trifle too pronounced. But the little Elaine was nature's darling. Her softly rounded person and countenance were instinct with charm. Even her little brown hands had delicacy and character. Her white-stockinged legs, from the fine ankles to the rounded knees at her skirt's edge, were turned to a sculptor's desire. Beside them, Enid's merely serviceable legs looked like sticks. The white bows in their hair shared the ensemble effect of each: Enid's perched precisely in the middle, its loops and ends vibrantly and decisively erect; Elaine's drooped a little at one side, its crispness at once confessing and defying evanescence and fragility.

Margaret thrilled with the child's loveliness, but for some subtle reason she smiled chiefly on Enid.

That little lady concluded she must be a person worthy of confidence.

"My doll's name is Clara," she imparted. "An' hers is Isabel, only she calls it 'Ithabel'!"

The color deepened in Elaine's dainty cheek. She was stung to protest; which she did with all the grace in the world, hanging her head at one side and speaking low.

"I don't either!" she murmured. "I thay Ithabel!"

"Either way is very nice," Margaret hastened to say.

"We've been to Miss Eaton's Sunday school children's party," Enid informed her. "These are our best dresses, and our white kid slippers. Don't you think they're pretty? Mine tie with ribbons, but hers only button like a baby's."

Elaine looked down grievingly at the offensively infantile slippers, turning her exquisite little foot.

"I'm going to speak a piece for Easter," Enid pursued, "all alone by myself; and she's going to speak one in concert with a class."

"Oh, I hope you will come and speak them for me some time," Margaret invited; "and bring Clara and Isabel."

"Maybe we will," answered Enid. "We must go now. Come on, Elaine."

Margaret watched them until they stopped beside a flowerbed along the sidewalk where the first tulips of the season were unfolding. Elaine bent over to examine them. Margaret reproached herself that, though Elaine had spoken but once, it was her image that lingered uppermost. Why should she add even the weight of her preference to that child in whose favor the dice were already so heavily loaded? For in Margaret's eyes, beauty was always the chief gift of the gods.

As she resumed her sewing, a sudden, fantastic fear shot across her thoughts—the fear that Elaine would die. She recognized it, in a moment, for the heart's old, sad prevision of impermanence in beauty, its rooted unbelief in fortune's constancy.

A quick glance up the street showed Elaine still stooping over the tulip bed, her stiff little skirts sticking out straight behind her. The grotesqueness was somehow reassuring. Margaret smiled, half at the absurd little figure, half at her own absurdly tragic fancy.

On the other porch Frank was taking his leave—a process of some duration. First he stood on the lower steps talking at length with Jean who stood on the top step. Then he raised his cap and started away, only to remember something before he reached the corner and to run back across the lawn. There he stood talking while Jean sat on the porch railing, suggesting a faint Romeo and Juliet effect. The next time, Jean called him back. They met halfway down the cement walk and conversed earnestly and lengthily.

With an exquisite sympathy Margaret watched these maneuvers from under discreet eyelids. She was glad for them both, with a clear-souled, generous joy. And yet she felt a sensitive pleasure that walked on the edge of pain. In the young man especially she took a quick delight—in his supple length of limb, the spread of his shoulders, his close-cropped black hair, his new clothes, the way he thrust his hands deep in his trousers' pockets while he swung on the balls of his feet, the attentive bend of his head toward Jean; she reveled in all his elastic, masculine youth which she knew for the garb of a straight, strong, kindly, honorable soul. But out of the revel grew a trouble, as if some strange spirit prisoned in her own struggled to tear itself free, to fling itself, wailing, in the dust.

"Egotism!" said Margaret to herself, curling her lip, sewing very fast. The fluttering spirit lay tombed and still.

When Frank was finally gone, Jean sauntered across the street to Margaret's porch. She perched on the rail and pulled at the leafless vine-stems beside her, talking idly and desultorily of things she was not interested in.

She was an attractive girl, more wholesome than beautiful. Her bronze-brown hair coiled stylishly about her head, gleamed in the late sun. There were some tiny freckles across her nose. She wore a pale blue summer-dress with short sleeves out of which her young arms emerged, fresh and tender from their winter seclusion.

The two maidens circled warily about the topic they were both longing to talk of. Margaret noted in Jean a new aloofness. Every time she threw Frank's name temptingly into the open Jean purposely let it lie.

At last, with a little gasp of laughter, looking straight before her, Jean exclaimed: "I guess I'm sort of scared!"

"What I like about Frank," said Margaret, "is that he's so true and reliable. He's a fellow you can trust!"

"Yes," assented Jean. "Don't you think he looks—nice in that new suit?"

"Splendid! Frank's a handsome boy."

"Isn't he?" sighed Jean.

"He'll always be constant to anyone he cares for. And, I think—he does care for someone."

"What makes *you* think so?" demanded Jean, her blue eyes suddenly intent on Margaret.

"What makes you think so?" Margaret parried.

Jean sat up instantly very straight and stiff.

"Who said I thought anything?"

"Oh, no, no!" Margaret disclaimed hastily. "I didn't mean that. I meant anyone would think so!"

Jean lapsed into a placated limpness, resting her lithe young figure in its summer blue against the dingy house-wall.

"Isn't it funny," she mused, "how you can resolve you won't think, and keep yourself from thinking, and really not think, because you've made up your mind you wouldn't—and all the time you *know*!"

Margaret was searching in her mind for some tenderest phrase of warning when Jean anticipated her.

"Well, it's a good thing I don't care!—I thought at first I didn't like his hair that way, but I do now—better than the other way. He was telling about college."

"He finishes this year, doesn't he?"

"Yes. He's going in with his father next year—unless he makes up his mind to go to Yale. But he doesn't think he will. His father wants him here; and he's about decided that's best."

"Marg'ret," called a thin, querulous, broken voice from within the house; "ain't it time you was gettin' supper?"

Margaret opened the door to call back in a loud, clear voice: "Not yet, Mother."

Jean slipped off the railing. "I must go."

"It really isn't time yet. Mother gets nervous, sitting all day. And she doesn't care to read any more. Stay a little longer."

These snatches of Jean's confidence were delicious to her.

"Oh, I've got to go."

Jean suddenly put both arms around Margaret's waist and clasped her in a swift embrace.

"I wish," she said, "some awfully nice old widower or bachelor would come along and marry you!"

As Jean crossed the street with the lowering sun making a nimbus in her chestnut-golden hair, she began to sing. The words sprang joyous and clear as a bobolink's note—

"What's this dull town to me?

Robin's not here!"

But a sudden waft of consciousness smote them to a vague humming that passed swiftly into—

"My Mary's asleep by thy murmuring stream;

Flow gently, sweet Afton, disturb not her dream."

In the scented dark of the spring evening, Margaret came to the porch again. A little curved moon sailed the sky—less a light-giver than a shining ornament on the breast of night. A while before children's laughter and skurrying footfalls had echoed down the sidewalks. Boys had played ball in the middle of the street, with running and violent contortions, and shouts and calls rejoicing in the release of their animal energies. But these sounds had ceded to silence as the soft darkness fell. Then young strollers, two and two, had passed; but these also were gone. A gentle wind rustled very softly in the dead vine-stalks. The world was alone with the fragrant wind and the dreaming dusk and the little silver scimitar of moon.

The house opposite was all dark, except for a line of lamplight beside the drawn blind of a side window. Earlier, Jean had turned on the porch lights and sat under them in the most graceful of the wicker chairs, reading, or affecting to read, and Frank, coming down the street, had seen her in all that glow. Then they had turned off the lights and gone away together, and the house had sunk into shadowy repose. Vague lines of wanness betrayed the place of the cement walks. The fruit-trees were dim, withdrawn, half-hinted shapes of whiteness, but their perfume, grown bolder in darkness, wandered the winds with poignant, sweet desire.

Margaret leaned against the weather-worn corner-post of the porch; her hand passed over its cracked, paint-blistered surface with, a soft, absent touch. She felt to her finger-tips the wooing lure of the night. In the spring of her pulses she was aware of Frank and Jean somewhere together in the dusky, fragrant, crescent-clasped folds of it. She seemed to draw in with her breath and gather subtly through the pores of her flesh all the shy, sweet, youthful yearning of the world—and, behind that, wordlessly she knew the driven sap, the life-call, the procreant urge. She sighed and stirred restlessly. The strand of pain that runs in the pleasure of such moods began to ache gently like an old wound touched with foreknowledge of evil weather. She shared the pang that lies at the heart of spring.

Words of poetry pressed into her mind, voices of the great interpreters. She was not a cultivated woman, hardly to be called educated; her horizon, even of books, was chance-formed and narrow; but what circumstance had given her she remembered well. The groping, vain longing that stirred in her fell on speech, and moved among the haunted echoes of the world.

"Bloomy the world, yet a blank all the same—

Framework that waits for a picture to frame."

And then, sudden as a cry:

"Never the time and the place,

And the loved one all together!"

She drew a long, shivering sigh, and deliberately thrust the lines out of her mind. Best not to remember them—on such a night! Their edges cut like young grass drawn through careless fingers.

The little new moon was rising higher in the deep, soft blue-darkness of the sky. Margaret looked up at its gleaming curve, and other words of poetry came to her, words she had read once in an old magazine—translated from the Persian:

"Quaffing Hadji-Kivam's wine-cup, there I saw by grace of him,

On the green sea of the night, the new moon's silver shallop swim!"

They swung on, like a familiar, wistful, passionate tune:

"Oh, my heart is like a tulip, closing up in time of cold!

When, at length, shy Bird of Fortune, shall my snare thy wings enfold?"

Footsteps sounded along the walk, the linked steps of two, lingering, yet with the springing fall of youth; then a murmur of voices, girl's and boy's interchanging, lingering, too, and low, weighted, like the footsteps, with the burden of their hour. Margaret drew back a little behind the sapless vine-stems. She knew that she could not be seen in the shadow of the porch, even by a passer far less absorbed than the two who drifted by. She had recognized Frank and Jean at once, and thrilled intimately at the quality of their voices. Both were changed from the careless tones of every day, Frank's husky and strained, Jean's vibrant and tremulous. What they said was quite inaudible—only that betraying *timbre*, conscious and unconscious, hung on the scented air. A single word in the girl's thrilled voice—a sharpened, quivering note of life at high tension—pierced the shadows of the porch:

"—— you ——"

"'You!'" Margaret leaned forward among her shadows, thrusting her clenched hands downward, then pressed them tight upon her heart. "You!" That little key unlocked the flood-gates. The barriers went down, and the tide of passionate loneliness swept her soul.

"You!" she whispered to the fragrant, shimmering, vitalizing night; and the word mocked her, and returned unto her void. She leaned her bosom against the angled surface of the porch-post; she pressed her face among the dry, unbudded vines. The cry went out from her into the empty spaces of the world—a voiceless, hopeless call: "You! you! you! Oh, you who never came to me!"

Her soul was ravaged by that mocking bitterness of loss which comes only to those who have not possessed. She, crying for a lover in the night, she who had never been sought! If ever her shy and homely girlhood might have attracted a youth, poor Margaret's love of poetry would have frightened him away. If the burdened poverty of her maturity might have admitted a suitor, her acquaintance numbered no man who would not have shunned an earnest-minded old maid. And she knew this utterly. A thousand old aches were in the sudden rush of anguish, and shame fought among them. She was shocked and startled at the drip of salt tears down her cheeks, at the heaving of her shaken breast.

She struggled to rebuild her old barriers against the woe—pride, and dignity, and the decent acceptance of one's lot. But those were for the eyes of men and women; and here were no eyes, only night, and the risen sap and the wild heart in her breast. Duty? She had never swerved in doing it, but she thrust the thought by with passionate rebellion at the waste of her in dull service to the outworn lives which neither asked nor could take from her anything but the daily drudgery. She groped for the old humble consolations, tender appreciations, generous friendships, the joy in others' joy. But there the wall had broken through. "I am nothing to them!" thought Margaret bitterly. "Jean will not care to talk to me after to-night. And I can't always kiss other people's babies! I want one of my own!"

The gauzy veil of dream that wrapped her often had fallen from before her eyes. Rent by the piercing beauty of the night, and soaked in her tears, that fragile fabric of vision served no more. Imagined blisses had betrayed her, naked and tender, to the unpitying lash of truth. The remote, the universal, mocked her sore longing for something near and real, of earth and flesh—oh, as welcome in sorrow as in joy!—to be imperiously her own! The river of life dashed by and would not fill her empty cup. The love she loved so had passed her by.

She faced the hollowest desolation known to humanity. She had committed no sin; she had been true and tender and faithful; she had not failed in the least and humblest dues of love: yet, now she stood wrapped in torment, and saw, across a great gulf fixed, the joys of love's elect. She stood utterly frustrate and alone—a shared frustration were happiness! Her mental life had been so intensely uncompanioned that she was tortured with doubts of her own reality. What warrant of Being had that soul which could not touch in all the blank, black spaces of the void another soul to give it assurance of itself? What if the aching throat and riven breast were but the phantom anguish of a dream Thing, unpurposed, unjustified, a Thing of ashes and emptiness!

There remained God—perhaps! Was God a dream too? Was there any *You* in all the empty worlds?

She stood quite still, questing the universe for God. She thought of her father's God—the savage Hebrew deity he thought he worshiped, the harsh Puritan formalist who ruled his creed, the hysterical, illogical sentimentalist who swayed his heart. She dropped them all out of her mind. God was not, for her, in the ancient earthquake or fire or whirlwind. But—perhaps—somewhere!

She sank to her knees in the darkness, and, laying her head upon her arms on the railing, sought in her soul for God.

"You are Love," she said. "They say it, but they do not believe it; but *I* believe it. You are Love that creates, and makes glad—and wounds. You are Love that rises in all creatures in spring, and would make all things beautiful and kind. You are Love that gives—and gives itself. You made me to love love and love's uses, and nothing else in the world! You made my life loveless. Why?"

She waited a moment, then, with a sobbing breath of remembrance, "Oh, one spring they nailed you on a cross because you loved too much!"

After that she was very still, her head bent upon her arms, her heart quiet, waiting for the still, small voice, the answer of God.

It came presently, and she knew it was the answer. She accepted it with comfort, and sad pride, and submission, and a slow, strange, white happiness of consecration. The answer came without any words. If there had been words, they might have been, perhaps, like these:

"Bear the pain patiently, my daughter, for life is wrought in pain, and there is no child born without sharp pangs. I have not shut thee out from my festival of spring. Thy part is thy pang. I have given thee a coronal of pain and made thee rich with loss and desire. I have made thee one of my vestals who guard perpetually the hearth-fire which shall not be lit for them. I have denied thee love that love shall be manifest in thee. Wherever love fails in my world, there shalt thou re-create it in beauty and kindness. The vision thou hast, and the passion, are of me, and I charge thee find some fair and sweet way that they perish not in thee. All ways are mine. Be thou in peace."

Margaret rose at length. The moon was gone from the sky, but out of its deep, tender darkness shone the far, dim light of stars. A cool wind touched her cheek, bearing a faint, ethereal odor of blossoms as from a great distance. And upon her face, if one might have seen for the darkness, shone a fine, ethereal beauty far-brought from that great distance which is nearer than hands and feet.

Against the shadowy front of the house opposite, two figures were vaguely discernible, the taller a little darker than the encompassing space, the other a little lighter. As Margaret looked, they melted together, and were no longer two but one.

She smiled in the darkness, very sweetly, and, holding her head high, turned and went quietly into the dark little house.

Work Is a Blessing

By Lafayette Young

Work is a blessing to the human race.

If this had remained a workless world, it would have been a homeless world. The progress of the human race began when work began. When work began, men began to wear clothes; thus progress commenced.

Industry and happiness go hand in hand.

Men who feel that they are doomed to daily toil, and that there is no so-called emancipation from the daily routine, imagine that happiness would be theirs if they did not have to work. The man whose employment compels him to get up at six o'clock in the morning imagines if he could just get out of that slavery he would ask for no greater happiness. But if he ever does reach that condition he will find out what true misery is.

Some years ago the warden of the Iowa penitentiary told me that he had a prisoner serving a long term, who begged a day off. He wanted to stop the regular routine. He wanted to be set free in the courtyard for one day. He wanted to look straight up at the sky, and to breathe the air of the outdoors. I was at the penitentiary the day the prisoner's request was granted, and at ten o'clock the prisoner had grown tired of idleness. The sky had lost its attraction. There was something missing. And he got word to the warden that he wished to be returned to labor.

There are millions of men toiling in factories and in mines, laying brick on tall buildings, swinging cranes in the great iron mills, tending the machines in cotton or woolen mills, who think that they would be perfectly happy if they were once perfectly idle. But their experience would be like that of the prisoner's.

What a wretched world this would be without work! How many things we have which are indispensable, that we would not have but for somebody's work. Work has built every great bridge, every great cathedral, every home, large or small. It has made every invention. Work found man in a cave, and put him into a good home. Work has made man decent and self-respecting.

The great nations are the working nations; the great peoples are the working peoples. Nations, like individuals, date their prosperity and happiness from the beginning of work. The start was made when man gave attention to the primal curse of the race recorded in the book of

Genesis: "By the sweat of thy face shalt thou eat bread, until thou return to the ground." This mandate has never been repealed. Lazy men in all parts of the world have undertaken to nullify it. The ambition for idleness fills jails and penitentiaries. It causes man to commit forgeries and murders. Every man slugged in a dark alley is put out of the way by some other man desiring money without working for it.

There has been a foolish notion in many countries in regard to labor. They do not consider it dignified. In some countries, missionary families learn that they cannot cook their own victuals without losing caste. In other countries a certain number of servants must be kept if the family would be respected. In our own country there is a false pride in regard to labor. Young men avoid the learning of trades because they do not wish to soil their hands. Laboring men themselves have been guilty of not sufficiently estimating their own callings. They demand the rights of their class, but fail to respect it themselves. This causes many young men to seek some employment which will not soil their hands. Many thousands of young men make the mistake of not having some regular calling, some work which they can do better than anybody else. The man who has a regular trade is never found walking the streets looking for a job. Even when he is called old, he can secure employment.

Industry is indispensable to happiness. Idleness destroys the souls of more young men, and leads to more forms of dissipation, than any other influence.

The experienced mechanic knows how rapidly and joyfully time passes when he is interested in his work. He never watches the clock; to him quitting time comes all too soon.

Labor can be made a joy if man wills it so.

An appreciation of what a man earns and the thought that he can do something with his money, ought to be a part of the happiness of labor. Work develops the man. It develops his appreciation of others. He is likely to be unhappy if he works solely for himself. The Indian hunter, returning from the chase, lays the evidence of his prowess at the feet of his squaw. He is glad that he has accomplished something, and in her eyes he is a hero.

Once I was driving in the Allegheny Mountains in the early summer. Unexpectedly I came to a little cottage almost covered with flowers and vines. A brown-faced woman with pruning shears was at her work. Around her bees were humming, and birds were twittering. I sought to buy some flowers. She said she never had sold a flower in her life. I asked her what induced her to work early and late, cultivating, planting and pruning. She said, "I do this work because I enjoy it, and because my husband and two sons will enjoy these flowers when they come home at night." This woman had the whole philosophy of human happiness. If there are women in heaven she will be there.

Work came as a blessing. It remains as a blessing. It makes us tired so that we can enjoy sleep. We awaken in the morning refreshed for a new day. When kings and queens shall be no more, when autocracy shall end, when the voices of intelligent men and women shall govern, then if work shall be universal, thus satisfying the energy, and giving direction to the ambitions of men, there will be no more wars.

To make work enjoyable, men and women must be proud of it; must not pretend that they are above it; must not apologize for it. Once I was in Holland. I saw women with a peculiar headdress as if they belonged to some lodge. They wore smiling faces. I inquired what their regalia meant, and was told that they were working women of the peasant or some other humble class. They were proud of their position. They were content, with plenty to do. They enjoyed the society of their families and friends. But their happiness consisted in being proud of, and satisfied with, the things they were doing. Who can say that they have not chosen the better part?

September

By Esse V. Hathaway

Blaze on blaze of scarlet sumach,
Roadsides lined with radiant gold,
Purple ironweed, regal, slender,
Rasping locust, shrill and bold.

Dusty smell in field and upland,
Sky of copper mixed with blue,
Life intense as is the weather—
Let's away, just me and you!

Host and Houseguest

"I say, old top, I wish you wouldn't be continually kissing the wife. I think once when you come and once when you go quite sufficient."

"But, my dear man, I can't wear myself out coming and going all the time just to please you."

—From *"Judge." Copyright by Leslie-Judge Co.*

The Poet of the Future

By Tacitus Hussey

Oh, the poet of the future. Will he come to us as comes
The beauty of the bugle's voice above the roar of drums—
The beauty of the bugle's voice above the roar and din
Of battle drums that pulse the time the victor marches in?

—James Whitcomb Riley.

"Oh, the poet of the future!" Can anybody guess
Whether he'll sound his bugle, or she'll wear them on her dress;
An' will they kinder get their themes from nature, second hand,
An' dish 'em up in language that plain folks can't understand?

There's a sight of this 'ere po'try stuff, each year, that goes to waste,
Jest a-waitin' fer a poet who has the time and taste
To tackle it just as it is, an' weave it into rhyme,
With warp and woof of hope and love, in life's swift loom of time.

An' mebbe the future poet, if he understands the thing,
Won't start the summer katydids to singin' in the spring,
Jest like the croakin' frog; but let the critter wait at most,
To announce to timid farmers that "it's jest six weeks till frost."

The katydid and goldenrod are partners in this way:
They sing and bloom where'er there's room, along life's sunny way;
So I warn you, future poet, jest let 'em bloom an' lilt
Together—don't divorce 'em. That's jest the way they're built.

In order to be perfect, the future poet should

Know every sound of nature, of river, lake an' wood,

Should know each whispered note and every answerin' call—

He should never set cock-pheasants to drummin' in the fall.

"Under the golden maples!" Not havin' voice to sing

They flap their love out on a log quite early in the spring;

For burnin' love will allus find expression in some way—

That's the style that *they've* adopted—don't change their natures, pray.

I cannot guess just what the future poet's themes may be;

Reckon they'll be pretty lofty, fer, as anyone can see,

The world of poetry's lookin' up an' poets climbin' higher;

With divine afflatus boostin' them, of course they must aspire.

The poets of the good old times were cruder with the pen;

Their idees weren't the same as ours—these good old-fashioned men—

Bet old Homer never writ, even in his palmiest day,

Such a soul-upliftin' poem as "Hosses Chawin' Hay."

"Hosses" don't know any better out in the Hawkeye State—

Down to Boston now, I reckon, they jest simply masticate.

The poet of the future'll blow a bugle, like as not—

Most all us modern poets had to blow fer what we've got.

To keep the pot a-b'ilin' we all have to raise a din

To make the public look our way—an' pass the shekels in.

The scarcity of bugles seems now the greatest lack

Though some of us keep blowin' 'thout a bugle to our back.

The poet of the future! When once he takes his theme

His pen will slip as smoothly as a canoe glides down stream.

He'll sing from overflowin' heart—his music will be free—

Would you take up a subscription fer a robin in a tree?

He'll never try to drive the Muse, if he doesn't want to go,
But will promptly take the harness off—er drive keerfull an' slow—
When po'try's forced, like winter pinks, the people's apt to know it
An' labor with it jest about as hard as did the poet.

Putting the Stars with the Bars

By Verne Marshall

Midnight beneath a low-hanging strip of amber-hued moon. Smoke in one's eyes and sulphur in his nostrils; the pounding of cannon in his ears and a hatred of war and its sponsors in his soul. A supply wagon piled high with dead men on one side of the road and a little ambulance waiting for its bruised load to emerge from the mouth of the communicating trench near by. Sharp tongues of fire darting into the night on every side as the guns of the French barked their challenge at the Crown Prince on the other bank of the Meuse. A lurid glare over there to the left where the smoke hung thickest under drifting yellow illuminating bombs and red and blue signal bombs that added their touch to the weird fantasy that wasn't a fantasy at all, but a hill in whose spelling men had changed one letter and turned it into hell.

It was Dead Man's Hill at Verdun—Le Cote Mort Homme. And Dead Man's Hill it truly was, for among the barbed wire entanglements and in some of the shell craters in No Man's Land there still lay the skeletons of Frenchmen and Germans who had been killed there months before and whose bodies it had been impossible to recover because the trenches had not changed positions and to venture out between them was to shake hands with Death.

Dead Man's Hill at Verdun—where ten thousand men have fought for a few feet of blood-soaked ground in vain effort to satiate the battle-thirst of a monarch and his son! The countryside for miles around is laid waste. Villages lie in tumbled masses, trees are uprooted or broken off, demolished wagons and motors litter the roads and fields, and dead horses, legs stiff in the air, dot the jagged landscape. Not a moving object is seen there by day except the crows that flutter above the uptorn ground and the aeroplanes that soar thousands of feet above. But, with the coming of night, long columns of men wind along the treacherous roads on their way to or from the trenches, hundreds of supply wagons lumber across the shell holes to the stations near the line, ammunition trains travel up to the lines and back and the ambulances ply their routes to dressing stations. Everything must be done under night's partially protecting cloak, for the German gunners seldom miss when daylight aids their vision.

A tiny American ambulance—a jitney—threads its way down from the Dead Man to ——, carrying a boy through whose breast a dum-dum bullet had torn its beastly way. Three hours before, the driver of that ambulance had talked with the boy who now lay behind him on a stretcher. Then the young Frenchman had been looking forward to the wondrous day when the war would end. He had planned to come to America to live, just as soon as he could get back to Paris and say good-bye to the mother from whom he had received a letter that very day.

"I will be lucky!" he had exclaimed to the American. "I will not be killed. I will not even be wounded. Ah, but won't I be glad when the war is over!"

But his life was slipping away, faster than the Red Cross car could carry him to aid. The checking station reached, two orderlies pulled the stretcher from the ambulance. There was a choking sound in the wounded soldier's throat and the driver, thinking to ease his breathing, lifted his head. The closed eyes fluttered open, the indescribable smile of the dying lighted his face and with his last faint breath he murmured those words that always still war momentarily—

"Ah, *mere! Ma mere!*"

"Oh, mother! My mother!"—and he was dead.

Just one little incident of war, just a single glimpse at the accomplishments of monarchial militarism.

That French boy has not come to America, but America has gone to him. He died for a flag that is red, white and blue—for the tricolor of France. And we have gone across the sea to place the stars of our flag with the bars of his. His fight was our fight and our fight is his. Together we fight against those who menace civilization in both old world and new. We fight against the army that outraged Belgium and devastated France, against the militaristic clique that sanctioned the slaughtering and crippling of little children, the maiming of women, against that order of militarists who decorated the commander of the submarine that sank the Lusitania with her babies and their mothers.

We are at war and we are Americans.... Enough.

Verne Marshall was the driver of that ambulance. Three months of his service were spent at Verdun.

The Kings of Saranazett

By Lewis Worthington Smith

A Scene From the First Act

A drama of the awakening of the nearer Orient. In this scene Nasrulla appears as the royal lover of the fig merchant's daughter, Nourmahal. She has learned something of the ways of the West, where even kings have but one acknowledged consort, and she is not willing to be merely one of a number of queens.

Before the wall and gate enclosing Nourmahal's Garden. It is early morning, just before dawn. Above the gleaming white of the wall's sun-baked clay there is the deep green of the trees—the plane, the poplar, the acacia, and, beyond the garden, mountains are visible through the purple mist of the hour that waits for dawn, slowly turning to rose as the rising sun warms their snowy heights. At the left the wall extends out of sight behind a clump of trees, but at the right it ends in a tower topped by a turret with a rounded dome passing into a point. The space under the dome is open, except for a railing, and is large enough for one or more persons. It may be entered from the broad top of the wall through a break in the railing. At the left, out from the trees and in front of the wall, there is a well marked out with roughly piled stones.

At the right, out of sight behind the trees that come almost to the tower at the corner of the wall, a man's voice is heard singing Shelley's "Indian Serenade."

"I arise from dreams of thee

In the first sweet sleep of night,

When the winds are breathing low,

And the stars are shining bright;

I arise from dreams of thee,

And a something in my feet

Hath led me—who knows how?

To thy chamber window, Sweet!

"The wandering airs they faint

On the dark, the silent stream—

The Champak odors fail

Like sweet thoughts in a dream;

The nightingale's complaint,

It dies upon her heart;—

As I must die on thine,

O! beloved as thou art!

"Oh lift me from the grass!

I die! I faint! I fail!

Let thy love in kisses rain

On my lips and eyelids pale.

My cheek is cold and white, alas!

My heart beats loud and fast;—

Oh! press it to thine own again,

Where it will break at last."

During the singing Nourmahal has come slowly out from the left, walking along the broad top of the wall until, coming to the tower, she drops down on the floor by the railing of the turret and listens, her veil falling from before her face. When the song has ended, Nasrulla comes forward and approaches the little tower. He leads a horse, a white horse with its tail dyed red in the Persian fashion.

Nourmahal. You turn the gray of the poplars in the darkness into the silver of running water.

King Nasrulla. The dawn is waiting under your veil. I see now only the morning star.

Nourmahal. I am but the moon, and I must not be seen when My Lord the Sun comes.

King Nasrulla. The Lord of the Sky rises to look on the gardens where the nightingales have been singing.

Nourmahal. But when he finds that the nightingales are silent, he passes to other gardens.

King Nasrulla. Following the song, as I follow the lisp of spring in your voice, the flutter of the wings of birds in the branches when buds are swelling.

Nourmahal. It is the flutter of wings and the song that you care for; it is not the bird.

King Nasrulla. It is the song of the bird that tells me where I shall find the bird herself. It is the oasis lifted up into the sky that guides the thirsty traveler across the desert.

Nourmahal (rising in agitation). When I am your queen, will you follow the voices of other nightingales?

King Nasrulla. You will be my first queen.

Nourmahal. I must be your only queen.

King Nasrulla. Always my first queen, and in your garden the fountains shall murmur day and night with a fuller flow of water than any others. The flowers there shall be more beautiful than anywhere else in all the world, and a hundred maidens shall serve you.

Nourmahal. And I shall not be your only queen?

King Nasrulla. It is not the way of the world.

Nourmahal. I have heard stories of places where the king has only one queen.

King Nasrulla. It has never been so in Saranazett.

Nourmahal. It has not been so in Saranazett, but does nothing change?

King Nasrulla. I must be king in the way of my ancestors.

Nourmahal (dropping down by the railing again). And we must live in the way of our ancestors, over and over again, sunrise and noon-glare and star-shine, as it was before our stars rose in the heavens, as it always will be?

King Nasrulla. Our ancestors have taught us that a king should not live too meanly.

Nourmahal. We cannot appeal to our ancestors. We cannot appeal to anything, and nothing can be undone. As the Persian poet says, "The moving finger writes," and what is written must be.

King Nasrulla. And if what is written is beautiful, and if you are to be a king's throne-mate, if all the treasures of all the world are to be sought out for you——

Nourmahal. It is nothing, nothing, if you must have another wife, if you must have two other wives, three.

King Nasrulla. My prime minister will choose the others. I choose you.

Nourmahal (passionately). But what shall we ever choose again—and get what we choose? Have not the hours been counted out for us from the beginning of the world? Can we stop the grains of sand in the hour-glass?

King Nasrulla. Each one will make a new pleasure as it falls.

Nourmahal. Yes, but it falls. We do not gather it up. It falls out of the heavens as the rain comes. We cannot make it rain.

King Nasrulla. But the drops are always pleasant.

Nourmahal. Yes, like a cup of water to a prisoner who dies of thirst and cannot know when his jailer comes. If we could bring the clouds up over the sun when the hot dust is flying, it would be really pleasant, but

"That inverted Bowl we call the Sky,

Whereunder crawling coop'd we live and die,

Lift not your hands to *It* for help—for It

As impotently moves as you or I."

You are my sky, and the old poet is right, if you must have four wives because your father had four wives, and his father.

King Nasrulla. They are but symbols of kingliness, and they shall bow in the dust before you, whom my heart chooses, as weeds by the roadside bow when you pass in your tahktiravan and the air follows its flying curtains.

Nourmahal. Why should anyone bow to me? Why should I care for bowing? It would make me a slave to the custom of bowing. Are you a king and must you be a slave too? Impotence is the name of such kingship, and why should I care to be a queen when my king cannot make me queenly?

King Nasrulla (advancing to the tower and leaving his horse standing). Come! The stars are paling, and there is only the light of your eyes to lift me out of the dust. Come!

In the side of the wall by the tower a sloping series of stout pegs has been driven, descending to the ground at short intervals. Nourmahal comes out of the tower, puts her foot on the highest of these pegs, takes Nasrulla's hand, and, with his help, comes slowly down the pegs, as if they were a flight of stairs, to the ground.

Nourmahal. How I love a horse! It is Samarcand and Delhi and Bokhara and Paris, even Paris.

King Nasrulla. Paris! What is Paris?

Nourmahal (standing in front of the horse and caressing its head). I don't know. I have never been there, but a horse makes me think of Paris. I don't know London, but a horse makes me think of London too. A horse could take me there. I could ride and ride, and every day there would be something new and something wonderful. There are cities beyond the water, too, marvelous cities, full of things more than we dream of here. A horse is swift, and the tapping of his feet on the stones is distance. When he lifts his head, when he curves his neck, already in his heart he is going on and on.

King Nasrulla. And these are the stories that you have heard, stories about Paris and London and the cities across the water?

Nourmahal. Stories? Perhaps not stories. Dreams, I think, imaginings dropped from the wings of falcons flying out of the west.

King Nasrulla. You shall sit on the horse, and you can seem to be riding. Then as your dreams come true, you can tell them to me. Let the horse be Paris in my fancies too, and London and the cities across the water.

The horse is still standing where he stopped when Nasrulla led him out from behind the trees with him. He faces toward the left, and Nasrulla is back of him. Nourmahal puts her foot into Nasrulla's hand, and he lifts her into the saddle. When she is comfortably seated, he stands beside her and in front of her, back of the horse, leaning against the horse's neck and caressing his shoulder.

King Nasrulla. Now we are on the road, and all the world is moving across the horizon. If it is all a dream, let me be in the dream.

Nourmahal (looking out and away from him and pausing a moment). Stories! Dreams!—What I have heard is only a whisper, but it seems so true and so beautiful. Somewhere a man loves one woman always and no other. Somewhere a king is not a manikin stalking through ceremonies. Somewhere he lives humanly as other men. Somewhere to-day is not like yesterday, and man has learned to break the cycle of what has been forever, of what seems dead and yet out of death comes back again and again. I have not seen it, but I know it. Somewhere you and I could be happy without being king or queen. Somewhere a woman thinks her own thoughts, and not the thoughts of her lord only. Somewhere men are not bound to a king, and somewhere kings are not bound to the words of their fathers' fathers.

King Nasrulla (slowly, after a pause). It is the way of the world, Nourmahal. What the world is, it is, and that is forever and ever, unless it should be the will of God to make a new world.

Nourmahal. A new world! (*She pauses dreamily.*) Yes, that is what I want, a new world. That is what men are making somewhere, I know it. That is what is in my heart, and the same thing must be in the hearts of other men and women. A new world! What would it be to wake up every morning with a fresh wonder, not knowing what the day would bring? What would it be every morning to take the saddle and follow a new road ahead of the sun?

King Nasrulla. If I could go with you——

Nourmahal. You have horses.

King Nasrulla. It is not so decreed. My place is here.

Nourmahal. Your place is here, and it is your place to have three or four queens as your ministers decide for you. One queen is to keep peace with the King of the South, another is to keep peace with the King of the West, and the third is to keep peace with the King of the East. The fourth queen you may choose for yourself from your own people—if you choose before some other king offers a daughter. You may make slaves of your queens so that your neighbor kings may make a slave of you.

King Nasrulla. Yes, if I would be king—and you would be queen.

Nourmahal. Queen!—in a world where the flowers that bloom to-day died centuries ago! Queen—in a world where queens may look out of grated windows and never walk the streets! Queen—in a world where My Lord the King may not come to my door too often lest the daughter of the King of the South put poison in the nectar that her slaves offer him to-morrow!

King Nasrulla. The world is the world, and its enduring is forever and ever. We are but shadows that change and break on the surface of running water. We may stand for a moment in the sun, but we cannot stop the rain that fills the stream. We cannot fix our images for a moment on the drops that are rushing out to the sea.

Nourmahal (looking away from him dreamily). "Ah Love! could you and I with Him conspire To grasp this sorry Scheme of Things Entire, Would we not shatter it to bits—and then Remould it nearer to the Heart's desire?"

He looks at her steadily, but she does not turn her head, and, while they are so silent a woman comes from the left with a water jar, fills it from the well, puts it on her head, and passes off again. The sun is now warming the tops of the mountains to a soft pink.

King Nasrulla. We must find the water where it flows—or go thirsty.

Nourmahal (more passionately). But somewhere the women do not carry water. The poet only thought of doing what somewhere men have done. Here a thousand years are but as yesterday and ten thousand as a watch in the night. I am not I, but an echo of the mad desires of dead men whose dust has been blown across the desert for countless centuries. Why should I not think of my own desires before my dust, too, flies forgotten before the passing caravans?

King Nasrulla. But you are to be my queen. Nothing more can anyone give you in Saranazett.

Nourmahal. And to-morrow or next week your ambassador to the King of the East comes back with letters and pledges of friendship. Perhaps he brings with him the King's daughter.

King Nasrulla. But she is only the official seal of a bond, only a hostage. She is not the rose that I pin over my heart. She is not the nightingale that I love to hear singing in my garden. She is not the face behind the lattice that draws my eager feet. She is not the fountain that will make me drink and drink again.

Nourmahal. But I shall not ride with you into the distance and leave the kings' daughters behind?

King Nasrulla. The King of the East——

Nourmahal. I know. The King of the East has a great army. I must stay in my garden, or I shall have to spend my life talking about the things he likes or dislikes, his angers and his fondnesses, with the women of his harem.

She puts her foot out for his hand, ready to be taken down from the horse.

King Nasrulla. Nourmahal!

Nourmahal. Yes, I must keep my veil before my face and stay within my garden.

He helps her down, and she turns the horse's head back to the right in the direction from which they came.

King Nasrulla. I shall take you, Nourmahal, and make you queen.

Nourmahal. Take me! Take the others and let them be queens. They will be happy enough, after the way of their mothers, but you cannot take the wind.

King Nasrulla. Being your lover is not ceasing to be king. May not the king ask of his subjects what he will? What is it to be king?

Nourmahal (turning as she is passing toward the gate). Sometimes it is making a fresher and happier world for those who come to kneel before the throne. Kings are not often so wise.

King Nasrulla. And when they are not so wise they think of their own happiness. They let love come into the palace, and the favorite queen has the riches of the earth heaped in jewels before her. The tenderness of the moon shines in the clasp of her girdle, and the splendor of the sun glitters in a circlet for her forehead.

Nourmahal. And sometimes, seeking their own pleasure, kings make the killing of those who are not kings their joy. They teach all men to be soldiers and all soldiers to be ruthless. Their women learn to delight in the echoes of battle, and the man who is not scarred by the marks of many fights they pity and despise. So women forget to be gentle, and the lords and masters of earth no longer watch over them and care for them, no longer shelter the weak and the defenseless, no longer think of right and justice, because they carry in their hands the javelins of might and they have learned to fling them far.

King Nasrulla. But I shall watch over you as the cloud watches over the garden where the roses are waiting for the rain.

Nourmahal. No, I shall not have a king to watch over me. Somewhere they have no kings. A queen dies daily with loneliness, or lives hourly in the burning hate of all her sister queens. To breathe the air where there are no queens would be an ecstasy. I will not be a king's first queen or his last queen or his concubine or any other creature whom he may cast aside for a new fancy whenever the fancy comes.

A messenger enters from the right, preceded by two attendants carrying each one of the long, melon-shaped lanterns that accompany royalty. The messenger bows before Nasrulla, dropping on one knee.

Messenger. Your Royal Highness, I am sent to beg that you will hear me.

King Nasrulla. It is my pleasure to listen to your message. Speak!

Messenger. It is not I speaking, Your Majesty, but your minister, Huseyn.

King Nasrulla. I listen to the words of Huseyn.

Messenger. Know, O Mighty Lord of the Great Center of Earth—the ambassador to the King of the East is reported returning by the long highway.

Nourmahal's father, Mehrab, comes out from the gate in the wall and stands listening.

King Nasrulla. Say to Huseyn that I will see him and make arrangements for his reception before nightfall.

Messenger. He brings very important tidings, Your Majesty. Pardon me, O Lord of the Lives of Your Servants. I speak but the words of Huseyn.

King Nasrulla. I hear the words of Huseyn.

Messenger. The ambassador should be received a early as may be, is the word of Huseyn. He knows the will of the King of the East, and the King of the East would know your will, O Mightiest of the Mighty.

Nourmahal (bowing to her knees before him). Let me beg of you also, King Nasrulla, that you give audience at once to the ambassador who comes with word from the King of the East.

King Nasrulla. I listen to the words of Nourmahal with the words of Huseyn.

Messenger. And I shall say to the Prime Minister Huseyn that His Majesty, the Lord of Everlasting Effulgence, will graciously consent to speak with him before the sun looks in at his image in the water jars.

Nourmahal. O King Nasrulla, for the sake of the rule that is thine from thy fathers, for the maintaining of peace in all thy borders, for the security of thy people, who harvest their hopes in fear, permit the approach of the ambassador who returns from the King of the East.

King Nasrulla. The wish of Nourmahal is a command. I go to make ready for the ambassador who comes with word from the King of the East.

Nourmahal. And for the daughter of the King of the East, give thanks, O King Nasrulla. It is said that she is very beautiful, and many wooers have sought her vainly. She has been kept for the joy and the splendor and the growing greatness of My Lord the King.

King Nasrulla. Announce my coming to my Prime Minister, Huseyn.

Messenger (rising). Your Noble Majesty is most gracious. I fly with your words to Huseyn.

King Nasrulla. As a king I go, but my thoughts are not a king's thoughts, and they stay here. It may be I shall look for them again, as one looks for love in his friend's heart at the home-returning. Farewell!

Nourmahal. I shall keep your thoughts forever, My Lord Nasrulla, but for the King and the ways of the King—farewell!

The two lantern carriers who have come with the messenger turn to the right to light the way for the King, and, as they pass off, he follows them. Nourmahal watches them until they are gone, while Mehrab, Nourmahal's father, comes forward slowly.

Mehrab. He threatened you, did he?

Nourmahal. Threaten! No, father, he did not threaten me.

Mehrab. Does he not mean to make you queen whether you wish to be or not?

Nourmahal. He will not dare.

Mehrab. I am only a merchant, only a dealer in figs and olives. I am not to be feared or considered by him or by those that are about him. It is the way of his kind to think that you are to be taken as he would take a pomegranate from the garden of one of his satraps.

Nourmahal. He will not take me.

Mehrab. They despise me because I go with the caravans, but I have learned something. I know the world. My camels have tracked the sands hundreds of miles from Saranazett, and there are places where the words of Nasrulla the King mean less than the words of Mehrab the merchant.

Nourmahal. They will have horses to follow us. Horses are swifter than camels.

Mehrab. We shall have horses too, and ours shall be the fleetest. The riders of the King's horses will put out their palms for my silver. They will know how to make their whips fall lightly.

Nourmahal (eagerly). Let us go to-morrow. Let us go before the daughter of the King of the East is carried in her palanquin to the palace. I want to see all the places where you have been. I want to know something of the strange things that you have seen.

Mehrab. The women of Saranazett have never traveled.

Nourmahal. But I will not be a woman of Saranazett. There are other worlds and other ways for me than the ways of Saranazett.

Mehrab. You shall not be queen one day and someone else queen in your place the next. I was not born to live in the world's high places, but also I was not born to bend the knee. You shall not suffer because you are not a king's daughter, and because those that are kings' daughters smile at you behind their curtains.

Nourmahal (more dreamily reluctant). If we could make Saranazett over into a new world.

Mehrab. A new world somewhere else, Nourmahal. The packs are being made ready for the camels. Have your women tie up your clothes as if they were bundles of figs. Day after to-morrow or the next day or the next, we shall take horse and follow. We shall go to a world that is an old, old world, wiser than our world, a world where men's thoughts are free and their women's eyes look wherever they will.

Nourmahal (passing to the gate). The women shall make ready.

Mehrab. At once, and tell Zuleika she goes with you.

Nourmahal. Zuleika shall make ready.

She passes out through the gate into the garden. Mehrab turns and sees the spikes driven into the wall by the tower. For a moment he looks at them in astonishment, observing that they pass down to the ground slopingly, and then, one by one, he pulls them out and flings them down on the ground violently.

The Old Cane Mill

By Nellie Gregg Tomlinson

"What's sorghum?" Don't you know sorghum?
My gran'son nigh sixteen,
Don't boys know nothin' nowadays?
Beats all I ever seen.
Why sorghum's the bulliest stuff
Wuz ever made ter eat.
You spread it thick on homemade bread;
It's most oncommon sweet.

"Come from?" Wall yer jist better bet
It don't come from no can.
Jus' b'iled down juice from sorghum cane,
Straight I'way 'lasses bran'.
"What's cane?" It's some like corn, yer know,
An' topped with plumes o' seed.
Grows straight an' tall on yaller clay
That wouldn't grow a weed.

Long in September when 'twuz ripe,
The cane-patch battle field
Wuz charged by boys with wooden swords,
Good temper wuz their shield.
They stripped the stalks of all their leaves,
Then men, with steel knives keen
Slashed off the heads and cut the stalks
An' piled them straight an' clean.

The tops wuz saved ter feed the hens,
Likewise fer nex' year's seed.
The farmer allus has ter save
Against the futur's need.
The neighbors cum from miles erbout
An' fetched the cane ter mill.
They stacked it high betwixt two trees,
At Gran'dads, on the hill.

An' ol' hoss turned the cane mill sweep,
He led hisself erroun.
The stalks wuz fed inter the press,
From them the sap wuz groun'.
This juice run through a little trough
Ter pans beneath a shed;
There it wuz b'iled an' skimmed and b'iled,
Till it wuz thick an' red.

Then it wuz cooled an' put in bar'ls
An' toted off to town
While us kids got ter lick the pan,
Which job wuz dun up brown.
Gee whiz! but we did hev good times
At taffy pullin' bees.
We woun' the taffy roun' girls' necks—
Bob wuz the biggest tease.

Inside the furnace, on live coals,
We het cane stalks red hot,
Then hit 'em hard out on the groun'—
Yer oughter hear 'em pop!

Sometimes a barefoot boy would step
Inter the skimmin's hole,
Er pinch his fingers in the mill,
Er fall off from the pole.

When winter winds went whis'lin' through
The door an' winder cracks,
An' piled up snow wuz driftin'
Till yer couldn't see yer tracks,
Then we all drawed roun' the table
An' passed the buckwheat cakes,
Er mebbe it wuz good corn bread.
"What's sorghum?" Good lan' sakes.

Wall, son, yer hev my symperthy;
Yer've missed a lot, I swan.
Oh, sure yer dance an' joy-ride
Frum ev'nin' untel dawn,
Yer've football, skates an' golf ter he'p
The passin' time ter kill,
But give me mem'ry's boyhood days,
Erroun' the ol' cane mill.

The Queer Little Thing

By Eleanor Hoyt Brainerd

Bonita Allen was a queer little thing. Everyone in the school, from Miss Ryder down to the chambermaid, had made remarks to that effect before the child had spent forty-eight hours in the house, yet no one seemed able to give a convincing reason for the general impression.

The new pupil was quiet, docile, moderately well dressed, fairly good looking. She did nothing extraordinary. In fact, she effaced herself as far as possible; yet from the first she caused a ripple in the placid current of the school, and her personality was distinctly felt.

"I think it's her eyes," hazarded Belinda, as she and Miss Barnes discussed the new-comer in the Youngest Teacher's room. "They aren't girl eyes at all."

"Fine eyes," asserted the teacher of mathematics with her usual curtness.

Belinda nodded emphatic assent. "Yes, of course; beautiful, but so big and pathetic and dumb. I feel ridiculously apologetic every time the child looks at me, and as for punishing her—I'd as soon shoot a deer at six paces. It's all wrong. A twelve-year-old girl hasn't any right to eyes like those. If the youngster is unhappy she ought to cry twenty-five handkerchiefs full of tears, as Evangeline Marie did when she came, and then get over it. And if she's happy she ought to smile with her eyes as well as with her lips. I can't stand self-repression in children."

"She'll be all right when she has been here longer and begins to feel at home," said Miss Barnes. But Belinda shook her head doubtfully as she went down to superintend study hour.

Seated at her desk in the big schoolroom she looked idly along the rows of girlish heads until she came to one bent stoically over a book. The new pupil was not fidgeting like her comrades. Apparently her every thought was concentrated upon the book before her. Her elbows were on her desk, and one lean little brown hand supported the head, whose masses of straight black hair were parted in an unerring white line and fell in two heavy braids. The face framed in the smooth shining hair was lean as the hand, yet held no suggestion of ill-health. It was clean cut, almost to sharpness, brown with the brownness that comes from wind and sun, oddly firm about chin and lips, high of cheekbones, straight of nose.

As Belinda looked two dark eyes were raised from the book and met her own—sombre eyes with a hurt in them—and an uncomfortable lump rose in the Youngest Teacher's throat. She smiled at the sad little face, but the smile was not a merry one. In some unaccountable way it spoke of the sympathetic lump in her throat, and the Queer Little Thing seemed to read the message, for the ghost of an answering smile flickered in the brown depths before the lids dropped over them.

When study hour was over the Youngest Teacher moved hastily to the door, with some vague idea of following up the successful smile, and establishing diplomatic relations with the new girl; but she was not quick enough. Bonita had slipped into the hall and hurried up the stair toward the shelter of her own room.

Shrugging her shoulders, Belinda turned toward the door of Miss Ryder's study and knocked.

"Come in."

The voice was not encouraging. Miss Lucilla objected to interruptions in the late evening hours, when she relaxed from immaculately fitted black silk to the undignified folds of a violet dressing gown.

When she recognized the intruder she thawed perceptibly.

"Oh, Miss Carewe! Come in. Nothing wrong, is there?"

Belinda dropped into a chair with a whimsical sigh.

"Nothing wrong except my curiosity. Miss Ryder, do tell me something about that Allen child."

Miss Lucilla eyed her subordinate questioningly.

"What has she been doing?"

"Nothing at all. I wish she would do something. It's what she doesn't do, and looks capable of doing, that bothers me. There's simply no getting at her. She's from Texas, isn't she?"

The principal regarded attentively one of the grapes she was eating, and there was an interval of silence.

"She is a queer little thing," Miss Lucilla admitted at last. "Yes, she's from Texas, but that's no reason why she should be odd. We've had a number of young ladies from Texas, and they were quite like other school girls only more so. Just between you and me, Miss Carewe, I think it must be the child's Indian blood that makes her seem different."

"Indian?" Belinda sat up, sniffing romance in the air.

"Yes, her father mentioned the strain quite casually when he wrote. It's rather far back in the family, but he seemed to think it might account for the girl's intense love for nature and dislike of conventions. Mrs. Allen died when the baby was born, and the father has brought the child up on a ranch. He's completely wrapped up in her, but he finally realized that she needed to be with women. He's worth several millions and he wants to educate her so that she'll enjoy the money—'be a fine lady,' as he puts it. I confess his description of the girl disturbed me at first, but he was so liberal in regard to terms that——"

Miss Lucilla left the sentence in the air and meditatively ate another bunch of grapes.

"Did her father come up with her?" Belinda asked.

"No, he sent her with friends who happened to be coming—highly respectable couple, but breezy, very breezy. They told me that Bonita could ride any broncho on the ranch and could shoot a jack-rabbit on the run. They seemed to think she would be a great addition to our school circle on that account. Personally I'm much relieved to find her so tractable and quiet, but I've noticed something—well—unusual about her."

As Belinda went up to bed she met a slim little figure in a barbaric red and yellow dressing gown crossing the hall. There was a shy challenge in the serious child face, although the little feet, clad in soft beaded moccasins, quickened their steps; and Belinda answered the furtive friendliness by slipping an arm around the girl's waist and drawing her into the tiny hall bedroom.

"You haven't been to see me. It's one of the rules that every girl shall have a cup of cocoa with me before she has been here three evenings," she said laughingly.

The Queer Little Thing accepted the overture soberly and, curled up in the one big chair, watched the teacher in silence.

The cocoa was soon under way. Then the hostess turned and smiled frankly at her guest. Belinda's smile is a reassuring thing.

"Homesick business, isn't it?" she said abruptly, with a warm note of comradeship in her voice.

The tense little figure in the big chair leaned forward with sudden, swift confidence.

"I'm going home," announced Bonita in a tone that made no reservations.

Belinda received the news without the quiver of an eyelash or a sign of incredulity.

"When?" she asked with interest warm enough to invite confession and not emphatic enough to rouse distrust.

"I don't know just when, but I have to go. I can't stand it and I've written to Daddy. He'll understand. Nobody here knows. They're all used to it. They've always lived in houses like this, with little back yards that have high walls around them, and sidewalks and streets right outside the front windows, and crowds of strange people going by all the time, and just rules, rules, rules, everywhere. Everybody has so many manners, and they talk about things I don't know anything about, and nobody would understand if I talked about the real things."

"Perhaps I'll understand a little bit," murmured Belinda. The Queer Little Thing put out one hand and touched the Youngest Teacher's knee gently in a shy, caressing fashion.

"No, you wouldn't understand, because you don't know; but you could learn. The others couldn't. The prairie wouldn't talk to them and they'd be lonesome—the way I am here. Dick says you have got to learn the language when you are little, or else have a gift for such languages, but that when you've once learned it you don't care to hear any other."

"Who's Dick?" Belinda asked.

"Dick? Oh he's just Dick. He taught me to ride and to shoot, and he used to read poetry to me, and he told me stories about everything. He used to go to a big school called Harvard, but he was lonesome there—the way I am here."

"The way I am here" dropped into the talk like a persistent refrain, and there was heartache in it.

"I want to go home," the child went on. Now that the dam of silence was down the pent-up feeling rushed out tumultuously. "I want to see Daddy and the boys and the horses and the cattle, and I want to watch the sun go down over the edge of the world, not just tumble down among the dirty houses, and I want to gallop over the prairie where there aren't any roads, and smell the grass and watch the birds and the sky. You ought to see the sky down there at night, Miss Carewe. It's so big and black and soft and full of bright stars, and you can see clear to where it touches the ground all around you, and there's a night breeze that's cool as cool, and the boys all play their banjos and guitars and sing, and Daddy and I sit over on our veranda and listen. There's only a little narrow strip of sky with two or three stars in it out of my window here, and it's so noisy and cluttered out in the back yards—and I hate walking in a procession on the ugly old streets, and doing things when bells ring. I hate it. I hate it."

Her voice hadn't risen at all, had only grown more and more vibrant with passionate rebellion. The sharp little face was drawn and pale, but there were no tears in the big tragic eyes.

Belinda had consoled many homesick little girls, but this was a different problem.

"I'm sorry," she said softly. "Don't you think It will be easier after a while?"

The small girl with the old face shook her head.

"No, it won't. It isn't in me to like all this. I'm so sorry, because Daddy wants me to be a lady. He said it was as hard for him to send me as it was for me to come, but that I couldn't learn to be a lady with lots of money to spend down there with only boys and him. There wasn't any lady there on the ranch at all, except Mammy Lou, the cook, and she didn't have lots of money to spend, so she wasn't the kind he meant. I thought I'd come and try, but I didn't know it would be like this. I don't want to be a lady, Miss Carewe. I don't believe they can be very happy. I've seen them in carriages and they don't look very happy. You're nice. I like you, and I'm most sure Daddy and Dick and the boys would like you, but then you haven't got lots of money, have you? And you were born up here and you don't know any better anyway. I'm going home."

The burst of confidence ended where it had begun. She was going home, and she was so firm in the faith that Belinda, listening, believed her.

"But if your father says no?"

The dark little face was quiet again, all but the great eyes.

"I'll have to go," the Queer Little Thing slowly said.

Four days later Miss Lucilla Ryder called the Youngest Teacher into the study.

"Miss Carewe, I'm puzzled about this little Miss Allen. I had a letter from her father this morning. He says that she has written that she is very homesick and unhappy and doesn't want to stay. He feels badly about it, of course, but he very wisely leaves the matter in our hands—says he realizes she'll have to be homesick and he'll have to be lonesome if she's to be a lady. But he wants us to do all we can to make her contented. He very generously sends a check for five hundred dollars, which we are to use for any extra expense incurred in entertaining her and making her happy. Now, I thought you might take her to the theater and the art museum, and the—a—the aquarium, and introduce her to the pleasures and advantages of city life. She'll soon be all right."

With sinking heart Belinda went in search of the girl. She found her practicing five-finger exercises drearily in one of the music-rooms. As Belinda entered the child looked up and met the friendly, sympathetic eyes. A mute appeal sprang into her own eyes, and Belinda understood. The thing was too bad to be talked about, and the Youngest Teacher said no word about the homesickness or the expected letter. In this way she clinched her friendship with the Queer Little Thing.

But, following the principal's orders, she endeavored to demonstrate to Bonita the joy and blessedness of life in New York. The child went, quietly wherever she was taken—a mute, pathetic little figure to whom the aquarium fish and the Old Masters and the latest matinee idol were all one—and unimportant. The other girls envied her her privileges and her pocket-money, but they did not understand. No one understood save Belinda, and she did her cheerful best to blot out old loves with new impressions; but from the first she felt in her heart that she was elected to failure. The child was fond of her, always respectful, always docile, always grave. Nothing brought a light into her eyes or a spontaneous smile to her lips. Anyone save Belinda would have grown impatient, angry. She only grew more tender—and more troubled. Day by day she watched the sad little face grow thinner. It was pale now, instead of brown, and the high cheek bones were strikingly prominent. The lips pressed closely together drooped plaintively at the corners and the big eyes were more full of shadow than ever; but the child made no protest or plea, and by tacit consent she and Belinda ignored their first conversation and never mentioned Texas.

Often Belinda made up her mind to put aside the restraint and talk freely as she would to any other girl, but there was something about the little Texan that forbade liberties, warned off intruders, and the Youngest Teacher feared losing what little ground she had gained.

Finally she went in despair to Miss Ryder.

"The Indian character is too much for me," she confessed with a groan half humorous, half earnest. "I give it up."

"What's the matter?" asked Miss Ryder.

"Well, I've dragged poor Bonita Allen all over the borough of Manhattan and the Bronx and spent many ducats in the process. She has been very polite about it, but just as sad over Sherry's tea hour as over Grant's tomb, and just as cheerful over the Cesnola collection as over the monkey cages at the Zoo. The poor little thing is so unhappy and miserable that she looks like a wild animal in a trap, and I think the best we can do with her is to send her home.

"Nonsense," said Miss Lucilla. "Her father is paying eighteen hundred dollars a year."

Belinda was defiant.

"I don't care. He ought to take her home."

"Miss Carewe, you are sentimentalizing. One would think you had never seen a homesick girl before."

"She's different from other girls."

"I'll talk with her myself," said Miss Lucilla sternly.

She did, but the situation remained unchanged, and when she next mentioned the Texan problem to Belinda, Miss Lucilla was less positive in her views.

"She's a very strange child, but we must do what we can to carry out her father's wishes."

"I'd send her home," said Belinda.

It was shortly after this that Katherine Holland, who sat beside Bonita at the table, confided to Belinda that that funny little Allen girl didn't eat a thing. The waitress came to Belinda with the same tale, and the Youngest Teacher sought out Bonita and reasoned with her.

"You really must eat, my dear," she urged.

"Why?"

"You'll be ill if you don't."

"How soon?"

Belinda looked dazed.

"I'm afraid I don't understand."

"How soon will I be sick?"

"Very soon, I'm afraid," the puzzled teacher answered.

"That's good. I don't feel as if I could wait much longer."

Belinda gasped.

"Do you mean to say you want to be ill?"

"If I get very sick Daddy will come for me."

The teacher looked helplessly at the quiet, great-eyed child, then launched into expostulation, argument, entreaty.

Bonita listened politely and was profoundly unimpressed.

"It's wicked, dear child. It would make your father wretchedly unhappy."

"He'd be awfully unhappy if he understood, anyway. He thinks I'm not really unhappy and that it's his duty to keep me here and make a lady of me, no matter how lonely he is without me. He wrote me so—but I know he'd be terribly glad if he had a real excuse for taking me home."

Belinda exhausted her own resources and appealed to Miss Lucilla, who stared incredulously over her nose-glasses and sent for Bonita.

After the interview she called for the Youngest Teacher, and the two failures looked at each other helplessly.

"It's an extraordinary thing," said Miss Lucilla in her most magisterial tone—"a most extraordinary thing. In all my experience I've seen nothing like it. Nothing seems to make the slightest impression upon the child. She's positively crazy."

"You will tell her father to send for her, won't you?"

Miss Lucilla shook her head stubbornly.

"Not at all. It would be the ruination of the child to give in to her whims and bad temper now. If she won't listen to reason she must be allowed to pay for her foolishness. When she gets hungry enough she will eat. It's a shame to talk about a child of twelve having the stoicism to starve herself into an illness just because she is homesick at boarding-school."

Belinda came back to her thread-worn argument.

"But Bonita is different, Miss Ryder."

"She's a very stubborn, selfish child," said Miss Ryder resentfully, and turning to her desk she changed the conversation.

Despite discipline, despite pleadings, despite cajolery, Bonita stood firm. Eat she would not, and when, on her way to class one morning the scrap of humanity with the set lips and the purple shadows round her eyes fainted quietly, Belinda felt that a masterly inactivity had ceased to be a virtue.

James, the house man, carried the girl upstairs, and the Youngest Teacher put her to bed, where she opened her eyes to look unseeingly at Belinda and then closed them wearily and lay quite still, a limp little creature whose pale face looked pitifully thin and lifeless against the white pillow. The

Queer Little Thing's wish had been fulfilled and illness had come without long delay.

For a moment Belinda looked down at the girl. Then she turned and went swiftly to Miss Ryder's study, her eyes blazing, her mouth so stern that Amelia Bowers, who met her on the stairs, hurried to spread the news that Miss Carewe "was perfectly hopping mad about something."

Once in the presence of the August One the little teacher lost no time in parley.

"Miss Ryder," she said crisply—and at the tone her employer looked up in amazement—"I've told you about Bonita Allen. I've been to you again and again about her. You knew that she was fretting her heart out and half sick, and then you knew that for several days she hasn't been eating a thing. I tried to make you understand that the matter was serious and that something radical needed to be done, but you insisted that the child would come around all right and that we mustn't give in to her. I begged you to send for her father and you said it wasn't necessary. I'm here to take your orders, Miss Ryder, but I can't stand this sort of thing. I know the girl better than any of the rest of you do, and I know it isn't badness that makes her act so. Now she is ill—really ill. I've just put her to bed, and honestly, Miss Ryder, if we don't send for her father we'll have a tragedy on our hands. It sounds foolish, but it is true. If nobody else telegraphs to Mr. Allen I am going to do it."

When the doctor came there were bright red spots on the Queer Little Thing's cheeks, and she was babbling incoherently about prairie flowers and horses and Dick and Daddy.

Meanwhile a telegram had gone to Daddy and the messenger who delivered it heard a volume of picturesque comment that was startling even on a Texas ranch.

"Am coming," ran the answering dispatch received by Miss Ryder that night; but it was not until morning that Bonita was able to understand the news.

"He's scared, but I know he's glad," she said and she swallowed without a murmur the broth against which even in her delirium she had fought.

One evening, three days later, a hansom dashed up to the school and out jumped a tall, square-shouldered man in a wide-brimmed hat, and clothes that bore only a family resemblance to the clothing of the New York millionaires, though they were good clothes in their own free-and-easy way.

A loud, hearty voice inquiring for "My baby" made itself heard even in the sickroom, and a sudden light flashed into the little patient's eyes—a light that was an illumination and a revelation.

"Daddy," she said wearily, and the word was a heart-throb.

Mr. Allen wasted no time in a polite interview with Miss Ryder. Hypnotized by his masterfulness, the servant led him directly up to the sick-room and opened the door.

The man filled the room; a high breeze seemed to come with him, and vitality flowed from him in tangible waves. Belinda smiled, but there were tears in her eyes, for the big man's heart was in his face.

"Baby!"

"Daddy!"

Belinda remembered an errand downstairs.

When she returned the big Texan was sitting on the side of the bed with both the lean little hands in one of his big brawny ones, while his other hand awkwardly smoothed the straight black hair.

"When will you take me home, Daddy?" said the child with the shining eyes.

"As soon as you're strong enough, Honey. The boys wanted me to let them charge New York in a bunch and get you. It's been mighty lonesome on that ranch. I wish to heaven I'd never been fool enough to let you come away."

He turned to Belinda with a quizzical smile sitting oddly on his anxious face.

"I reckon she might as well go, miss. I sent her to a finishing school, and by thunder, she's just about finished."

There was a certain hint of pride in his voice as he added reflectively:

"I might have known if she said she'd have to come home she meant it. Harder to change her mind than to bust any broncho I ever tackled. Queer Little Thing, Baby is."

Copyrighted by Doubleday, Page & Co.

An American Wake

By Rose A. Crow

This was the last night in the old home, which had sheltered the family for five generations. The day had been full of excitement, as by a merciful ordinance last days usually are. The final packing had been done, the chests and boxes securely fastened and carefully labeled. This was all looked after by Margaret, herself, amidst interruptions by her brood of young children. Visits from friends and relatives, living at a distance, occupied much of the day; attending to countless minor things kept them all busy until nightfall. Even then there was no time allowed to visit the shrine.

Margaret had a fairy shrine, to which she carried the cares of the day and the hopes of the morrow. This charmed place was a stile over the ivy-clad walls of the garden. There she brought her childish joys and sorrows, and in the quiet received consolation. She had fought the fiercest battles of her womanhood with her head resting against the ivy-covered pillar. To-night, when she was parting from her country and friends, there was no time to commune with her silent friend.

Shortly after dusk, in accordance with local etiquette, very stringent on such momentous occasions, the relatives, friends and neighbors of a lifetime began to drop in by twos and threes until every inch of wall space was filled.

Who of all this gathering was more welcome than "John, the Fiddler"? He was a great favorite with young and old. The sight of him carrying his fiddle caused a feeling of emotion in the hearts of the older people. It recalled the tragic story of John's father who years before left for America intending to send for his wife and crippled son. A fever contracted on shipboard deprived them of a husband and father. It was then that John Doyle became "John, the Fiddler."

John was beckoned into the "room," where with Father O'Connell and a few trusty friends, he was treated to a small measure of potheen. Dan Monahan had donated a very small jug for this special occasion. To be given the first shot from Dan's still was no small favor, as those present knew. Before taking his seat at the end of the room, John drank Margaret's health, wishing herself and family a safe voyage across the water, and a happy home on the prairies of Iowa.

Each guest realized the strain of parting and generously made an effort to conceal the gloom with a brave semblance of mirth. There was dancing, singing of songs, and elaborate drinking of healths. With persistent calls for Margaret's brother James, the dancing stopped. The floor was cleared, and he was borne in on the shoulders of the leaders, who had found him leaning against the ivy-covered wall, gazing at the moon, floating over his old home which, alas! he would never see again.

James MacNevin was a magnificent specimen of Irish manhood and a charming singer. He was about twenty-three years old, tall and broad-shouldered, with a fine head of curly auburn hair. His clear blue eyes reflected the sadness of the group around him, while his white teeth flashed a smile. In one hand he crushed his handkerchief, while with the other he nervously twirled a sprig of ivy. A few measures of "Good Night and Joy Be with You All" came from the violin. For an instant he wavered, then throwing back his head he sang the song, not with full volume, but with intense feeling, emphasis and a clear ringing tone. The song seemed to voice his own feelings as his chest rose and fell. He was no longer just James MacNevin, but a pilgrim traveling to a strange country. His whole soul was filled with the sentiment, and there was such pathos in its heart-throb that the whole company was moved to tears. The last verse ended, he stood a moment with gaze transfixed—then rousing himself, bowed, smiled and with one hand in his sister Margaret's, the other clutching the sprig of ivy, he passed out of the home forever.

Rochester, Minn.

(With apologies to the Mayos)
By Marie G. Stapp

Mr. Smith had gallstones,

Mr. Jones had gout,

Bad appendices had the Browns

But now they've been cut out.

Rachel had a goitre,

Susan a queer spleen,

A tumor worried Mrs. Wright

Though it could not be seen.

Robert had large tonsils

And Dick had adenoids, too,

Bill Green had never had an ear,

He did when *they* got through.

Peggy had a leaky heart,

Her father had no hair,

Both heart and head are now fixed up

And what a happy pair!

And I—well I have nothing wrong—

That's why I don't feel right;

I'll pay my bill at this hotel

And go back home to-night.

God's Back Yard

By Jessie Welborn Smith

AN EPISODE FROM ACT THREE

Place, Tim Murphy's saloon.   Time, evening.

Men are crowding about the bar, drinking and laughing coarsely. The wives are huddled together on a long bench at one side of the room. The children keep close to their mothers, but stretch their little necks to watch the dancing in the back of the room, where a group of painted women are tangoing to the wheezy accompaniment of an old accordion. Over in the corner a man sprawls drunkenly across a broken-down faro table.

Dick Long (hammering the bar with his mug and singing). Oh, I'm goin' to hell, and I don't give a damn. I'm goin' to hell. I'm goin' to—hell.

Murphy (knocking a board from the crate that holds the new nickel-in-the-slot gramaphone). You're going a damn sight faster than that, Dickie Bird, but you'll have to speed up a bit to get in on the concert. The program begins at eight o'clock sharp, like it says on the card in the window, and everybody gets an invite, but Caruso don't sing this time.

First Painted Lady (stopping the dance and coming down beside Murphy). Let 'er go, Murph. Give us "Too Much Mustard." The piano player down at the Gulch plays that just fine, and a piece about a girl that didn't want to love him, but he made her do it. That machine was long on personal history, Murph. I heard them all through three times. Let 'er go. We're all here.

First Wife (leaning over and speaking eagerly). Mrs. Long won't be able to come, Murphy, and Old Moll is settin' up with her to-night. I met Doc as I came across. The young-un died. I don't see no use in waitin' when we're all here.

Rosie Phelan (reaching over and pulling Long's sleeve). Did you hear that, Dick? Your kid is dead. Your kid is—d-e-a-d. Do you get me?

Man at the Bar. Aw, break it to him gentle. He don't know he is a father yet. Have a heart.

Rosie Phelan (disgustedly). "Have a heart." Well, what do you think of that? For a man who guzzles all day you are mighty strong on the heart-throb slush. "Speak kindly to the erring." Didn't know you had got religion. Was it you got the revivalist to come up from the Gulch?

Nell (shifting her wad of gum). Well, he was sitting over at Benton's rather lonesome-like as I came along. I allus follow the crowd.

Murphy (hotly). And that is what that preacher will have to do if he makes any converts up here at the mine. I reckon that, with that music machine, I'm equipped to compete with any preacher that comes larking around here until kingdom come. He said he'd save me, if he had to chase me to hell and back, did he? Well, that guy should worry. That pale chicken-liver chase me to—Pour out the drinks, Bob. It's my treat.

Bob slops a little whiskey into every glass and mug on the bar and passes it round. As it comes to the wives they smile, but shake their heads. Murphy lifts his glass.

Murphy. Won't you women drink the minister's health. How about you females, Bett? Nell? Rosie? Mollie? You girls never turn down free liquor, do you? Ready? To hell with the minister.

Barkeeper. To hell with every denatured female that comes round here praying for our souls' salvation. I reckon a feller can do what he damn pleases with his own soul.

First Lounger (lazily boastful). I told my old woman that if I ketched her or the kids hanging round listening to that mollycoddle letting off steam, I'd——

First Wife (spitefully). Us women ain't got no call to get religion. We're too meek already. My man knows that he'll have a wildcat at his head when he comes in with that O'Grady woman, but it don't do no good. He ain't afeared o' nothin' short o' the devil. You don't ketch me joinin' while my old man is alive. You gotta have some protection. Safety first, I say.

Second Wife (meekly). They say the "Blue Ridge Mountains" is a mighty tuneful piece. My sister heard it over at Smarty's las' Thanksgiving. Can you tell whether your pianoler plays that, Murphy?

Second Painted Lady (patronizingly). How would you expect Murphy to know what is stored in that machine? You pays your money and your choice is whatever it happens to grind out. If you place your money on a "Harem" and draws an "Apple Blossom Time in Normandy," you got to take your medicine. What you waiting for, Murph? My gentleman friend is coming over from the Pass this evening, and I can't hang around here all night.

Rosie (excitedly, turning from the window that looks upon the street). The light is out at Benton's. The minister is coming over here. Remember and give him hell. Let him turn the other cheek.

Murphy. No prayer meeting virgin is going to interfere with my business.

The door opens and the minister steps inside. Murphy goes over and greets him with mock politeness.

Murphy. Rosie, you are chief usher to-night. Will you find the minister a seat? Sit over, Nell. There's room enough between you and Bett for any sky pilot that ever hit the trail. Bob, give the preacher a drink. He looks sort of fagged. It's hard work saving sinners in God's Back Yard. I hope this little concert ain't going to interfere with your meeting, parson.

Minister (standing at the bar, whiskey glass in hand). Not at all, friend. What is the bill of fare?

Rosie (coming forward in her low-cut red gown and swinging her full skirts from side to side). For Gawd's sake, why didn't you tell me it was going to be religious? I'd forgot it was prayer-meetin' night, Murph. *(She carefully tucks her handkerchief over her bosom in pretense of modesty.)* I'd dressed up more, if I'd remembered.

Nell (holding out a string of glittering beads). Here, take these, Rosie. These'll cover up some. I ain't takin' an active part, so I don't mind.

Rosie (lifting her arms to fasten the beads). Not takin' an active part? You don't know what you're sayin'. I heard of a minister once who could make hell look so darned nice you wanted to fall for it right away. Couldn't such a fellah give the heavenly gates a jar? *(She turns to the minister.)* Where d'you want to sit? Up there by Mollie? Take your choice.

Old Moll's Daughter (jumping down from her perch at one end of the bar and walking over brazenly to drop the first nickel in the slot). Clear the way, can't you? I'm praying for the "Bunny Hug" and the minister is backing me. For Gawd's sake, can't you clear the floor? Do you want the music to be half done before you find your partners? I'll be obliged to you, parson, if you'll save this dance for me. *(She pauses a moment, nickel in hand.)*

First Card Player. I'll stake you ten to one it'll be "The Pullman Porters on Parade."

Second Player (doggedly). They always play "A Great Big Blue-Eyed Baby."

Rosie (shaking her head and singing, hands on hips). "My harem, my harem, my roly, poly harem."

Nell (with mock sentiment). "For it's Apple Blossom Time in Normandy, in Normandy, in Normandy."

The nickel jangles in the slot. The disk begins to revolve. It grates and begins its introductory mechanical clinkety-clinkety clink. A small child wails dismally as the music shivers through the room.

"Jesus, lover of my soul,

Let me to Thy bosom fly.

While the nearer waters roll,

While the tempest still is high.

Hide me, O, my Saviour, hide

Till the storm of life is past.

Safe into the haven guide,

O, receive my soul at last."

Rosie's hands drop from her hips as the song begins. The dancing impulse passes from her limbs. Even the muscles of her face harden convulsively.

Rosie (hysterically). Oh, I can't stand that, Murphy. For Gawd's sake, can't you stop it?

She starts over toward the machine impulsively. Then something catches her, she pauses and is held a moment while a superstitious awe makes her eyes again the big roundness of childhood's wonder. She draws the back of her hand across her forehead in an endeavor to bring herself out of the daze.

Rosie (falling sobbing beside the bench). "O, receive my soul at last." Why did you leave your little Rosie? Mother, Oh, mother. I ain't fit to come to you no more, mother—I ain't fit, I ain't fit.

One of the mothers reaches over and strokes her hair.

Old Moll's Daughter (opening the door and stepping out into the lonely street as she laughs madly). Old Murphy in cahoots with the minister. Oh, hell!

The door slams shut. The glasses on the bar jangle harshly. A snatch of song boldly defiant rings in from the street: "Don't tell me that you've lost your dog." Murphy walks over and stands looking at the music box. It is still grinding out the music.

"Other refuge have I none.

Hangs my helpless soul on Thee.

Leave, ah, leave me not alone.

Still support and comfort me.

All my trust on Thee is staid.

All my help from Thee I bring.

Cover my defenseless head

With the shadow of Thy wing."

The wives are all crying quietly. Rosie and Bett are sobbing with the wild abandon that such natures know. Tears are falling upon the idle hands at the card table. The men at the bar are strangely quiet.

Man at the Faro Table (lifting himself up on his elbow). I ushe shing—I ushe shing zhat—I ushe shing Jeshus—Jeshus—I ushe shing—(*He drops his head over on the table and weeps drunkenly.*)

Little Child (pulling at her mother's shoulders and whining peevishly). Who is Jesus, mamma? Do we know Jesus? (*Happily.*) Will he cover my head with a pretty birdie's wing? (*The mother shakes with sobs and the child speaks more caressingly.*) Don't cry, mother. I like my hat with the posies on it. You can have the feathers, nice, good mamma. Don't cry.

Murphy (absently, looking at the minister). They sang that at the funeral. Sally didn't have no call to hide anything. She was that white and pure. I always felt her slippin'—slippin' away. She worried so them last days because of the little kid. "Take him back home, Murph," she kept sayin'. "A little child has got to have some raisin'. A kid has got to go to Sunday school, Tim, dear, and there ain't never no meetin's in God's Back Yard."

Man at the Bar (dejectedly, going over to the door). It's all right for the young-uns, but when a man has got a thirst and is down on his luck, I don't allow that God is going to help much. You got to get 'em young, parson, and keep 'em headed straight. It's hell turning back. I tried it, and I couldn't make it go.

Minister (gently, as if speaking to someone very near). Oh, Jesus, lover of all these misguided souls, come down to this little room to-night, for it is dark here, and, Oh, so cold and dreary. Speak to them, Jesus, as you did to me. Let them see the glory of Thy face. Will someone pray?

Murphy (looking across at the loafers and speaking half as an invitation, half as a command). Are you staying, boys?

One of the Men (doggedly, as they look at one another sheepishly and no one moves to go). Ain't we always stayin' till closin' time?

Murphy (warmly). You sure do, boys. (*He buries his head in his crossed arms over the music-box.*) It's your lead, parson.

The Wild Crab Apple

By Julia Ellen Rogers

The wild, sweet-scented crab apple! The bare mention of its name is enough to make the heart leap up, though spring be months away, and barriers of brick hem us in. In the corner of the back pasture stands a clump of these trees, huddled together like cattle. Their flat, matted tops reach out sidewise until the stubby limbs of neighboring trees meet. It would not occur to anyone to call them handsome trees. But wait! The twigs silver over with young foliage, then coral buds appear, thickly sprinkling the green leaves. Now all their asperity is softened, and a great burst of rose-colored bloom overspreads the treetops and fills the air with perfume. It is not mere sweetness, but an exquisite, spicy, stimulating fragrance that belongs only to wild crab-apple flowers. Linnæus probably never saw more than a dried specimen, but he named this tree most worthily, *coronaria*, "fit for crowns and garlands."

Break off an armful of these blossoming twigs and take them home. They will never be missed. Be thankful that your friends in distant parts of the country may share your pleasure, for though this particular species does not cover the whole United States, yet there is a wild crab apple for each region.

In the fall the tree is covered with hard little yellow apples. They have a delightful fragrance, but they are neither sweet nor mellow. Take a few home and make them into jelly. Then you will understand why the early settlers gathered them for winter use. The jelly has a wild tang in it, an indescribable piquancy of flavor as different from common apple jelly as the flowers are in their way more charming than ordinary appleblossoms. It is the rare gamy taste of a primitive apple.

Well-meaning horticulturists have tried what they could do toward domesticating this *Malus coronaria*. The effort has not been a success. The fruit remains acerb and hard; the tree declines to be "ameliorated" for the good of mankind. Isn't it, after all, a gratuitous office? Do we not need our wild crab apple just as it is, as much as we need more kinds of orchard trees? How spirited and fine is its resistance! It seems as if this wayward beauty of our woodside thickets considered that the best way to serve mankind was to keep inviolate those charms that set it apart from other trees and make its remotest haunt the Mecca of eager pilgrims every spring.

The wild crab apple is not a tree to plant by itself in park or garden. Plant it in companies on the edge of woods, or in obscure and ugly fence corners, where there is a background, or where, at least, each tree can lose its individuality in the mass. Now, go away and let them alone. They do not need mulching nor pruning. Let them gang their ain gait, and in a few years you will have a crab-apple thicket. You will also have succeeded in bringing home with these trees something of the spirit of the wild woods where you found them.

—From *The Tree Book*.

A Ballad of the Corn

By S. H. M. Byers

Oh, the undulating prairies,
And the fields of yellow corn,
Like a million soldiers waiting for the fray.
Oh, the rustling of the corn leaves
Like a distant fairy's horn
And the notes the fairy bugles seem to play.

"We have risen from the bosom
Of the beauteous mother earth,
Where the farmer plowed his furrow straight and long.
There was gladness and rejoicing
When the summer gave us birth,
In the tumult and the dancing and the song.

"When the sumach turns to scarlet,
And the vines along the lane
Are garmented in autumn's golden wine—
Then the land shall smile for plenty,
And the toiler for his pain,
When the soldiers of our army stand in line.

"With our shining blades before us,
And our banners flaming far,
Want and hunger shall be slain forevermore.
And the cornfield's lord of plenty
In his golden-covered car
Then shall stop at every happy toiler's door."

Oh, the sunshine and the beauty

On the fields of ripened corn,

And the wigwams and the corn-rows where they stand.

In the lanes I hear the music

Of the faintly blowing horn

And the blessed Indian summer's on the land.

The Children's Blessing

By Virginia Roderick

On the slope of a hill, beneath silvery olives, a group was gathered about the young stranger. He had entered the village only that morning, seeking the companionship of such Nazarenes as might be there. And they had brought him out here in the open to receive his message. But though he carried them greetings, and news from the distant groups of the Christ's followers, it was plain that he had not been sent to them on a mission.

They waited until he should be ready to explain his quest.

"You did not see Him, then?"

Into the young man's eyes there came a great, yearning sadness. "No," he answered. "But you," he asked eagerly, "did none of you see Him?"

They shook their heads, all of them.

"We were too far away," one murmured.

"But I had for spiritual father one who had seen Him," the traveler offered, his face lighting. "You know how He blessed a company of little children? How He put His hands upon them?" He paused and they nodded silently. "My teacher was one of those children," he said, his dark eyes aglow with reverent pride.

A quick glance flashed about the group; but no one spoke and the traveler went on, the radiance of his face blotted out again in sadness. "It is because he is gone that I am a wanderer now. I was always with him, and we went about together, preaching the Kingdom. It was all so clear to my teacher because he had seen Him. He told me of His wonderful look."

They fell silent, brooding and thoughtful.

Then one asked: "What was it like—the blessing He gave your teacher? Did he gain goods and store?"

The young traveler's eyes opened in amazement. "Why no! How could that be? My teacher was like Him," he explained simply.

Again the quick look passed about the circle. At last one spoke, slowly: "There is a man here in the village who was also blessed with the children."

The young traveler started up joyously. "Take me to him," he entreated. "Let me talk with him; that is what I have come here seeking—another teacher."

"Nay, friend——" began one; but another hurriedly whispered: "Let us not tell him. Perhaps he can help." And so the first speaker finished: "I fear you will not find him like your teacher, but you shall go; it is only a step."

And they guided him, all but impatient, to a mean hovel just within the town. There they left him.

It was a man with a dark, bitter face that answered his knock. "May I speak with Nemuel?" the stranger asked courteously.

"I am Nemuel," growled the man curtly.

"But I mean Nemuel who was one of the children that Jesus blessed," persisted the young traveler, his face softly alight as the name passed his lips.

"Come in; I am the man." He straightened proudly. "I was a child seven years old when I saw Him——"

He stopped, for the young stranger, pale and gasping, broke in: "You saw Him! He touched you! You have seen His face, and yet your own—forgive me, friend. But my master was also one of the children blessed by the Christ, and he was ... different." He hesitated, still looking at the somber face in puzzled distress.

The man caught the young stranger's arm. "You knew another of those He blessed? Tell me, did he have great wealth, palaces, honors? Did he wait long? Did the blessing tarry so long in the fulfilment as with me?"

The young stranger shook his head in deep bewilderment. "I do not understand. No, he had no wealth, no palaces, no honors. He followed the Christ. He was blessed by His spirit. Why, how could one want goods and honors when one had seen His wonderful smile, when His arms—" He broke off, gazing at his host in appalled incomprehension.

Nemuel's dark face grew darker, more bitter. "Then there *is* no blessing, after all," he said slowly. "I have waited, believing, trusting. I have kept my life clean. I have kept myself holy—away from those He had not touched—" The stranger drew a quick breath and his eyes softened with pity. "I have never forgotten that I was blessed above others. And now there *is* no blessing." And he covered his face with his hands.

There was a silence and then the young stranger spoke very gently: "The blessing my master taught me, was for all children—for all childlike faith and trust and purity. It was a sanctification of the child spirit."

Nemuel had lifted his head and was listening, his eyes fastened wonderingly on the stranger's face.

"And it was not a blessing to be wrapped up in a napkin. It was not one to bring you good fortune, as if it had been a sorcerer's charm. It was a blessing for you to take and to make—to use it—to give it to others. Through you He blessed *all* children.... And yet—" the stranger's voice deepened—"yet there *was* something special too."

"What was it?" Nemuel breathed.

The stranger bent on him a gaze full of yearning. "Have you not remembered His face?" he asked. "His wonderful look—just for you?" There was a pleading note of reproach in his voice as he leaned toward Nemuel, but his face was all love and tenderness.

Nemuel began to shake his head slowly, still fixing the stranger with his gaze.

"No," he confessed. "I haven't been able to remember—not for years. At first I did. Afterward I *knew* His face was wonderful, but I could not *see* it. But now—now I begin to remember——"

The young stranger waited for the halting words, his face lighting softly with a holy hope and joy.

"Why, your face—" Nemuel still hesitated, groping, and then suddenly his voice rang out in triumph, and memory dawned clearly in his eyes—"why, *your face*—is—like—*His*! Oh, I do remember!—and—I begin to understand."

Kitchener's Mob

From The Atlantic Monthly

By James Norman Hall

Trench-mortaring was more to our liking. That is an infantryman's game, and while extremely hazardous, the men in the trenches have a sporting chance. Everyone forgot breakfast when word was passed down the line that we were going to "mortarfy" Fritzie. Our projectiles were immense balls of hollow steel, filled with high explosive. Eagerly, expectantly, the boys gathered in the first-line trenches to watch the fun. First a dull boom from the reserve trench in rear where the mortar was operated.

"There she is!" "See 'er?" "Goin' true as a die!" All the boys would be shouting at once.

Up it goes, turning over and over, rising to a height of several hundred feet. Then, if well aimed, it reaches the end of its upward journey directly over the enemy's line, and falls straight into his trench. There is a moment of silence, followed by a terrific explosion which throws dirt and débris high in the air. By this time, the Tommies all along the line are standing on the firing benches, head and shoulders above the parapet, forgetting their danger in their excitement, and shouting at the top of their voices:

"'Ow's that one, Fritzie boy?"

"Guten morgen, you Proosian sausage wallopers!"

"Tyke a bit o' that there 'ome to yer missus!"

But Fritzie kept up his end of the game, always. He gave us just as good as we sent, and often he added something for good measure. His surprise packages were sausage-shaped missiles which came wobbling toward us, slowly, almost awkwardly; but they dropped with lightning speed. The explosion was terrible, and alas for any Tommy who misjudged the place of its fall! However, everyone had a chance. Trench-mortar projectiles are so large, and they describe so leisurely an arc before they fall, that men have time to run.

I've always admired Tommy Atkins for his sense of fair play. He loved giving Fritz "a little bit of all right," but he never resented it when Fritz had his own fun at our expense. I used to believe, in the far-off days of peace, that men had lost their old primal love for dangerous sport, their native ignorance of fear. But on those trench-mortaring days, when I watched boys playing with death with right good zest, heard them shouting and laughing as they tumbled over one another in their eagerness to escape being killed, I was convinced that I was wrong. Daily I saw men going through the test of fire triumphantly, and at the last, what a fearful test it was, and how splendidly they met it! During six months, continuously in the firing line, I met less than a dozen natural-born cowards; and my experience was largely among clerks, barbers, plumbers, shopkeepers, men who had no fighting tradition to back them up, to make them heroic in spite of themselves.

The better I knew Tommy, the better I liked him. He hasn't a shred of sentimentality in his make-up. There is plenty of sentiment, sincere feeling, but it is very well concealed. I had been a soldier of the King for many months before I realized that the men with whom I was living, sharing rations and hardships, were anything other than the healthy animals they looked. They seemed to live for their food. They talked of it, anticipated it with the zest of men who were experiencing for the first time the joy of being genuinely hungry. They watched their muscles harden with the satisfaction known to every normal man when he is becoming physically fit for the first time. But they said nothing about patriotism, or the duty of Englishmen in wartime. And if I tried to start a conversation on that line, they walked right over me with their boots on.

This was a great disappointment at first. I would never have known, from anything that was said, that a man of them was stirred at the thought of fighting for old England. England was all right, but, "I ain't a-goin' balmy about the old flag and all that stuff." Many of them insisted that they were in the army for personal and selfish reasons alone. They went out of their way to ridicule any and every indication of sentiment.

There was the matter of talk about mothers, for example. I can't imagine this being the case in a volunteer army of American boys; but never, during sixteen months of British army life, did I hear a discussion of mothers. When the weekly parcels post from England arrived, and the boys were sharing their cake and chocolate and tobacco, one of them would say, "Good old mum. She ain't a bad sort," to be answered with reluctant, mouth-filled grunts, or grudging nods of approval. As for fathers, I often thought to myself, "This is certainly a tremendous army of posthumous sons!" Months before I should have been astonished at this reticence. But I had learned to understand Tommy. His silences were as eloquent as any splendid outbursts or glowing tributes could have been. It was a matter of constant wonder to me that men living in the daily and hourly presence of death could so control and conceal their feelings. Their talk was of anything but home; and yet I knew that they thought of little else.

One of our boys was killed, and there was a letter to be written to his parents. Three Tommies who knew him best were to attempt this. They made innumerable beginnings. Each of them was afraid of blundering, of causing unnecessary pain by an indelicate revelation of the facts. There was a feminine fineness about their concern which was beautiful to see. The final draft of the letter was a masterpiece, not of English, but of insight; such a letter as any one of us would have liked his own parents to receive under similar circumstances. Nothing was forgotten which could make the news in the slightest degree more endurable. Every trifling personal belonging was carefully saved up and packed in a little box to follow the letter. All this was done amid much boisterous jesting; and there was hilarious singing to the wheezing accompaniment of an old mouth-organ. But of reference to home, or mothers, or comradeship, not a word.

Rarely a night passed without its burial parties. "Digging in the garden," Tommy calls the grave-making. The bodies, wrapped in blankets or waterproof ground-sheets, are lifted over the parados and carried back a convenient twenty yards or more. The desolation of that garden was indescribable. It was strewn with wreckage, gaping with shell-holes, billowing with numberless nameless graves, a waste land speechlessly pathetic. The poplars and willow hedges had been blasted and splintered by shell-fire. Tommy calls these "Kaiser Bill's flowers." Coming from England, he feels more deeply than he would care to admit the crimes done to trees in the name of war.

Our chaplain was a devout man, but prudent to a fault. He never visited us in the trenches; therefore our burial parties proceeded without the rites of the church. This arrangement was highly satisfactory to Tommy. He liked to "get the planting done" with the least possible delay or fuss. His whispered conversations, while the graves were being scooped, were, to say the least, quite out of the spirit of the occasion. Once we were burying two boys with whom we had been having a supper a few hours before. There was an artillery duel in progress, the shells whistling high over our heads and bursting in great splotches of white fire, far in rear of the opposing lines of trenches. The grave-making went speedily on while the diggers argued in whispers as to the calibre of the guns. Some said they were six-inch, while others thought nine-inch. Discussion was momentarily suspended when trench-rockets went soaring up from the enemy's line. We crouched motionless until the welcome darkness spread again. And then, in loud whispers—

"'Ere! If they was nine-inch they would 'ave more screech."

And one of different opinion would reply:

"Don't talk so bloomin' silly! Ain't I a-tellin' you you can't always size 'em by the screech?"

Not a prayer. Not a word either of censure or praise for the boys who had gone. Not an expression of opinion as to the meaning of the great change which had come to them and which might come as suddenly to any or all of us. And yet I knew that every man was thinking of these things.

There were days when the front was really quiet. The thin trickle of rifle-fire only accentuated the stillness of an early summer morning. Far down the line many a Tommy could be heard singing to himself as he sat in the door of his dug-out, cleaning his rifle. There would be the pleasant crackle of burning pine sticks, the sizzle of frying bacon, the lazy buzzing of swarms of bluebottle flies. Occasionally, across a pool of noonday silence, we heard the birds singing; for they didn't desert us. When we gave them a hearing, they did their cheery little best to assure us that everything would come right in the end. Once we heard a skylark, an English skylark, and for a while it made the world beautiful again. It was a fine thing to watch the faces of those English lads as they listened. I was deeply touched when one of them said, "Ain't 'e a plucky little chap, singin' right in front of Fritzie's trenches fer us English blokes?"

It was a sincere and beautiful tribute.

The Professor

By Calista Halsey Patchin

The professor had been dead two months. He had left the world very quietly, at that precise hour of the early evening when he was accustomed to say that his "spirit friends" came to him. The hospital nurse had noticed that there was always a time at twilight when the patient had a good hour; when pain and restlessness seemed to be charmed away, and he did not mind being left alone, and did not care whether or not there was a light in the room. Then it was that those who had gone came back to him with quiet, friendly ways and loving touch. He said nothing of this to the nurse. It was an old friend who told me that this had been his belief and solace for years.

When the professor had first come to town he had spoken of the wife who would follow him shortly, from the East. He did not display her picture, he did not talk about her enough so that the town, though it made an honest effort, ever really visualized her. She would come—without a doubt she would come—but not just yet. It was only that the East still held her. Gradually, he spoke of her less and less often, with a dignified reserve that brooked no inquiry, and finally not at all.

The town forgot. It was only when his illness became so serious that all felt someone should be written to, that it was discovered there was no one. The professor, when he was appealed to, said so. Then also, the hospital nurse noticed that at the twilight hour, when he talked quietly to his unseen friends, there was always One who stayed longer than the rest.

But he had been dead two months now, and the undertaker was pressing his bill, and there were other expenses which had been cheerfully borne by friends at the time, and indeed if there had been no other reason, it remains that something must become of the personal possessions of a man who leaves neither will nor known heirs. So the professor's effects were appraised, and a brief local appeared in the daily paper until it had made a dent in the memory of the public, apprising them that his personal property would be offered at public auction at two p.m. of a Thursday, in his rooms on the third floor of the Eureka Block.

It was the merest thread of curiosity that drew me to this sale. I did not want to buy anything. It was a sort of posthumous curiosity, and it concerned itself solely with the individuality of the dead man. Not having had the opportunity of knowing him well in life, and never having known until I read his obituary what I had missed, I took this last chance of trying to evolve the man from his belongings. All I did know was that he was a teacher of music of the past generation in a Western town which grew so fast that it made a man seem older than he was. More than this, he was a composer, a music master, who took crude young voices, shrill with the tension of the Western winds and the electric air, and tamed and trained them till they fell in love with harmony. When he heard a voice he knew it. One of his contraltos is singing now in grand opera across the sea. A tenor that he discovered has charmed the world with an "upper note."

All the same, the professor had grown old—a new generation had arisen which knew not Joseph; he failed to advertise, and every young girl who "gave lessons" crowded him closer to the wall. Now and then there would appear in the daily paper—not the next morning, but a few days after the presentation of some opera—a column of musical criticism, keen, delicate, reminiscent—fragrant with the rosemary that is for remembrance. When "Elijah" was given by home talent with soloists imported from Chicago, it was the professor who kindly wrote, beforehand this time, luminous articles full of sympathetic interpretation of the great masters. And at rare intervals there would appear a communication from him on the beauty of the woods and the fields, the suburbs of the town and the country, as though he were some simple prophet of nature who stood by the wayside. And this was no affectation. Long, solitary walks were his recreation.

It was a good deal of a rookery, up the flights of narrow, dirty stairs to the third floor of the Eureka Block. And here the professor had lived and taught. Two rooms were made from one by the sort of partition which does not reach to the ceiling—a ceiling which for some inexplicable reason was higher in some places than in others.

The voice of the auctioneer came down that winding way in professional cadences. There were in the room about as many people as might come to a funeral where only friends of the family are invited. It was very still. The auctioneer took an easy conversational tone. There was a silent, forlorn sort of dignity about the five pianos standing in a row that put professional banter and cheap little jokes out of the question. The pianos went without much trouble—a big one of the best make, an old-fashioned cottage piano, a piano with an iron frame. One of the appraisers, himself a musician, became an assistant auctioneer, and kindly played a little—judiciously very little—on each instrument in turn.

Then came the bric-a-brac of personal effects—all the flotsam and jetsam that had floated into these rooms for years. The walls were pockmarked with pictures, big and little. There was no attempt at high art; the professor had bought a picture as a child might buy one—because he thought it was pretty. It was a curious showing of how one artistic faculty may be dormant while another is cultivated to its highest point. But no matter how cheap the picture, it was always conscientiously framed. And this was a great help to the auctioneer. Indeed, it was difficult to see how he could have cried the pictures at all without the frames.

By this time the rooms were fuller of people. There were ladies who had come in quietly, just to get some little thing for a remembrance of their old friend and teacher. These mostly went directly over to the corner where the music lay and began looking for something of "his." If it were manuscript music so much the better. But there was little of this. It appeared that with the professor, as with most of us, early and middle manhood had been his most productive time, and that was long enough ago for everything to have been duly published in sheet and book form—long enough, indeed, for the books themselves to have gone out of date.

There they were—long, green notebooks, bearing the familiar names of well known publishers, and with such a hydra-head of title as "The Celestina, or New Sacred Minstrel; a Repository of Music adapted to every variety of taste and grade of capacity, from the million to the amateur or professor."

There were four or five of these. There was sheet music by the pile. There was an opera, "Joseph," the production of which had been a musical event.

Presently the auctioneer came that way. He had just sold a large oleograph, framed, one of those gorgeous historical pictures which are an apotheosis of good clothes. He approached an engraving of an old-fashioned lady in voluminous muslin draperies, with her hair looped away from her face in a "Book of Beauty" style.

"*He* liked that," murmured a lady.

"What do I hear!" cries the auctioneer, softly. "Oh, such a little bid as that—I can't see it at all in this dark corner. Suppose we throw these peaches in—awfully pretty thing for dining room—and this flower piece—shall we group these three?—now, how much for all? Ah, there they go!"

"Here, ladies and gentlemen, is a gold-headed cane which was presented to the deceased by his admiring friends. It is pure gold—you *know* they would not give him anything else. How much for this? How much? No—his name is *not* engraved on it—so much the better—what do I hear?"

"Look at this telescope, gentlemen—a good one—you know the professor was quite an astronomer in his way—and this telescope is all right—sound and in good condition"—the auctioneer had officiated at a stock sale the day before. "You can look right into futurity through this tube. Five dollars' worth of futurity? Five—five and a half? Case and all complete."

There was a pocketful of odds and ends; gold pens, lead pencils, some odd pocket knives; these inconsiderable trifles brought more in proportion than articles of greater intrinsic value. Evidently this was an auction of memories, of emotion, of sentiment.

There was a bit of the beam of the barn that was burned down when the cow kicked over the historic lamp that inaugurated the Chicago fire—no less than three persons were ready to testify to their belief in the genuineness of the relic, had anyone been disposed to question it. But no one was. Nearly all the people in the room were the dead music teacher's personal friends; they had heard the story of all these things; they knew who had sent him the stuffed brown prairie chicken that perched like a raven above the door—the little old-fashioned decanter and wine glasses of gilded glass—the artificial begonias—that clever imitation that goes far toward making one forswear begonias forevermore. There were lamps of various shapes and sizes, there was a kit of burglarious looking tools for piano tuning, there was a little globe—"Who wants the earth?" said the auctioneer. "You all want it."

There was a metronome, which, set to go, began to count time in a metallic whisper for some invisible pupil. Over in the corner just beyond the music were the professor's books. Now we shall find him out, for what a man reads he is, or wishes to be. There was a good deal of spiritualistic literature of the better sort. There was a "History of Christianity and Paganism by the Roman Emperor Julian," a copy of "She," a long shelf full of *North American Reviews*, a dozen or so of almanacs, a copy of Bluebeard. There were none of the "popular" magazines, and if there had been newspapers—those vagrants of literature—they had gone their way. There was a manuscript play for parlor presentation, with each part written out in legible script, entitled, "The Winning Card."

All these and many more things which only the patient appraisers can fully know were sold or set aside as unsalable, until all was done. And then those who had known and loved him and those who had not known or cared for him came down the stairs together.

Fate stood on the landing. As always, Fate ran true to form. She was a woman; a little tired, as a woman might well be who had come a thousand miles; a little out of breath from the two flights of stairs. Her old-fashioned draperies clung about her; her hair was looped away from her face in a "Book of Beauty" style. The man who stood aside to let her pass was talking. "Of course," he was saying, "he was a side-tracked man. But I believe he stands the biggest chance of being remembered of any man in Iowa."

Swift protest at his first words clouded her face; sheer gratitude for his last words illumined it. She bent forward a little and went on up the stairs alone.

She faltered in the doorway, her hand fumbling at her throat. One of the men who had been talking below hastened to her side.

"It's all over," he said, then added, at the dumb misery that grayed her face: "—the auction."

"I—I—didn't come for that," the apathy in her voice holding it steady. "I—I am his wife. His last letter—he sent for me." A sob broke her speech. "It came last week—two months too late."

What the Iowa Boy Hears in the Wind in the Corn

My Baby's Horse

By Emilie Blackmore Stapp

My baby's horse is Daddy's knee;
When nighttime comes he rides away
To Sleepytown by Dreamland Sea;
I love to hear their laughter gay.

Ride, baby, ride, the Sandman bold
Is following close behind you, dear,
But Daddy's arms will you enfold
And so for you I have no fear.

Your prancing steed is slowing down;
The Sandman's riding very fast.
Oh, here you are at Sleepytown;
The Sandman's caught you, dear, at last.

He'll tie your steed by Dreamland Sea,
And on its shores all night you'll play,
Then you'll come riding home to me
To make life sweet another day.

The Call of the Race

By Elizabeth Cooper

It was the last day of September, the maple trees were turning to red and gold, the mist of purple haze was in the air, and all Japan was going to the parks and woods to revel in the colors they loved so well.

Three men came out of the American Embassy, and looked for a moment over the roofs below them, half conscious of the beauty of this autumn time. They chatted for a few moments, then one of them motioned to a servant to put his mail bag in the jinrickshaw and slowly stepping into the tiny carriage he was whirled away.

The other men watched him for a few moments in silence, then as they turned to go to the English club, the elder shook his head slowly as he rather viciously bit the end from his cigar.

"Freeman's made a big fool of himself," he said. "Nice man, too."

The younger man looked after the fast disappearing jinrickshaw and asked after a moment's hesitation:

"He's married a Jap, hasn't he? I'm new here but I have heard something about him that's queer."

"Yes," the Ambassador replied. "Married her, preacher, ring, the whole thing."

"How did it happen? Why did he *marry* her?" the younger man asked with a laugh.

"We all talked to him. I talked to him like a father, but he wouldn't listen to reason. Saw her at the mission school, fell head and heels in love with her and wouldn't take anyone's advice. Even the missionary was against it. Told him that mixed marriages never came out right; that the girl always reverted to type," said the Ambassador a little bitterly.

"Well, has it turned out as they predicted?" inquired the secretary interestedly.

"Well, no," admitted the Ambassador. "It's been two years, and everything seems to be all right so far. No one ever sees much of either of them. You meet her with him once in a while in some garden admiring the wistaria, or the lotus. She's a beauty—a real beauty—and belongs to one of the old Samurai families up north somewhere."

"How did the mission get her? I thought they went in more for the lower classes," asked the secretary.

"Well, it seems that some missionary up north saw her and was attracted by her cleverness and her pretty face, and she persuaded the girl's parents to send her to school here. They're as poor as Job's turkey; but they live in a great old palace and observe all the old time Jap customs. Haven't changed a bit for centuries. The real thing in old-time aristocracy. But the missionary got past them some way and the girl came down—when was it?—six years ago, I think. Missionary says she's clever, has become a Christian, and evidently forgotten that she's a Jap."

"It'll perhaps be the exception that proves that all mixed marriages are not failures," said the optimistic secretary.

"No," said the older man, "I know Japan and the Japanese. There's something in them that never changes—the call of the blood or whatever it is. No matter how much education they have, change of religion, life in foreign countries—anything—they're Japanese, and in a crisis they go back to their gods and the instincts of their race. We all told Freeman this—the missionary, myself, everybody took a hit at him when we found he really meant business, but he only laughed. He said Yuki was as European as he was. Never thought of the gods, hardly remembered her people, and all that rot. He ought to know better: this is his second post in Japan. Was out here twelve years ago and got in some kind of trouble. I was surprised when the government sent him back; but I suppose they thought it had all blown over, and I presume it has, although the Japs don't forget."

The Ambassador was quiet for a few moments, then he said:

"No, I don't believe at all in intermarriage between the Oriental and the Occidental. Their traditions, customs, everything is different. They have no common meeting ground, and that racial instinct, that inherent something is stronger in the Oriental than in the Westerner. A woman here in this country, for example, is taught from babyhood that she must obey her parents, her clan, *absolutely*. Her family is first, and she must sacrifice her life if necessary for them, and they will go to any lengths in this obedience. I told this to Freeman, everyone did, but he just gave his happy laugh, and said that his wife-to-be was no more Japanese in feeling and sentiment than he was—that she had outgrown the old religion, the old beliefs. He laughed at the idea that her family would have any influence over her after she was his wife. Yet—I know these people—and have always been a little worried——"

The two men chatted until they entered the doors of the English club.

Morris Freeman with his fast runner was drawn swiftly through the modern streets of new Japan, then more slowly through the little alleys, where the shops were purely native. Finally he drew up at an entrance and stopped under the tiny roof of a gateway. He had been expected, evidently, because no sooner had he stopped than the great gate was swung open and a smiling servant stood in the entrance. Freeman handed him the mail bag and said:

"Tell the Ok San that I will be back in about an hour," and was taken swiftly up the street. The coolie at the gate was still watching the disappearing jinrickshaw when a Japanese approached, and bowing to the servant asked: "Is your mistress within?" The servant answered in the affirmative, looking at him interestedly, as he was different from the average man one sees in Tokio. He was dressed in an old-time costume that immediately told the city-bred servant that the man was from some distant province.

The visitor went to the veranda, dropped his clogs, and entered the doorway. A young girl was kneeling before a koto lightly strumming its strings and did not hear the entrance of the man. He stood for a moment looking around the room; then he saw Yuki and walking over to her sat down facing her. Yuki stared at him first in astonishment; then a look of fear came into her black eyes. He was silent for many minutes, then he coolly remarked:

"You do not speak to your uncle. You do not care to make me welcome in this your home." He looked down at her contemptuously.

She saluted him, touching her head to her folded hands upon the floor. After a few polite phrases she rose, went to the hibachi, fanned the flame a moment, poured water from the kettle into the teapot, and brought a tiny tray on which was a cup and the pot of tea. She poured out the tea, and, taking the cup in both hands, slid it across the floor to him; when he took it, she again touched her head to the floor, and inquired:

"I trust my honorable Uncle is in the enjoyment of good health?"

The man sipped the tea slowly, gazing around the room, taking in all its details. His eyes especially rested upon the shrine in the corner. Then he regarded her long and intently.

"I see you have brought your family shrine to the house of the foreigner with whom you live—the man who has made you forget your people. Have you opened it; do you offer the daily incense; or is it simply an article of furniture for your foreign husband to admire?"

Yuki said nothing; she could not explain to this old man that the shrine had meant nothing to her, but having come from her old home she had kept it simply as a remembrance of the past.

Not receiving an answer the man continued:

"The foreigner is kind to you?"

Yuki smiled and said softly to herself: "Kind—kind—my Dana San." Then seeing her uncle expected an answer, she said in a quiet tone:

"Most kind, my honorable Uncle."

"You wonder why I come to you to-night?" he inquired.

Yuki took the tea-things and put them behind her, then remarked:

"My humble house is honored by your presence."

"Honored, yes," sneered the uncle. "But still you wonder. I will tell you why I came to you to-night. Once upon a time there was a family in Japan—happy, honored—proud of their title, of their history—and, more than all, proud of their overlord. He was impetuous, and like many of the older Japanese, resentful of the foreigner's intrusion. Here, one day on a visit to his capital, he met a stranger, one of that hated race who spoke slightingly of his country, of his gods. There was the quick retort, the blow, and he our lord went to the Land of Shadows. The evil gods of the foreigner protected the man who gave the blow. His name was never discovered—it was claimed he did the cowardly act in self-defense and he got safely away."

Yuki leaned forward eagerly.

"Oh, it is of my honorable father you speak?"

"Yes, it is of your father I speak," said the man in a low, bitter voice. "Since his death the gods have not favored our house; we have lost position, money, everything. But at last—at last our prayers to the gods have been answered. The enemy of our house is delivered into our hands—into *your* hands."

Yuki looked bewildered.

"*My* hands? What do you mean, my honorable Uncle?"

"Yuki San, we have learned the name of the man who struck your father!" he exclaimed in a low, tense voice.

Yuki looked at the tragic face before her a moment, then she said: "At last, at last you know?"

"Yes," replied her uncle. "At last, after all these years of patience, revenge is in our hands. Oh, Yuki San, the foreigner, your husband, is the man who killed your father."

Yuki drew back, her face pallid, her body trembling.

"Morris, my Dana San?"

"Yes, your Dana San."

Yuki sat for a moment in bewilderment, then the color came back to her face and she leaned forward eagerly.

"But, my lord, my lord, he could not have done it! He is so kind, so good, he never hurt a thing in all his life."

The man leaned forward, gazing intently into her eyes.

"Has this stranger made you forget your father? Have you forgotten your oath, *your* oath? Have you forgotten why your father is now in the Land of Shadows?" He pointed to the shrine.

"Look, there is his tablet within that shrine. But the doors are closed. In our home, in our family temple are tablets. The doors of the shrines have never been opened. His spirit has not had the incense to help him on the way. The morning offering has not been his. He has been compelled to travel alone on the way to the gods, because we, his family—you and I—have not avenged his death.

"No, do not speak," he continued, as Yuki was about to interrupt. "He was murdered, and until the man who sent him on his way joins him in his journey, his spirit can have no peace. And you, his daughter, dare not, for fear of the gods, open the shrine to make the offering that the poorest peasant makes to his dead! But to-night I bring you the final word of the clan. To give you the honor of doing the deed that will wash the stain from our name. You know that a servant must avenge the death of his master, a son that of his father, a Samurai the death of his overlord, and I come to give you—a girl, an inheritance that will make you envied of men."

"I do not understand—my lord, you mean——"

"Yuki San, he killed your father, the head of our house, and he must die to-night."

Yuki rose and went to the man. Taking him by the arms she looked up into his face piteously, with wide, frightened eyes.

"My lord, my lord, you can not mean it—that he shall die—Morris die!"

The old man looked down into the pale face, the searching, pitiful eyes; but there shone no mercy in the hard eyes that met the ones raised pleadingly to his.

"Yes, and you, the only child of the man he killed, shall fulfill the sacred oath, and bring peace to your father's honorable soul."

Yuki was utterly bewildered and said falteringly: "I do not understand—I do not understand."

With the monotonous voice of the fatalist the uncle continued:

"It would have been better if a man-child had been born to our lord, as his arm would not falter; but you will take as sure a way, if not as honorable as the sword. Here is the means." He drew a little bottle from the sleeve of his kimono. "A little of this and he sleeps instantly and well."

Yuki held out her hands to the man sitting like fate before her.

"My lord, how can I? We have been so happy! My Dana San has never given me an unkind look, never caused me a moment's sorrow. I love him, Uncle, not as a Japanese woman loves her lord, but as a foreign woman from over the seas loves the man whom she has chosen from all the world. For two years we have been in this little house, for two years he has been my every breath. My first thought in the morning was for Morris, my Dana San, my last thought at night was joy in the thought that I was his and that he loved me. Sometimes I waken and look at him, and wonder how such a great man can care for such a simple Japanese girl as I am. And now you ask me to hurt him?" She drew her head up proudly. "I can not and I will not. He is my husband, and no matter what he has done I will protect him—even from you."

The man rose, and striding to her, grasped her roughly by the arm.

"Woman, you will do as we say. You are a Japanese and you know even unto death you must obey. I have no fear. It will be done—and by you—to-night."

He released her arm, and she, looking down upon the tatami, moved her foot silently to and fro, absorbed with this tragedy that had come into her happy life. Then she had a thought that brought hope to her, and she looked up eagerly. "Perhaps it is not true—perhaps it was not really Morris——"

"Listen," said the man roughly. "It was he. We *know*. But you—if you do not believe—make him confess to-night. If it was not he, then you are free. If it is, you will know what to do—and it will be done to-night—remember."

Yuki looked into the hard black eyes staring at her, fascinating her, taking all the life from her, and she said slowly as if under a spell:

"Yes—if he confesses—if it was he—I know it will be done. But—if the gods take him, they will also take me."

The uncle shook her roughly by the arm.

"*No!* Listen to me. Your work is not yet done. You must live. It would be too much happiness to have your spirit travel with him the lonely road. He must walk the path alone, without love to guide him. You will return to me to-night, return to your home and family who await you. Our vengeance would be only half complete if we allowed you to journey to the Land of Shadows with him. Come to me—" and he drew her to him. "Look at me. I will await you at the Willow Tea House."

He took her face in his hands and gazed steadily into her eyes, saying in a low, tense voice:

"I do not fear—you will obey. Are you not a Japanese? I expect—you—to—come—to—me—after your work is done—and the gods will be with you. Sayonara."

He put on his clogs at the entrance and went away, his form scarcely distinguishable in the gloom as he went down the pathway. Yuki looked after him, then threw herself on her face on the floor with a little moan, beating her hands in the manner of an Eastern woman.

It was absolutely quiet in the room, no noise coming from the street outside, except from a far distance a woman's voice chanting in a tone of singular sweetness words that sounded in their minor key like the soft tones of a flute: "*Amma Konitchi Wahyak Mo*," then between these sweet calls a plaintive whistle—one long-drawn note, then two shorter ones—the cry of the blind massage woman, making her rounds for her evening's toil.

The cry died away, and only the low moan was heard within the little room. Morris opened the gate and came lightly up the pathway, whistling a few bars of the latest popular song. He came inside the room, and, hardly able to distinguish the objects, looked about wonderingly, then seeing Yuki lying where she had thrown herself, he went over to her and picked her up.

"My sweetheart, what is it? What has happened?" He sat down upon the long chair and held her against him. "Tell me, dear one, tell me."

Morris went over to the lamp after a few moments and lighted it, then came back and showed Yuki a little gift he had brought her. She took it and looked at it with eyes filled with tragic grief; then, pressing it against her face, put her head on his shoulder and began sobbing in a heartbroken way that amazed Morris.

She lay with her face hidden, he softly caressing her hair. Finally she said:

"Morris, we have been here two years. Tell me—have I made you happy?"

Morris threw back his head and laughed happily.

"Happy, Yuki, happy? Dear heart, I had a long time ago put aside the thought that love meant happiness and happiness meant love. Now you have taught me that one cannot exist without the other. I love you, I live with you, you are mine. That tells everything. When you came into my life, into my heart, I was soured and embittered. Life meant only work and duties done; after that, comfort and a cigar—that was all. But now, I love my work as well, I do it as thoroughly, but there is something more. I know when I shut the office-door, I can come here where no one can enter. I can be alone with the woman I love and who loves me. There is no question of society or dinners, but just us two alone, you and me—and," turning up her face, "you are happy with me, my Yuki San? You love me?"

Yuki did not reply at once. Then in a low, sweet voice she replied:

"Morris, we Japanese women never speak of love. It is to us a subject left to singing girls and geishas. Without it we marry, and without it we live, and it is, unless by chance, a closed book to us. I do not know if I love you as the women of your race love their Dana Sans—I know I think of you by day, and I dream of you by night. I live only for you—to be what you wish me to be—and when you take me in your arms and say, 'My Yuki San, my sweetheart,' it seems to me that my heart with its happiness will break! I do not know if that is love—but if it be—I love you, my Dana San, I love you."

She lay quietly, and he rested his face against her hair, caressing it from time to time. After a silence, he inquired lightly:

"What about supper, Yuki?"

Yuki drew him to her again, for he moved as if he would rise.

"Wait, dear, let us talk a little. Tell me, when you to Tokio came—the first time——"

"Twelve years ago, when O Yuki San was a little girl."

"Twelve years ago—there was much trouble then between foreigners and Japanese. You and your friends—had—had trouble."

Morris looked at her quickly and his eyes darkened.

"Where did you hear that?" he asked.

Yuki, carelessly: "Oh, they gossip in the market-place."

Morris rose and walked up and down the room.

"I don't know what you have heard, but I might as well tell you the whole story. I did have trouble here in Japan. One night some of us got in a mix-up—a sort of quarrel with a Japanese, and I don't know how it happened—I never have known—but I struck and killed him. It was in the dark, and I could hardly see him."

After a silence Yuki stammered: "You—killed him?"

"In self-defense, O Yuki San," Morris defended eagerly; "it was in self-defense. But afterwards, what a time it was! Shall I ever forget that night getting back to my ship?" He passed his hand over his face, and then came back to his place beside her on the couch. "Don't speak of it any more; I don't want to think of it."

Yuki slipped down to the floor and sat there with her head against his knee. She sat very quietly, then finally put her hand up to the flower in her dress and slowly took it out and let it fall to the floor, petal by petal, watching the leaves as they fell. Then, after a long silence, she rose and started towards the tea table, hesitated, went a little way, and then came back to him. She knelt by the couch and said, in a low voice:

"Morris, no matter what happens, what you learn, what the gods may teach you soon—remember, I love you with all the love of my life. That I would give that life for you—oh, so willingly, if I only could! That through whatever you pass, I would gladly be with you; but I will come to you soon. I will not send you where I may not follow. I will come. I am yours, and the gods cannot let you go alone. You need me, and I would not be afraid. I love you—I want to go with you—but I am a Japanese—and I understand."

She let her face fall upon her hands and knelt there quietly. Morris looked at her blankly, thinking she was worried about something. Finally he lifted her face and kissed her.

"Never mind, dear one. I don't know what is troubling you, but of course you shall go with me wherever I go. I need you, and could not be without my Yuki San."

He started to read the papers; she rose and stood by the couch a moment, then taking a step toward the tea-things:

"Would my Dana San—like—a cup of tea?"

Morris, absorbed in his papers, assented. "Why, yes, I don't mind if I do."

She turned and walked slowly to the hibachi, knelt beside it, fanned the fire a moment, then poured the water from the iron kettle into the tiny teapot, let it stand a moment, looking over towards Morris. Then she took the bottle from her sleeve and poured a few drops into the cup, filling it with tea. She rose slowly and walked over to the long chair. She looked down at him as he lay half-reclining, hesitated, then handed him the cup. He took it, and looking up at her half laughing, exclaimed:

"To you, sweetheart!" and drank.

He fell back on the chair; the cup dropped from his hands. Yuki looked down at him in silence; then she bent over him, and lovingly crossed his hands upon his breast, touched his face caressingly with her fingers; then bent down and kissed him.

She turned slowly, and, in turning, her eyes fell upon the shrine. She looked at it intently, slowly crossed the room and knelt in front of it, bowed her head to the floor; then opened the doors, and bowed her head again.

She took out two candlesticks, two little jars of incense, a small bowl for rice, and another for water. She lighted the candles, lighted the incense, poured water in one bowl and rice in the other. Then she again touched her head to the floor, once—twice—thrice—rose, and walked backward to the open shojii.

She stood a moment looking around the room that she had loved so well; then turned her face to her lover lying so quietly in the chair. She knelt down facing him, touched her head to the floor and rising in the kneeling position, said, stretching out her arms towards Morris:

"Sayonara, my Dana San, good-bye, good-bye."

One Wreath of Rue

By Cynthia Westover Alden

The brawny lad in khaki clad,
We rightly cheer. Alas,
My eyes grow dim! I weigh with him,
The boy
Who failed
To pass.

A heart more brave no man could have,
His soul as clear as glass.
He faced with zest the doctor-test—
The boy
Who failed
To pass.

And now the blow is hurting so,
He sees the legions mass.
They go to war. Be sorry for
The boy
Who failed
To pass.

The future grim is flouting him
As in the weakling class.
Though fine and true, his years are few—
The boy
Who failed
To pass.

For warriors proud blow bugles loud,
Of silver or of brass;
One wreath of rue is due unto
The boy
Who failed
To pass.

Woodrow Wilson and Wells, War's Great Authors

An Interview with Honoré Willsie

"The war has thus far produced two great pieces of literature. One of these is H. G. Wells' 'Mr. Britling Sees It Through.' The other is President Wilson's War Message. I was curiously moved by 'Mr. Britling Sees It Through.' The effect of that novel on me was to move me away from the war, to let me get a picture of the war as a great procession against the horizon.

"Every code that I had—in government, in religion, in ethics—had been obliterated by the events of the last three years. But this novel showed me that there could be a code—that something coherent and true must come out of the chaos. Reading as many manuscripts as I do, I grow stale on ideas. I want to read out-and-out trash or else something that will give me a new philosophy of life. And Wells, at any rate, showed me that there could be a new philosophy.

"The great task before our writers to-day is to do for the individual what President Wilson's Declaration of War did for the nations of the world. This is the most important thing a writer can do—to make a new code for mankind. I can't think of any American writer able to do it. But did any of us expect Wells to write such a book as 'Mr. Britling Sees It Through'?

"One significant thing about President Wilson's message is that its author is absolutely sure of the hereafter. He is convinced that God is Eternal Goodness. All his utterances are the utterances of a man with a deep faith that never has been disturbed. And that sort of man is essentially the man for statesmanship.

"Religious fervor was the driving force of the fathers of our country. For an agnostic like myself to witness an exhibition of this force is to look wistfully at a power that cannot be understood. It is the spirit of the little red schoolhouse, of the meeting-house, of the town meeting—the spirit of American statesmanship and of American democracy.

"Human beings aren't big enough to get along without religion. Somehow or other we moderns have got to have some faith—as Lincoln had it, and Adams, and Washington—as Wilson has it. We need a new religion. For Wilson won't happen again very often.

"President Wilson's message formulates a new philosophy of government. His message came on Europe like a flash of light in the darkness of battle.

"President Wilson seems to have started his message with a definite conviction as to the existence of God. Mr. Wells must have started his novel with the hope of finding God through it. I size Wells up as a modern with the modern craving for God. Wells does not lead you to God, but he gives you the idea that God exists, and is just over beyond.

"But then religion is a favorite theme of the novelist. Winston Churchill's 'The Inside of the Cup' indicated that social service would take the place of religion. Well, maybe it would for some people. But nowadays most people need a religion that says that there is a hereafter.

"I think that I am the only human being in captivity who has read all of Holt's book on the cosmic relations. And what I got out of it was not a belief in spiritualism, but a realization of the fact that every one, high and low, rich and poor, educated and illiterate, has a craving for knowledge of life after death, has a craving for belief in life after death. And the war has raised this feeling to the nth power. We feel that we shall go mad if there is no hereafter. Mr. Wells leads us to believe that he will find that there is a hereafter. President Wilson shows us that he is sure there is one.

"This craving for conviction of the hereafter, increased by the war, inevitably makes our literature more spiritual. So we are seeing the last for awhile of the sex novel and of sordid realism. We no longer find people who believe that since you are an artist you should describe the contents of a garbage can. The soul of man as well as the body of man is coming into its own as the theme of the novelist.

"And the war is responsible. You can't stick out your tongue and make a face at God when a shell may momentarily hurl you from the earth. And who cares to read a sex novel now? What do the little bedroom scandals of the flimsy novels matter when the womanhood of Belgium has been despoiled?

"I am asked if our writers have deteriorated of late years. I think that the rank and file of our serial writers are way below those of forty or fifty years ago. Then our novelists were fewer and better. Look at the files of the old magazines and you will find that the novels that appeared serially in those days were much better than those that are appearing to-day. But one or two of our best novelists are just as fine as any of our writers of a bygone generation—Margaret Deland and Gertrude Atherton, for instance.

"And in other branches of literature I think we have improved on our forefathers. American poets have never before done such exquisite things as they are doing to-day, and one or two short story writers are doing better things than were ever done before in this country. If you compare the short stories in old issues of the magazines with those in the current issues you will find that the old short stories are as much inferior to the new short stories as the old novels—the serialized novels—are superior to the new ones."

A Field

By Minnie Stichter

Sometime I expect to turn a sharp corner and come face to face with myself, according to the ancient maxim, "extremes meet." For, did I not vow to the Four Great Walls that had imprisoned me for nine months, that I would fly to the uttermost parts of the earth so soon as vacation should open the doors? And did I not spend almost my entire summer within sight of my home, and in a field of a few acres dimension?

I caught sight of some flowers, just inside the barbed wire fencing the track, that were fairer than any I had yet gathered for my vases. As the old song has it, "O, brighter the flowers on the other side seem!" No one saw me get under that six-stranded barbed-wire fence, and I am not going to tell how I did it. But when I got through I felt as well guarded as though attended by a retinue of soldiers. And I found myself in another world—a dream-world!

It was a large field rosy with red clover and waving with tall timothy. A single tree glistened and rustled invitingly. In its shade I rested, refreshing myself with the field sights and sounds and fragrances. It was delightful to be the center of so much beauty as circled round about me. Then I had only to rest on the rosy clover-carpet at the foot of the tree, and the tall grass eclipsed all things earthly save the tree, and the sky overhead, and the round mat of clover under the tree which the grass ringed about. I had often wished for Siegfried's magic cloak. Well, here was something quite as good, which, if it did not render me invisible to the world, made the world invisible to me. Who of you would not be glad to have the old world with its "everyday endeavors and desires," its folly, its pride and its tears, drop out of sight for a while, leaving you in a flowery zone of perfect quiet and beauty, hedged in by a wall of grass!

There were many "afterwards." And the marvel of it all was that, for all I could do, the field retained its virgin splendor and kept the secret of my goings-in and comings-out most completely.

After the daisies, there came a season of black-eyed Susans. That was when the grasses were tallest and the feeling of mystery did most abound. I know I had been there many days before I discovered the myriads of wild roses near the crabtree thicket—those fairies' flowers so exquisite in their pink frailty that mortal breath is rude. Only when I reached the hedge, bounding the remote side of the field, did I enter into my full inheritance. Along a barbed-wire fence had grown up sumac, elderberry, crabtrees and nameless brambles, while over all trailed the wild grapevine, bearing the most perfect miniature clusters, fit to be sculptured by Trentanove into immortal beauty. And this hedge was the source of ever increasing wonder the whole summer long. I depended on it alone for sensational denouements after the grass was cut for hay. When the field lay shorn, like other fields about it far and wide, I could not have been lured hitherward but for the hedge. There the hard green berries of a peculiar bramble ripened into wax-white pellet-sized drops clustered together on a woody stem by the most coral-pink pedicles ever designed by sea-sprites.

In its time came the elderberry bloom, and its purple fruit; the garnet fruit of the sumach and its flaming foliage; the lengths of vines and their purple clusters—all these and more also ministered to my delight.

About goldenrod time, the school-bell rang me in from the field, but I managed to take recesses long enough to behold the kaleidoscopic views brought before me by the turning of nature's hand. The smooth velvety green of the field with its border of gold and lavender—great widths of thistle and goldenrod following the line of fence—was like the broidered mantle of some celestial Sir Walter Raleigh, spread for the queens of earth. I was no queen; but I did not envy royalty, since I doubted if it had any such cherished possessions as my field in its various phases.

In the November days, the brightness of the fields seemed to be inverted and to be seen in the opalescent tints of the sky. Then, the clearness of the atmosphere, the wider horizon, the less hidden homes and doings of men, had this message for the children of men: "If there is any secret in your life, leave it out."

When it is December and the fields are too snowy and wind-swept for pleasure-grounds, where the only bits of brightness are the embroideries of the scarlet pips of the wild-rose, it is good to nestle by the cozy fireside and conjure it all up again, and nourish a feeling of expectancy for the spring and summer that shall come. Again, the flowers and waving grass and drowsy warmth of the summer day; again, the songs of flitting birds, the scented sweets of the new-mown hay. Again the work of the fields goes on before me like a play in pantomime! Again, with my eyes, I follow home the boys with their cows, to the purple rim of the hill beyond which only my fancy has ever gone. Again I quit work with the tired laborer. Again I dream of the open, free, unfettered song that life might be if it were lived more simply, with less of artificiality. And again, for the sake of one patient toiler in the town, whose life-task admits of no holiday, I have the grace to return thither and begin where I left off—the life common to you and to me, the life ordained for us from the beginning.

Your Lad, and My Lad

By Randall Parrish

Down toward the deep blue water, marching to the throb of drum,
From city street and country lane the lines of khaki come;
The rumbling guns, the sturdy tread, are full of grim appeal,
While rays of western sunshine flash back from burnished steel.
With eager eyes and cheeks aflame the serried ranks advance;
And your dear lad, and my dear lad, are on their way to France.

A sob clings choking in the throat, as file on file sweep by,
Between those cheering multitudes, to where the great ships lie;
The batteries halt, the columns wheel, to clear-toned bugle call,
With shoulders squared and faces front they stand a khaki wall.
Tears shine on every watcher's cheek, love speaks in every glance;
For your dear lad, and my dear lad, are on their way to France.

Before them, through a mist of years, in soldier buff or blue,
Brave comrades from a thousand fields watch now in proud review;
The same old Flag, the same old Faith—the Freedom of the World—
Spells Duty in those flapping folds above long ranks unfurled.
Strong are the hearts which bear along Democracy's advance,
As your dear lad, and my dear lad, go on their way to France.

Peace and Then—?

By Detlev Fredrik Tillisch

Suburb of London. Three months after declaration of peace. Time: Noon.

CAST

Mrs. Claire Hamilton—about 35 years of age—portly—simply dressed.

Master Hal Hamilton—her son—about 10 years of age—full of life—dressed in Boy Scout uniform.

Mr. John Hamilton—soldier—botanist—about 39 years of age—tall—well built.

Sergeant, soldiers and pedestrians.

Claire Hamilton is seen fixing her corner flower stand and endeavoring to sell her plants to passers-by, but after three futile attempts she becomes tired of standing and takes seat on wooden bench in front of her stand. Takes letter from pocket—sighs and begins to read letter aloud.

Mrs. Hamilton (reading). "Dearest Love and Hal Boy—We are still in the bowels of hell—but even this would be nothing if I but knew my loved ones were well and happy. (*She wipes away a tear and continues reading.*) Nothing but a miracle can end this terrible war. Give my own dear Hallie boy a kiss from his longing papa." (*She lays letter on her lap and meditates.*) Peace (*shakes her head—looks at date of letter.*) February 16th—six months past and now it's all over—three months ago—Oh, God, bring him back to me and my boy. (*She goes back of flower stand and brings out box of mignonettes. Hal comes running in with bundle of newspapers and very much excited—his sleeve is torn. He stands still and looks at mother rather proudly and defiantly.*)

Mrs. Hamilton. Hal Boy—what's the trouble?

Hal. I licked Fritz.

Mrs. Hamilton. What for?

Hal. He said it took the whole world to lick the Germans.

Mrs. Hamilton. But, Hal, my boy—the war is over—you mustn't be hateful—be kind and forgiving.

Hal. Make them bring back my daddy then.

Mrs. Hamilton. You still have your mother—(*Hal runs to mother and embraces her tenderly.*)

Mrs. Hamilton. Whose birthday is it to-day? (*He thinks—pause.*) This is the 20th of August—now think hard. (*She awaits answer—silence—then takes box of mignonettes.*) Whose favorite flower is the mignonette?

Hal. Papa's! Papa's! (*Claps his hands boyishly.*)

Mrs. Hamilton. Yes, Hal—it's papa's birthday and mother is remembering the day by decorating our little stand with the flowers your papa has grown. (*He caresses the mignonettes tenderly.*)

Hal. Dear daddy—dear flowers—aren't they lovely, mother?

Mrs. Hamilton. Yes, Hal. (*She wipes away a tear, trying to conceal her emotions from her son.*)

Hal. Maybe some day I'll be a famous botanist like papa and then you'll have two boxes. (*Mother is silent trying to keep back the tears and Hal notices it.*) Papa is coming home soon, isn't he, mother? (*She just shakes her head.*)

Mrs. Hamilton. We must be brave.

Hal. When I get big I'm going to be a soldier and be brave like daddy.

Mrs. Hamilton. That won't be necessary any more—it isn't the people who want to fight.

Hal. But daddy did and you bet if anybody makes me sore I'll fight too.

Mrs. Hamilton. No, my boy—daddy didn't want to fight——

Hal. Then why did he go?

Mrs. Hamilton. Hal, you're a little boy and wouldn't understand—but just remember what your mother tells you: Don't be selfish—be tolerant, honest and charitable to all the peoples of the world, the big and the small alike. (*Enter passer-by who stops to look over plants. After Mrs. Hamilton has shown several and given him prices, he picks up the box of mignonettes.*)

Man. I'll take this box.

Mrs. Hamilton (*confused, not knowing whether to tell stranger about that particular box of flowers or sell it, as she sorely needs money. Then she picks up another plant to show it.*) Here's a very sturdy plant, sir.

Man. But I want this one. (*Pointing to box of mignonettes.*) How much is it? I'm in a hurry.

Hal (*goes to stranger and takes box from his hands*). You can't have them—they're daddy's.

Man (pushing him to one side). Get away from here, you little ruffian.

Mrs. Hamilton. That's my son, sir—he's not a ruffian. His father has not returned from the front and that——

Man (interrupting). Oh, yes—yes—we hear those stories every day now on every corner—it's the beggar's capital. (*He walks away hurriedly, but Hal starts after with clenched fist.*)

Mrs. Hamilton. Hal! Hal! What did mother tell you a few moments ago?

Hal (coming back). But he made me sore.

Mrs. Hamilton. What's the news—(*Hal hands her a paper, kisses her and starts up street.*)

Hal. Paper—extra—paper! (*He disappears.*)

Mrs. Hamilton (is attracted by headlines in paper and begins to read aloud). "Fifty men return to-day from the front to be placed in the asylum." (*She buries her face in her hands.*) Better that he were dead. (*Sound of footsteps is heard. Enter detachment of ten men in uniform in charge of a sergeant. They swing corner of flower stand and Mrs. Hamilton watches every man and there is a tense silence. Suddenly Mrs. Hamilton rushes toward them.*)

Mrs. Hamilton. John! John! My boy! (*They halt. Mrs. Hamilton swoons. Sergeant goes to her and assists her to bench in front of stand. She becomes calm and goes toward husband with out-stretched arms.*) Don't you know me? Claire, your wife! (*He stares at her, but shows no signs of recognition.*) You remember Hal—Hal, your own boy—our little boy—John! (*He just looks at her and smiles foolishly. Sergeant takes her gently by the arm to lead her away, thinking her hysterically mistaken as many others have been.*)

Sergeant. Are you quite sure, madam, that he is your husband?

Mrs. Hamilton. Yes—John Hamilton—have you no record——

Sergeant. Not yet. But time will clear away any doubts——

Mrs. Hamilton. Time—time! I've waited long enough on time. He's mine and I want him. (*Turns toward husband.*) You want to stay here with me and our boy—don't you, John? (*Pause.*) Sergeant, let me have him.

Sergeant (trying to hide his emotion). You're quite sure, madam—(*Mrs. Hamilton nods and sergeant takes John from ranks. John just stares. Mrs. Hamilton leads him tenderly to seat. Sergeant starts others to march.*)

Sergeant. I'll return for him after delivering these men. (*Mrs. Hamilton takes no notice of his remarks and they march off.*)

Mrs. Hamilton *(kissing his hands tenderly and giving him all signs of love and affection)*. Doesn't it seem good to be with us again? *(He smiles foolishly.)* And our boy Hal—He is so large now—You'll see him soon. Think of it—he's ten years old. *(Hal enters and without noticing father rushes toward his mother, holding a package in his hand. His father sees him and notices his uniform—rises quickly and rushes toward him but mother grabs his arm and holds him back. Hal remains standing.)*

Mrs. Hamilton. That's Hal—your own boy. Hal—your son.

Mr. Hamilton *(looks at Hal fiercely)*. Attention! *(Hal looks perplexed.)*

Mrs. Hamilton. This is your own papa—my boy. *(Hal runs toward him but stops.)*

Mr. Hamilton. Attention! *(His hands grab his pocket for revolver but finds none.)* You scullion—this is my girl! *(Turns and puts arms around Mrs. Hamilton.)* Aren't you, Sissy? *(Mrs. Hamilton realizes situation and plays her part—leads him to seat—strokes his hair and caresses him.)*

Mrs. Hamilton. What have you, Hal?

Hal. I sold all my papers and brought you a little cake for daddy's birthday.

Mrs. Hamilton *(smiles and shakes her head. She takes box of mignonettes and shows them to Mr. Hamilton.)*. You surely remember these—your own mignonettes—your prize? *(She is silent. He smells flowers—she anxiously awaits any signs of recognition—long pause—a slight spark of intelligence comes over him as he fondles the flowers—Mrs. Hamilton very tense but says nothing. Hal remains standing as if rooted to the spot. Enter sergeant.)*

Sergeant. I must deliver him with the others, madam. *(No reply.)* It's my duty. *(He goes to take Mr. Hamilton by the arm, but Mrs. Hamilton interferes.)*

Mrs. Hamilton. Duty! Duty! It has been my duty to slave and starve—my husband has done his duty—he volunteered his services—I willingly let him go—for what? For whom? *(Pause.)* Now it's all over. This is the result to me—to thousands, but now—*(stands between Mr. Hamilton and sergeant)*—God has brought him back to me and God will keep him with me!

Mr. Hamilton *(in a whisper)*. God—*(rubs hands over eyes)*—God—— *(Smells fragrance of the mignonettes. He takes Mrs. Hamilton's hand and Hal runs to him and kneels beside him.)* My mignonette. *(Smiles to Mrs. Hamilton and Hal.)* My mignonettes.

Semper Fidelis

By Addie B. Billington

When free from earthly toil and thrall of pain,
Time's transient guest,
One large of heart and finely quick of brain
Found early rest.
Kind friends ordained that on his coffin lid,
Bedecked with flowers,
His last Romance should lie, forever hid
From sight of ours.
Th' unfinished page no other hand might press,
Where his had wrought,
Nor Fancy weave strange threads—to match by guess
The strands he sought.
The motives worthy and the action grand,
In faithful trust,
To bury what they could not understand,
With fleeting dust.
And if within the years there treasured lies,
'Neath Memory's trance,
Wreathed in forget-me-nots, my sacred prize—
A life's Romance—
Heav'n grant no ruthless hand the pages turn,
When I am gone,
Striving its inmost meaning to discern;
'Tis mine alone.

Our Bird Friends

By Margaret Coulson Walker

Lovers of birds will doubtless be pleased to know that some of the most agreeable and interesting legends of the past were centered about these guests of our groves, whose actions formed the basis of innumerable fancies and superstitions. An acquaintance with the literature as well as with the life history of our feathered friends will not only increase our interest in the bird life about us but it will broaden our sympathies as well.

Birds exercised a strong influence on prehistoric religion, having been worshipped as gods in the earlier days and later looked upon as representatives of the higher powers. The Greeks went so far as to attribute the origin of the world itself to the egg of some mysterious bird. To others, these small creatures flitting about among our trees, represented the visible spirits of departed friends. The Aztecs believed that the good, as a reward of merit, were metamorphosed at the close of life into feathered songsters, and as such were permitted to pass a certain term in the beautiful groves of Paradise. To them, as to all North American Indians, thunder was the cloud bird flapping his mighty wings, while the lightning was the flash of his eye. The people of other countries believed that higher powers showed their displeasure by transforming wrong-doers into birds and animals as a punishment for their crimes.

In all lands birds were invested with the power of prophecy. They were believed to possess superior intelligence through being twice-born, once as an egg, and again as an animal. Because of their wisdom, not only they, but their graven images also, were consulted on all important affairs of life. Many nations, notably the Japanese, are still believers in the direct communication between man and unseen beings, through birds and other agents. In their country, birds are regarded as sacred, and for this reason the agriculturist gladly shares with them the fruit of his toil.

While we of to-day attach no supernatural significance to the presence of these feathered songsters, and even though to us they possess no powers of prophecy, we can find a great deal of pleasure in observing these beings whose boding cries were regarded as omens by the greatest of earth—beings whose actions in Vespasian's time were considered of vital national importance.

Aside from their historic and literary interest, these multitudinous, and often contradictory, legends and superstitions are of interest to us as a part of the faith of our fathers, much of which, combined with other and higher things, is in us yet. These beliefs of theirs, like many of what we are pleased to think are original ideas and opinions to-day, were hereditary and largely a matter of geography.

In ancient times the chief birds of portent were the raven or crow, the owl and the woodpecker, though there were a number of others on the prophetic list.

As an example of interest let us consider our friend the raven and his congener the crow, who are so confused in literature, as well as in the minds of those not familiar with ornithological classification, that it is almost impossible to treat them separately. The raven is a larger bird and not quite so widely distributed as the crow, but in general appearance and habits they are practically the same.

If tradition is to be credited, we are more indebted to this bird of ancient family than to any other feathered creature, for he has played an important part in history, sacred and profane, in literature, and in art.

On the authority of the Koran we know that it was he who first taught man to bury his dead. When Cain did not know what disposition to make of the body of his slain brother, "God sent a raven, who killed another raven in his presence and then dug a pit with his beak and claws and buried him therein." It was the raven whom Noah sent forth to learn whether the waters had abated—one of the rare instances wherein he ever proved faithless to his trust—and it was he who gave sustenance to the prophet Elijah.

In Norse mythology, Odin, the greatest of all the gods, the raven's God, had for his chief advisers two ravens, Hugin and Munin (Mind and Memory), who were sent out by him each morning on newsgathering journeys, and who returned to him at nightfall to perch on his shoulders and whisper into his ears intelligence of the day. When news of unusual importance was desired, Odin himself in raven guise went forth to seek it, and when the Norse armies went into battle they followed the raven standard, a banner under which William the Conqueror fought. When bellied by the breezes it betokened success, but when it hung limp, only defeat was expected.

Norse navigators took with them a pair of ravens to be liberated and followed as guides; if the bird returned it was known that land did not lie in that direction; if they did not, they were followed. The discoveries of both Iceland and Greenland are attributed to their leadership.

To the Romans and Greeks the raven was the chief bird of omen, whose effigy was borne on their banners, and whose auguries were followed with greatest confidence, while to the German mind he was his satanic majesty made manifest in feathers. In some parts of Germany these birds are believed to hold the souls of the damned, while in other European sections priests only are believed to be so reincarnated.

In Sweden the ravens croaking at night in the swamps are said to be the ghosts of murdered persons who have been denied Christian burial, and whom on this account Charon has refused ferriage across the River Styx.

As a companion of saints this bird has had too many experiences to mention.

By some nations he was regarded as the bearer of propitious news from the gods—and sacrosanct, to others he was the precursor of evil and an object of dread. With divining power, which enabled him for ages to tell the farmer of coming rain, the maiden of the coming of her lover and the invalid of the coming of death, he was received with joy or sadness, according to the messages he bore.

In England he was looked upon with greater favor; there the mere presence of the home of a raven in a tree-top was enough to insure the continuance in power of the family owning the estate.

The wealth of raven literature bears indubitable testimony to the interest people of all times and all localities have felt in this remarkable bird—an interest certain to increase with acquaintance.

To one with mind open to rural charm, this picturesque bird, solemnly stalking about the fields, or majestically flapping his way to the treetops, is as much a part of the landscape as the fields themselves, or the trees upon their borders; it possesses an interest different from that of any other creature of the feathered race. Though he no longer pursues the craft of the augur, his superior intelligence, great dignity and general air of mystery inspire confidence in his abilities in that line.

What powers were his in the old days! Foolish maidens and ignorant sailors might put their faith in the divining powers of the flighty wren; others might consult the swallow and the kingfisher; but it was to the "many-wintered crow" that kings and the great ones of earth applied for advice, and it was he who never failed them. According to Pliny, he was the only bird capable of realizing the meaning of his portents.

In the early morning light the worthy successors of the ancient Hugin and Munin go forth to-day in quest of news of interest to their clan, just as those historic messengers did in the days when the mighty Norse gods awaited their return, that they might act on the intelligence gathered by them during the daylight hours; and when slanting beams call forth the vesper songs of more tuneful birds, they return, followed by long lines of other crows, to their usual haunts on the borders of the marshes. Singly or in long lines, never in loose flocks like blackbirds, they arrive from all directions, till what must be the whole tribe is gathered together—a united family—for the night's repose.

As there in the treetops in the early evening, in convention assembled, they discuss important affairs, who can doubt that certain ones of their number are recognized as leaders, and that they have some form of government among themselves? One after another delivers himself of a harangue, then the whole assemblage joins in noisy applause—or is it disapproval? At other times sociability seems to be the sole object of the gathering.

As one old crow, more meditative than the rest, at the close of the conclave always betakes himself to the same perch, the lonely, up-thrust shaft of a lightning-shattered tree on the hillside, we decide that here is old Munin, who has selected this perch as one favorable to meditation—a place where he may ponder undisturbed over the occurrences of the day.

Others among the group have habits as fixed and noticeable. Even though approaching his perch from the opposite direction, one will be seen to circle and draw near it from the accustomed side; some of the more decided ones will invariably remain just where they alight; others will turn around and arrange themselves on their perches indefinitely. In the fields it will be noticed that some are socially inclined and forage in groups, while others, either from personal choice or that of their neighbors, are more solitary. Like members of the human family, each has his own individual characteristic.

While the chief charm of the crow is his intelligence, his dignity also claims our attention. Who ever saw one of his tribe do anything foolish or unbecoming to the funeral director he has been ever since the birth of time, and that he must ever be while time endures? The ancients believed him to be able to scent a funeral several days before death occurred, so sensitive was he to mortuary influences, and there is little doubt he still possesses the power to discern approaching death in many creatures smaller than himself—and to whom he expects to extend the rite of sepulchre. Inside and out he is clothed in deepest black; even his tongue and the inside of his mouth are in mourning. Seeming to think it incumbent on him to live up to his funeral garb and occupation, faithful to his trust, with clerical solemnity he goes about his everyday duties.

Gazing on them from his watchtower in the tree tops, what does this grave creature think of the gayer birds that dwell in the meadows and groves round about? What thinks he of the clownish bobolink, in motley nuptial livery, pouring out his silly soul in gurgling, rollicking song, in his efforts to please a possible mate, then quarreling with both her and his rivals, who also have donned cap and bell to win her favor? What of the unpretentious home—a mere hollow in the ground—where the care-free pair go to housekeeping? What of the redwings building their nests among the reeds in the midst of the marsh—so low as almost to touch the water? Of the fitful wren, incessantly singing of love to his mate, yet who fails to assist her in nest-building, and who proves but an indifferent provider for his young family? Of the lonely phoebe, calling in plaintive, mysterious tones to a mate unresponsive to his sorrowful beseechings? Of the robin, who makes of the grove a sanctuary? He doubtless has his opinions concerning every one of them, for he views them all with interest. Hearing all the other birds singing their love and seeing them winning favor with their brilliant colors, does he envy them?

On the theory of compensation, his sterling qualities render accomplishments and decorative raiment unnecessary. With no song in which to tell his story, and no garments gay to captivate the eye, the crow must needs live his love—and he does—to the end. Seriously he wins the mate to whom he remains true forever. To him the marital bond is not the mere tie of a season, but one that holds through life. He assists the dusky bride of his choice in establishing a commodious home in the most commanding situation available—the top of the tallest tree in the edge of the wood, and which may have been planted by one of his ancestors. He assists her in giving warmth to their eggs in the nest. He carries food to her while she broods over them. He braves every danger in protecting both her and them against predatory hawks and owls and frolicking squirrels, to whom he is known as the "warrior crow." With tenderest solicitude he relieves his mate as far as he can in ministering to their nestlings.

And what of the young crows in the nest? When their elders are away on commissary tours, the young ones, bewailing the absence of parents almost constantly, are always found, on the return, in attitudes of expectancy. To them the approach of older crows, even though it be from the left, is never ominous of anything but good. And when after many excursions baby appetites have been satisfied, in their lofty cradles in the tree tops, the infant crows are rocked by the breezes, and though the tuneless throats of the parents yield no songs they are not without music, for soft æolian lullabies soothe them to sleep.

On hearing farmers talk, one would think that the diet of the crow is entirely granivorous, while no bird has a more adaptable appetite; everything eatable is perfectly acceptable—harmful grubs, beetles, worms, young rats, mice, snakes and moles, as well as mollusks, acorns, nuts, wild fruit and berries are among his staple articles of diet. And, though it is no longer believed that "he shakes contagion from his ominous wing," he occasions a lamentable amount of infant mortality among rabbits, and squirrels, and even among weak-limbed lambs, depriving them of health, strength and happiness—but not through magic. These last he attacks in the eye, as the most vulnerable point. In the old days he is reputed to have met with great success as an oculist; in these his patients never recover.

In winter, when cereal stores and acorns which supply the season's want lie buried in the snow, and when such animals as in youth were ready prey have grown to a more formidable majority, crows frequently suffer and perish from hunger, and when snows lie long on the ground many of them are found dead beneath their roosting places.

The voice of the crow when heard distinctly has in it something of the winter's harshness and seems to harmonize best with winter sounds—creaking boughs and shrieking winds—but when modulated by distance it is not unmusical. In the twilight, when calling to his belated brethren across the marshes, his uncanny call might well be taken for the cry of a lost soul craving Christian burial. Yet this might depend on one's mood. To each he seems to speak a different language. To St. Athanasius he said: "Cras, cras!" (To-morrow, to-morrow). To the sympathetic Tennyson he always called, in tenderest accents, the name "Maud."

Though this bird is said to have no tongue for expressing the happier emotions, the voice of the mother crow when soothing her nestlings, with gurgling notes of endearment, is tender as the robin's; and the head of the family, though croaking savagely when his mate is molested, and though able to send an exultant "caw" after a retreating enemy, never lowers himself by scolding as the jay does.

Whatever his faults may be—and they are many—to anyone taking the trouble to study the crow, either in captivity or in his native environment, he will prove the most interesting example of his race, an agreeable companion, an ideal home-maker, a thrifty being, a liberal provider, an able defender of his family, a destroyer of harmful insect and animal life, a burier of the dead, a creature of dignity, a keen observer, and the intellectual marvel of the bird world.

A Load of Hay

By James B. Weaver

Hard paved streets and hurrying feet,
Where it's oft but a nod when old friends meet,
Rattle of cart and shriek of horn,
Laughing Youth and Age forlorn,
Bound for the office I speed away,
When my auto brushes—a load of hay!

Chauffeur curses, I scarcely hear,
For things I loved as a boy seem near:
Scent of meadows at early morn,
Miles of waving fields of corn,
Lowing cattle and colts at play—
Far have I drifted another way!

Hark, the bell as it calls the noon!
Boys at their chores, hear them whistle a tune!
Barn doors creaking on rusty locks,
Rattle of corn in the old feed-box,
Answering nicker at toss of hay—
Old sweet sounds of a far-off day.

There, my driver stops with a jerk;
Then far aloft to the scene of my work;
But all day long midst the city's roar
My heart is the heart of a boy once more,
My feet in old-time fields astray,
Lured—by the scent from a load of hay!

Iowa as a Literary Field

By Johnson Brigham [1]

LITERARY IOWA IN THE NINETEENTH CENTURY

Late in the last century readers of books awoke to the fact that the world-including, world-inviting prairies of the Mississippi Valley were no longer inarticulate; that in this great "Heart of the World's Heart," among the millions who have been drawn to these prairie states, there are lives as rich—in all that really enriches—as those immortalized in the literature of New England, or of the Pacific slope. It was not to be expected that the westward-moving impulse to create would cease on reaching the Mississippi River.

In Iowa's pioneer days but little original matter found its way into print except contributions to the rough and ready journalism of the period. A few pioneer writers, possessed of the historiographer's instinct, performed a rare service to the young commonwealth by passing on to future generations their first-hand knowledge of the prominent men and events of the first half of the century. Chief among these are Theodore S. Parvin, William Salter, Alexander R. Fulton, Samuel S. Howe and Charles Aldrich. The two last named published several series of "The Annals of Iowa" which remain unfailing reservoirs of information to later historians and students of Iowa history. Iowa Masonry is specially indebted to Professor Parvin for his invaluable contributions to the history of the order in Iowa. Dr. Salter wrote the first notable Iowa biography, that of James W. Grimes, published in 1876. Fulton's "Red Men of Iowa" is as valuable as it is rare, for, though written as late as 1882, it is the first exhaustive attempt to describe the tribes originally inhabiting Iowa.

The war period—1861-5—developed "Iowa in War Times," by S. H. M. Byers, and "Iowa Colonels and Regiments," by A. A. Stuart, also many valuable personal sketches and regimental histories.

Long before the close of the century, the name of Samuel Hawkins Marshall Byers had grown familiar to the people of Iowa, because of the popularity of his song entitled "Sherman's March to the Sea," and because contemporary historians, attracted by its suggestive title, adapted it as especially appropriate for the most dramatic event in the history of the war for the Union.

Major Byers' most lasting contribution to literature is his poem "The March to the Sea," epic in character and interspersed with lyrics of the war. Reading this, one can hear the thrilling bugle call, and "see once again the bivouacs in the wood."

Looking again, one can see the army in motion—

"A sight it was! that sea of army blue,

The sloping guns of the swift tramping host,

Winding its way the fields and forests through,

As winds some river slowly to the coast.

The snow-white trains, the batteries grim, and then

The steady tramp of sixty thousand men."

Passing over pages filled with stories of the camp and march, and with moving pictures of the dusky throng of camp-followers who saw in the coming of Sherman's men "God's new exodus," we come to the dramatic climax:

"But on a day, while tired and sore they went,

Across some hills wherefrom the view was free,

A sudden shouting down the lines was sent;

They looked and cried, 'This is the sea! the sea!'

And all at once a thousand cheers were heard

And all the army shout the glorious word.

"Bronzed soldiers stood and shook each other's hands;

Some wept for joy, as for a brother found;

And down the slopes, and from the far-off sands,

They thought they heard already the glad sound

Of the old ocean welcoming them on

To that great goal they had so fairly won."

I would not be unmindful of our Iowa poet's other contributions. Before the century's close, Mr. Byers had written "Switzerland and the Swiss," and "What I saw in Dixie," also a book of verse entitled "Happy Isles and Other Poems," besides much occasional verse in celebration of events in

Iowa history. So many and excellent are Major Byers' contributions to such occasions that their author has fitly been styled the "uncrowned poet laureate of Iowa." The title is strengthened by two distinctively Iowa songs, one, "The Wild Rose of Iowa," a tribute to our State Flower; the other entitled "Iowa," sung to the air of "My Maryland."

One of Iowa's pioneer poets was signally honored by public insistence that his "swan song" was the song of another and greater. In July, 1863, John L. McCreery, of Delhi, Iowa, published in *Arthur's Home Magazine* a poem entitled "There Is No Death." The poem went the round of the press attributed to Bulwer Lytton. A newspaper controversy followed, the result of which was that the Iowa poet was generally awarded the palm of authorship. But error sometimes seems to possess more vitality than truth! Every few years thereafter, the McCreery poem would make another round of the press with Bulwer Lytton's name attached! Finally, in response to urgent request, the modest author published his story of the poem.

It is interesting to note the circumstances under which the first and best stanza was conceived. The author was riding over the prairie on horseback when night overtook him. Orion was "riding in triumph down the western sky." The "subdued and tranquil radiance of the heavenly host" imparted a hopeful tinge to his somber meditations on life and death, and under the inspiration of the scene he composed the lines:

"There is no death; the stars go down

To rise upon some other shore;

And bright in heaven's jeweled crown

They shine forever more."

The next morning he wrote other stanzas, the last of which reads:

"And ever near us, though unseen,

The dear, immortal spirits tread;

For all the boundless universe

Is life—there are no dead."

One of the curiosities of literature is the fact that the substitution of Bulwer's name for that of the author arose from the inclusion of McCreery's poem (without credit) in an article on "Immortality" signed by one "E. Bulmer." An exchange copied the poem with the name Bulmer "corrected" to Bulwer—and thus it started on its rounds. As late as 1870, Harper's "Fifth Reader" credited the poem to Lord Lytton! The Granger "Index to Poetry" (1904) duly credits it to the Iowa author.

It is interesting to recall, in passing, the fact that nowhere in or out of the state is there to be found a copy of McCreery's little volume of "Songs of Toil and Triumph," published by Putnam's Sons in 1883, the unsold copies of which the author says he bought, "thus acquiring a library of several hundred volumes."

It seems to have been the fate of Iowa's pioneer poets to find their verse attributed to others. So it was with Belle E. Smith's well-known poem, "If I Should Die To-night." Under the reflex action of Ben King's clever parody, it has been the habit of newspaper critics to smile at Miss Smith's poem. But when we recall the fact that several poets thought well enough of it to stake their reputation on it; and that, in the course of its odyssey to all parts of the English-reading world, it was variously attributed to Henry Ward Beecher, F. K. Crosby, Robert C. V. Myers, Lucy Hooper, Letitia E. Landon, and others, and that Rider Haggard used it, in a mutilated form, in "Jess," leaving the reader to infer that it was part of his own literary creation, may we not conclude that the verse is a real poem worthy of its place in the anthologies? In the Granger Index (1904) it is credited to Robert C. V. Myers,—the credit followed by the words: "Attributed to Arabella E. Smith"!

If support of Miss Smith's unasserted but now indisputable claim to the poem be desired, it can be found in Professor W. W. Gist's contribution on the subject entitled "Is It Unconscious Assimilation?" [2] Miss Smith—long a resident of Newton, Iowa, and later a sojourner in California until her recent death—was of a singularly retiring nature. She lived much within herself and thought profoundly, as her poetical contributions to the *Midland Monthly* reveal. In none of her other poems did she reveal herself quite as clearly as in the poem under consideration. It is in four stanzas. In the first is this fine line referring to her own face, calm in death: "And deem that death had left it almost fair."

The poem concludes with the pathetic word to the living:

"Oh! friends, I pray to-night,

Keep not your kisses for my dead, cold brow—

The way is lonely, let me feel them now.

Think gently of me; I am travel-worn;

My faltering feet are pierced with many a thorn.

Forgive, O hearts estranged; forgive, I plead!

When dreamless rest is mine I shall not need

The tenderness for which I long to-night!"

I like to think of the veteran Tacitus Hussey, of Des Moines, as that octogenarian with the heart of youth. This genial poet and quaint philosopher made a substantial contribution to the century's output of literature, a collection of poems of humor and sentiment entitled "The River Bend and Other Poems." This author has contributed the words of a song which is reasonably sure of immortality. I refer to "Iowa, Beautiful Land," set to music by Congressman H. M. Towner. It fairly sings itself into the melody.

"The corn-fields of billowy gold,

In Iowa, 'Beautiful Land,'

Are smiling with treasure untold,

In Iowa,'Beautiful Land.'"

The next stanza, though including one prosaic line, has taken on a new poetic significance since the war-stricken nations of the old world are turning to America for food. The stanza concludes:

"The food hope of nations is she—

With love overflowing and free

And her rivers which run to the sea,

In Iowa, 'Beautiful Land.'"

Among Iowans in middle-life and older, the name of Robert J. Burdette, or "Bob" Burdette as he was familiarly called, brings vividly to mind a genial, sunny little man from Burlington, who went about doing good, making people forget their woes by accepting his philosophy—a simple philosophy, that of looking upon the sunny side of life. The "Chimes from a Jester's Bells" still ring in our ears, though the jester has passed on.

Reference has been made to the pioneer magazine of Iowa, the *Midland Monthly*, of Des Moines. As its eleven volumes include the first contributions of a considerable number of Iowa authors who have since become famous, this publication may be said to have inaugurated an era of intellectual activity in Iowa. Its first number contained an original story, "The Canada Thistle," by "Octave Thanet" (Miss French), a group of poems by Hamlin Garland from advance proofs of his "Prairie Songs," an original story by S. H. M. Byers, and other inviting contributions.

Looking back over the Iowa field from the viewpoint of 1894, when the *Iowa Magazine* entered upon its short-lived career (1894-99), I find, in addition to the authors and works already mentioned, a nationally interesting episode of the John Brown raid, by Governor B. F. Gue. Maud Meredith (Mrs. Dwight Smith), Calista Halsey Patchin and Alice Ilgenfritz Jones, the three pioneer novelists of Iowa, were among the magazine's contributors. In 1879, the Lippincotts published "High-water Mark" by Mrs. Jones. In 1881 appeared Maud Meredith's "Rivulet and Clover Blossoms," and two years later her "St. Julien's Daughter." Mrs. Patchin's "Two of Us" appeared at about the same time.

Miss Alice French, "Octave Thanet" to the literary world, has been a known quantity since 1887, when her fine group of short stories, "Knitters in the Sun," put Iowa on the literary map. "Expiation," "We All," a book for boys, "Stories of a Western Town" and "An Adventure in Photography" followed. Miss French has continued to write novels and short stories well on into the new century. In fact some of her strongest creations bear the twentieth century stamp.

Hamlin Garland was also known and read by many as early as the eighties. His, too, was the short-story route to fame, and Iowa was his field. From his literary vantage ground in Boston, the young author wrote in the guise of fiction his vivid memories of boy life and the life of youth in northeastern Iowa and southwestern Wisconsin. His "Main Traveled Roads," the first of many editions appearing in 1891, made him famous. Though the stories contained flashes of humor, the dominant note was serious, as befitted the West in the Seventies in which the author as boy and man struggled with adverse conditions. But the joy of youth would rise superior to circumstance, as is evidenced in the charming sketch of "Boy Life in the West." [3] I like to recall the prose-poem with which it concludes:

"I wonder if, far out in Iowa, the boys are still playing 'Hi Spy' around the straw-piles.... That runic chant, with its endless repetitions, doubtless is heard on any moonlight night in far-off Iowa. I wish I might join once more in the game—I fear I could not enjoy 'Hi Spy' even were I invited to join. But I sigh with a curious longing for something that was mine in those days on the snowy Iowa plains. What was it? Was it sparkle of winter days? Was it stately march of moon? Was it the presence of dear friends? Yes; all these and more—it was Youth!"

Before the century closed, this transplanted Iowan had also written "Jason Edwards," a story of Iowa politics, "Wayside Courtships," "Prairie Folks," "Spirit of Sweetwater," "Trail of the Gold-seekers," and scores of short stories first published in the magazines.

Mr. Garland's twentieth century output has been prolific of popular novels and short stories. His latest book, "A Son of the Middle Border," is pronounced by William Dean Howells a unique achievement and ranking well up with the world's best autobiographies.

A new name associated with Iowa at the close of the last century was that of Emerson Hough. "The Story of the Cowboy" (1897) can hardly be classed as fiction, and yet it "reads like a romance." Mr. Hough, long a roving correspondent of *Forest and Stream*, first tried "his 'prentice han'" as a story-writer in "Belle's Roses," a tense story of army life on the plains. [4] This was followed by several promising short stories and, in 1902, by "The Mississippi Bubble," a historical romance of quality founded upon the adventurous career of John Law, pioneer in the fields of frenzied finance. Three years later came his "Heart's Desire," a beautiful love story of the Southwest. In 1907 appeared his "Way of a Man" and "Story of the Outlaw." Several other novels have come from his facile pen. The most severely criticized and best seller of the series is his "54-40 or Fight," a historical novel based on the diplomatic controversy over Oregon in 1845-6. Mr. Hough is the most successful alumnus of Iowa State University in the difficult field of fiction.

Lingering over the index to the eleven volumes of Iowa's pioneer magazine, I am tempted to mention in passing several other names that stand out prominently in the memory of *Midland* readers.

Mrs. Virginia H. Reichard contributed an interesting paper, "A Glimpse of Arcadia." Mrs. Caroline M. Hawley gave a valuable illustrated paper on "American Pottery." Mrs. Addie B. Billington, Mrs. Virginia K. Berryhill, Mrs. Clara Adele Neidig, and other Iowans contributed to the poetry in the magazine's columns. Hon. Jonathan P. Dolliver, Hon. William B. Allison, Gen. James B. Weaver, and many other men prominent in the public life of Iowa contributed articles of permanent value. Mrs. Cora Bussey Hillis was the author of "Madame Deserée's Spirit Rival." Editor Ingham, of the *Register*, then of Algona, Editor Moorhead, then of Keokuk, now a Des Moines journalist, Minnie Stichter (Mrs. C. J. Fulton of Fairfield), Mrs. Harriet C. Towner, of Corning, Charles Eugene Banks, born in Clinton County, now a prominent journalist and *litterateur* in Seattle, Dr. J. Foster Bain, then assistant state geologist, now a resident of

London, and one of the world's most famous consulting geologists, Barthinius L. Wick, of Cedar Rapids, a voluminous historiographer, are among the many who, during the last five years of the old century, did their bit toward putting Iowa on the literary map.

Irving Berdine Richman, of Muscatine, had already written "Appenzell," a study of the Swiss, with whom, as consul-general, he had lived for several years. His *Midland* sketch, "The Battle of the Stoss," was followed by a little volume, "John Brown Among the Quakers, and Other Sketches." But the two great historical works to which he gave years of enthusiastic research were not published until well on in the twentieth century. The first of these, "Rhode Island; a Study of Separation," was honored with an introduction by John Bryce. It was so well received that the "study" was amplified into a two-volume work, "Rhode Island; Its Making and Meaning." The second, a work compelling years of research in old Mexico and Spain, is entitled "California Under Spain and Mexico." These alone give the Iowa historian an enviable world-reputation.

Literary Iowa in the Twentieth Century

Our study of the high places in Iowa literature has already been somewhat extended into the new century. The transfer of the Iowa magazine to St. Louis, in 1898, and its speedy suspension thereafter did not deter many Iowans from continuing to write. Difficult as it was for our unknowns to find a market for their wares in Eastern magazines and publishing houses, the persistent few, who knew they had what the public should want, "knocked" again and again "at the golden gates of the morning," and in due time the gates were opened unto them.

Edwin Legrange Sabin's first essay in *Midland* fiction was "A Ghostly Carouse,"—full of promise. His first book, "The Magic Mashie and other Golfish Stories," in common with all his other works, throbs with the heart of youth. His magazine verse, mainly humorous, has the same quality. Latterly he has been illuminating history, and especially the fast-dissolving wild life of the West, with stories closely adhering to fact and yet rampant with adventure—the kind of books our outdoor boys take to bed with them! To his readers Kit Carson, Fremont, Buffalo Bill, are as much alive as are the heroes of the stadium, the tennis court and the links. But underneath this delightfully light literature there is well-nigh concealed a poet of the Swinburne type, as witness this bit of verse:

"Upon the purple hillside, vintage-stained,

In drowsy langour brown October lies,

Like one who has the banquet goblet drained,

And looks abroad with dream enchanted eyes." [5]

Mrs. Bertha M. Shambaugh's *Midland* sketch of "Amana Colony; a Glimpse of the Community of True Inspiration," [6] suggested something more than "a glimpse," and in 1908 appeared an exhaustive study of that "peculiar people," entitled "Amana, the Community of True Inspiration," a valuable contribution to Iowa history.

Professor Selden L. Whitcomb, of Grinnell, had previously published several outlines for the study of literature, but his first volume of "Lyrical Verse" appeared in 1898. Two other books of poems followed, one in 1912, the other in 1914. His verse is marked by delicacy of poetical suggestion and perfection of rhyme and rhythm.

George Meason Whicher, of New York, whose name is now often seen in *The Continent* of Chicago, is the author of "From Muscatine and Other Poems" and of recent prose with Italian and Latin background. Mr. Whicher is the author of four poems in the *Midland*, all harking back to the poet's boyhood days in Muscatine, Iowa.

Dr. Frank Irving Herriott, dean of sociology at Drake University, a voluminous writer on historical and sociological themes, has a long list of works to his credit, all bearing twentieth century dates except one published by the American Academy which appeared in 1892. He wrote for the *Midland* a strong plea for public libraries, a plea which, doubtless, had its influence in inaugurating the library movement in Iowa beginning with the new century.

Another scholar in the sociological field who has made his impression upon thousands of students and adult readers is Dr. Frank L. McVey, president of the University of North Dakota. His historical sketch in the *Midland*, "The Contest in the Maumee Valley," was followed by other published papers and these by several books on sociological themes, among them "Modern Industrialism" and "The Making of a Town."

There are few more scholarly literary critics than Welker Given, of Clinton, Iowa. His Shakespearean and classical studies have won for him an enviable place among students of the classics.

Mrs. Anna Howell Clarkson, of New York, wife of Hon. J. S. Clarkson, long prominent in Iowa journalism and in national politics, followed up her *Midland* article on "The Evolution of Iowa Politics" with a book entitled "A Beautiful Life and Its Associations," a tribute of loving regard to a former teacher and friend, Mrs. Drusilla Alden Stoddard.

A *critique* on "Our Later Literature and Robert Browning" in the Iowa magazine in April, 1897, may, or may not, have turned the current of Lewis Worthington Smith's whole life; but its critical power made friends for the Nebraska professor and warmed the welcome given him when, in 1902, he took up his work in the English department of Drake University of Des Moines. While Professor Smith has published several works on language and literature and an acting drama entitled "The Art of Life," his literary reputation rests mainly upon his poetry. Since the opening of the new century, volume has followed volume; first "God's Sunlight," then "In the Furrow," and, in 1916, "The English Tongue," and "Ships in Port." Many of the poems in the two last named evince the impact of the World War upon a soul of strong sensibilities. Tempted to quote whole poems, as showing the wide range of this poet's vision, I will limit myself to the first stanza of "The English Tongue":

On to where Indus and Ganges pour down to the tide.

Words that have lived, that have felt, that have gathered and grown.

Words! Is it nothing that no other people have known

Speech of such myriad voices, so full and so free,

Song by the fireside and crash of the thunders at sea?"

Jessie Welborn Smith, wife of Professor Smith, is a frequent contributor of short stories and sketches to popular magazines.

The late Henry Wallace, though for many years an agricultural editor in Iowa, modestly began his contribution to general literature in the *Midland* with a pen-picture of the Scotch-Irish in America. Subsequently he wrote his "Uncle Henry's Letters to a Farm Boy," which has run through many editions; also "Trusts and How to Deal With Them" and "Letters to the Farm-Folk."

Eugene Secor, of Forest City, published poems in the *Midland* which were followed by "Verses for Little Folk and Others," "A Glimpse of Elysium" and "Voices of the Trees."

Helen Hoyt Sherman's modest "Village Romance" led to a long list of popular books, published since her marriage and under her married name, Helen Sherman Griffiths. Born in Des Moines, her present home is in Cincinnati.

Herbert Bashford, born in Sioux City, now living in Washington and California, contributed to the *Midland* a half-dozen poems of much promise. Mr. Bashford is now literary editor of the *San Francisco Bulletin* and has several books of poems and several popular dramas to his credit.

Mrs. Ella Hamilton Durley, of Los Angeles, formerly of Des Moines, a pioneer president of our Press and Authors' Club, and a prolific writer for the press, followed her journal and magazine successes with two novels, "My Soldier Lady" and "Standpatter," a novel of Southern California love and politics.

Caroline M. Sheldon, Professor of Romance Languages in Grinnell College, has followed up her *Midland* study of American poetry with "Princess and Pilgrim in England," and a translation and study of Echegary's play, "The Great Galeoto."

Many still recall with interest the realistic serial which ran in the *Midland*, entitled "The Young Homesteaders," also a number of short sketches and stories of pioneer life in the West, by Frank Welles Calkins, then of Spencer, Iowa, now a Minnesotan. Mr. Calkins has since become a frequent contributor to magazines, and a writer of books of outdoor life and adventure. His latest novel, "The Wooing of Takala," appeared in 1907.

One of the marked successes in the world of books and periodicals is Julia Ellen Rogers, long a teacher of science in Iowa high schools. While a resident of Des Moines she contributed to the *Midland* a descriptive article, "Camping and Climbing in the Big Horn," which evinced her love of "all outdoors" and her ability to describe what she saw. Her editorial connection with *Country Life in America* and her popular series of nature studies, "Among Green Trees," "Trees Every Child Should Know," "Earth and Sky," "Wild Animals Every Child Should Know," have given their author and her books a warm welcome from Maine to California.

One of the bright particular stars in our firmament, remaining almost undiscovered until near the close of the century's first decade, is Arthur Davison Ficke, of Davenport. Circumstances—his father's eminence at the bar—conspired to make the young poet a lawyer; but he could not—long at a time—close his ears to the wooing of the muse, and off he went, at frequent intervals, in hot pursuit of the elusive Euterpe. Though still a lawyer of record, the inward call of the soul must soon become too strong to be resisted. *Poeta nascitur.* I can see the young lawyer-poet in his own "Dream Harbor," and can feel his glad response to the call from the dream-world:

"Winds of the South from the sunny beaches

Under the headland call to me;

And I am sick for the purple reaches,

Olive-fringed, by an idle sea.

"Where low waves of the South are calling

Out of the silent sapphire bay,

And slow tides are rising, falling,

Under the cliffs where the ripples play."

It was natural that the sons of the late Henry Sabin should write acceptably. Though slightly older in years, Elbridge H. Sabin is younger in literature than his brother "Ed." The first decade of the new century was well advanced before Elbridge turned his attention from law to literature. The brief touch of life in the open given him while soldiering during the Spanish-American war may have suggested the change in his career. His first essay in authorship was "Early American History for Young Americans" (1904). He then turned his gaze skyward and in 1907 appeared "Stella's Adventures in Starland." Fairyland next invited him and in 1910 appeared "The Magical Man of Mirth," soon followed by "The Queen of the City of Mirth." In 1913 appeared his "Prince Trixie."

James B. Weaver, son of General Weaver, another lawyer with the poet soul, but with a somewhat firmer hold on "the things that are," has written much prose which only requires the touch of the *vers libre* editor to turn it into poetry. His appreciation of Kipling and other poets and his fine character-sketches, as for example that of Martin Burke, pioneer stage-driver and farmer, are remembered with delight. Just once, many years ago, when, a happy father, he looked for the first time upon his "Baby Boy," the poet in his nature obtained the upper hand of the lawyer and he wrote:

"O golden head! O sunny heart!

Forever joyous be thy part

In this fair world; and may no care

Cut short thy youth, and may no snare

Entrap thy feet! I pray thee, God,

For smoother paths than I have trod." [7]

Mr. Weaver was president of the Iowa Press and Authors Club in 1914-15 and the success of the famous Iowa Authors' Homecoming in October, 1914, was in large measure due to his untiring efforts.

In that Great American Desert of "free verse," the Chicago magazine, *Poetry*, the persistent seeker can find here and there an oasis that will well repay his search. One of these surprises is a poem entitled "The Wife," [8] by Mrs. Helen Cowles LeCron, of Des Moines. It is the plea of a longing soul for relief from the "sullen silence," and the "great gaunt shadows" of the "shaggy mountains," and for a return to "the gentle land," and to "the careless hours when life was very sweet." Mrs. LeCron is a prolific writer of clever and timely verse for the press, and is a poet of many possibilities.

Honoré Willsie (whose maiden name is Dunbar) was born in Ottumwa, Iowa, is a graduate of the University of Wisconsin, and is a resident of New York City. To her able editorship may be attributed the new literary quality of *The Delineator*. It was Mrs. Willsie's varied successes as a writer of papers on social problems, sketches, short stories and serials which won for her the literary editorship of that popular periodical. Her success as a novelist mainly rests upon "Heart of the Desert," "Still Jim," and "Lydia of the Pines," all published within the last four years, and each stronger than its predecessor.

A successful art publisher and an enthusiastic traveler, Thomas D. Murphy, a native Iowan, long a resident of Red Oak, is the author of a group of well-written and profusely illustrated books of travel, all written within the last decade, as follows: "British Highways and Byways"; "In Unfamiliar England"; "Three Wonderlands of the American West"; "On Old-World Highways"; and "On Sunset Highways."

Allan Updegraff is a born Iowan whose fame has come early in life. His "Second Youth" (1917) is winning praise from the critics as "an agreeable contrast with the stuffy bedroom atmosphere" of many books of the period, as refreshingly "modest humor," and as having "touches of characterization and serious feeling" which keep up the interest to the close.

Among the native Iowans who have distinguished themselves in literature is Willis George Emerson, of Denver, born near Blakesburg, Iowa. Mr. Emerson is author of "Buell Hampton," and a half-dozen other novels, the latest, "The Treasure of Hidden Mountain," also a hundred or more sketches and stories of travel.

Of the well-known authors who, during the impressionable years of their youth resided for a time in Iowa, the most famous is "Mark Twain" (Samuel L. Clemens) who, after his *wanderjahr*, in the late summer of 1854, took the "Keokuk Packet" and landed in Muscatine, Iowa, and there became the guest of his brother, Orrin, and his sister, Jane. Early in the spring of '55, his brother meantime having married and removed to Keokuk, Iowa, he paid his brother another visit. Orrin offered him five dollars a week and board to remain and help him in his printing office. The offer was promptly accepted. The Keokuk episode extended over a period of nearly two years, "two vital years, no doubt, if all the bearings could be known." Here he made his first after-dinner speech, which delighted his audience. Here he made a record in a debating society. Unable to pay his brother his wages, Orrin took him in as a partner! A lucky find of a fifty-dollar bill enabled Twain to start on his travels. Meanwhile he contracted to write travel sketches for the Keokuk *Saturday Post*. His first letter was dated "Cincinnati, November 14, 1856." "It was written in the exaggerated dialect then considered humorous. The genius that a little more than ten years later would delight the world flickered feebly enough at twenty-one." [9] A second letter concluded the series! Years later, just before he joined the Holy Land excursion out of which grew his "Innocents Abroad," he visited Keokuk and delivered a lecture. He came again after his return from the trip, on his triumphal lecture tour across the continent. Years later he and Cable gave readings in Keokuk, and while there he arranged a permanent residence for his mother. In 1886, with his wife and daughter, he paid his mother a visit, renewing old acquaintances and making new friends. In August, 1890, he was called to Keokuk by the last illness of his mother. It will thus be seen that, next to his home in Elmira, New York, his "heart's home" was Keokuk.

Nixon Waterman, author, journalist and lecturer, born in Newark, Illinois, and long a resident of Boston, was for several years an attaché of a small daily paper in Creston, Iowa. Among his published works is a comedy entitled "Io, from Iowa." In his several books of verse are many poems evidently inspired by memories of old times on the prairies of southwestern Iowa. Here is an echo from the poet's lost youth:

"Strange how Memory will fling her

Arms about some scenes we bring her,

And the fleeting years but make them fonder grow;

Though I wander far and sadly

From that dear old home, how gladly

I recall the cherished scenes of long ago!" [10]

William Otis Lillibridge, of Sioux Falls, whose brilliant career as a novelist was closed by death in 1909, was graduated from the College of Dentistry, State University of Iowa, in 1898. His "Ben Blair" and "Where the Trail Divides," gave abundant promise.

Randall Parish, though born in Illinois, was admitted to the bar in Iowa, and for a time was engaged in newspaper work in Sioux City. Since 1904, when he leaped into fame by his historical novel, "When Wilderness Was King," volume after volume has come from the press and every one has met with quick response from the public.

It is hard to account for Herbert Quick. Born on a farm in Grundy County, Iowa, a teacher in Mason City and elsewhere in Iowa, a lawyer in Sioux City, mayor of Sioux City for three terms, a telephone manager, editor of *La Follette's Weekly*, editor of *Farm and Fireside*, democratic politician, at present an active member of the Federal Farm Loan Board—with all this record of service, Mr. Quick has somehow found time, since 1904, to make for himself a name and fame as a magazine contributor, and, too, as a novelist who writes novels so novel that they find thousands of readers! Among his best known books are "Aladdin & Co," "Virginia of the Air Lanes," and "On Board the Good Ship Earth." Mr. Quick is preeminently a twentieth century man of affairs. Immersed as he now is in farm loans, it would not surprise his friends at any time if he were to issue another compelling novel!

Rupert Hughes, eminently successful as a novelist and dramatist, though Missouri-born, was for years a resident of Keokuk, Iowa, and his Iowa associations were so strong that he dropped everything to come halfway across the continent that he might participate in the reunion of Iowa authors in 1914. Mr. Hughes' books are among the best-selling and his plays among the best-drawing. This popular author has turned soldier. He was an officer of the New York National Guards in Mexico and again when war against Germany was declared he was among the first to respond to the call for troops.

Dr. Edward A. Steiner, of Grinnell, Iowa, a sociologist with a vision, has done more than any other man to bring together in friendly working relationship our native-born and foreign-born Americans. He has not only gone up and down the earth preaching an applied Christianity, but he has also written into nearly a dozen books, all of which have had many readers, his own experiences in the old world and the new, and his valuable observations—those of a trained sociologist bent upon righting the wrongs of ignorance and selfishness as he has found them embedded in customs and laws. The World War has opened a large field of usefulness for the Grinnell preacher of national and international righteousness.

Newell Dwight Hillis, the popular Brooklyn preacher, lecturer and author, was born in Maquoketa, Iowa, but has spent most of his life outside the state.

A new name in fictional literature is that of Ethel Powelson Hueston. Mrs. Hueston was reared in a family of eleven children, and her popular first book, "Prudence of the Parsonage," written on a claim in Idaho while caring for her invalid husband—who died in 1915—is the story of her own experience in a parsonage in Mt. Pleasant, Iowa. "Prudence Says So" is a continuation of the story. Mrs. Hueston was recently married to Lieutenant Edward J. Best, at Golden, Colorado.

Margaret Coulson Walker and Ida M. Huntington, both of Des Moines, have added to the information and delight of children by a number of illustrated books. Miss Walker's "Bird Legends and Life," and "Lady Hollyhock and Her Friends," and Miss Huntington's "Garden of Heart's Delight," and "Peter Pumpkin in Wonderland" are favorites with many.

Miss Emilie Blackmore Stapp, literary editor of the *Des Moines Capital*, has written a number of popular stories for children. Her "Squaw Lady," "Uncle Peter Heathen," and "The Trail of the Go-Hawks" have found many readers. She has done more than write stories. She has organized a national club called the "Go-Hawks Happy Tribe," and the Tribe has undertaken to raise a million pennies to help buy food for starving children in France and Belgium. The grand total of pennies reported September, 1917, was 255,000!

Edna Ferber, of "Emma McChesney" fame, and the author of a half-dozen clever novels, the latest of which is "Fanny Herself," was born in Wisconsin, but spent much of her youth in Ottumwa, Iowa, where her father was a successful merchant.

Oney Fred Sweet, born in Hampton, Iowa, and sometime a journalist in Des Moines, has made a national reputation as a feature writer on the *Chicago Tribune* and as a contributor of verse and sketches to the magazines.

Laura L. Hinckley, of Mount Vernon, Iowa, is a frequent contributor to the leading magazines. Recent stories in the *Saturday Evening Post* and in the *Woman's Home Companion* attest her ability in a difficult field.

A promising young claimant for literary honors is (Lotta) Allen Meachem, of New York, born in Washington County, Iowa. Following several good stories in the magazines, comes her "Belle Jones—A Story of Fulfilment," published by Dutton.

Eleanor Hoyt Brainerd, born in Iowa City, now a resident of New York, was in early life a teacher, but since 1898 has been on the staff of the *New York Sun*. Her "Misdemeanors of Nancy," in 1892, was the beginning of a successful career in authorship. Her "Nancy," "Bettina" and "Belinda" are better known to many than are their own next door neighbors.

Men who have not learned to deny the eternal boy in their nature find as much enjoyment as boys themselves in reading "Widow O'Callahan's Boys," and everybody enjoys "Maggie McLanehan," both creations of Gulielma Zollinger, of Newton, Iowa. Three other books, not so well known, are added to the list of Miss Zollinger's achievements in literature.

Mrs. Elizabeth (Eslick) Cooper, born in Homer, Iowa, has spent most of her adult life in the Orient and is an authority on the status of women in Oriental lands. She is the author of "Sayonara," a play produced by Maxine Elliot, of many magazine articles, and of a half dozen books, all published since 1910. Her books are vivid pictures of life in China, Egypt, Turkey and Japan.

Among the most prominent magazine writers and journalists of the period is Judson Welliver. He several years ago graduated from Iowa journalism to the larger field, the national capital, and has latterly become one of the regular contributors to *Munsey's*, and a frequent contributor to other periodicals.

Another prominent magazine writer is Joe Mitchell Chapple, early in life editor of a La Porte, Iowa, weekly. Mr. Chapple is the founder, publisher and editor of the *National Magazine*, Boston, and the author of "Boss Bart," a novel, and editor of a popular collection of verse.

One of the youngest magazine writers forging to the front is Horace M. Towner, Jr., of Corning, Iowa, son of Congressman Towner. A long list might be made of his recent contributions to the leading magazines.

A group of new writers, some of them Iowans, have happily been given a medium for reaching the public through the new *Midland*, of Iowa City. Mr. Frederick, the editor, has in the main evinced excellent judgment in the selection of stories, sketches and verse, and has won commendation from our severest Eastern critics. The new *Midland* has, doubtless, started not a few middle-western authors on their way to the front in the field of literature.

The World War has already added the names of several Iowans to the literature of the great struggle. The best known is James Norman Hall, of

Colfax, Iowa, whose "Kitchener's Mob" and articles in the *Atlantic* have added greatly to popular knowledge of conditions at the front. Already twice wounded, the first time in the trenches; the latest—may it be the last!—in the air, this brave young American can well say with Virgil, "all of which I saw and part of which I was." After his discharge from the English army, Mr. Hall went abroad commissioned to do literary work for Houghton, Mifflin & Company; but his zeal for the cause of the Allies, combined possibly with a young man's love of adventure, led him to re-enter the service, this time in the Aviation Corps. He is now (in September, 1917) slowly recovering from a shot which penetrated his left lung.

The Gleasons, Mr. and Mrs. Arthur Gleason, of Cedar Rapids, Iowa, and of New York City, have both won honors in the Red Cross work in Belgium and incidentally have made valuable contributions to the "human interest" story of the World War. Mrs. Helen Hayes Gleason was the first American woman knighted by King Albert for meritorious service at the front. Mr. Gleason in his "Young Hilda at the Wars" begins his charming story of Hilda with this tribute to the state in which his wife first saw the light:

"She was an American girl from the very prosperous State of Iowa, which if not as yet the mother of presidents, is at least the parent of many exuberant and useful persons. Will power is grown out yonder as one of the crops."

"Golden Lads," by Mr. and Mrs. Gleason, is a vivid recital of experiences with the Hector Munro Ambulance Corps at the front in Belgium.

Though the evaluations in this review are confined chiefly to *belles lettres*, it would not be fair to the reader to omit the state's large indebtedness to Dr. B. F. Shambaugh and his scholarly associates of the State Historical Society, of Iowa City, for their many valuable contributions to the general, social and economic history of Iowa; to Dr. Jesse Macy, of Grinnell, for his valuable studies in the science of government; to the late Samuel Calvin, also to Dr. Thomas H. McBride, of the State University, Dr. Louis H. Pammel, of the State College, and Dr. Charles Keyes, of Des Moines, for their contributions to science; to Dr. Charles H. Weller, of the State University, for his "Athens and Its Monuments," and other works throwing light upon an ancient civilization; to George E. Roberts, of New York, a native Iowan, for his clear elucidation of national and world problems; to the late Judges Kinne, Deemer and MacLean, and other jurists for standard works on jurisprudence; to Carl Snyder, Woods Hutchinson and a host of other Iowans who are contributing to the current literature of our time.

This review, incomplete at best, would be unfair to the president of the Iowa Press and Authors Club were it to conclude without mention of the inspiration of her leadership. Mrs. Alice Wilson Weitz began life as a journalist at the Iowa State Capital. In the course of her busy and successful later career as wife, mother and public-spirited citizen, she has somehow found time to write on literary and timely themes. Her latest contribution to the state of her birth is a scenario entitled "The Wild Rose of Iowa" which was to have been produced on the screen in all the cities of the state; but, unfortunately, the film, prepared with great labor and expense, and with the aid of some of the best dramatic talent in Iowa, was destroyed or lost on the way from Chicago to Des Moines. It is to be hoped that this may soon be reproduced, for Mrs. Weitz' scenario admirably presented in symbol the whole story of Iowa's wonderful development from savagery to twentieth-century civilization.

A list of Iowa State University publications—a pamphlet of forty-one pages—includes hundreds of monographs, dissertations, etc., covering a wide range of original research.

It must have become evident from this incomplete review that Iowa is literarily, to say the least, no longer inarticulate. It is equally apparent, to those who really know their Iowa, that, far from being a dead level of uninteresting prosperity, our state is rich in suggestive literary material, ready and waiting for the authors of the future. Topographically, Iowa abounds in surprises. In the midst of her empire of rich rolling prairie are lakes and rivers, rugged cliffs and wooded hills, villages and cities set upon hills overlooking beautiful valleys through which streams wind their way seaward, her east and west borders defended by castellated rocks overlooking our two great rivers. Ethnologically, within these borders are communities of blanket Indians still living in wigwams, surrounded by communities in which are practiced all the arts of an advanced civilization. Sociologically, side by side with her native-born and native-bred citizens, are communities of Christian Socialists, also remnants of a French experiment in Communism, Quakers, Mennonites, anti-polygamous Mormons, and whole regions in which emigrants from Holland, Germany and Scandinavia are slowly and surely acquiring American habits of thought and life. Historically speaking, we have the early and late pioneer period with its rapid adjustment to new conditions, with its multiform perils developing latent heroism, its opportunities for character-building and for public service. Later the heroic period, during which a peace-loving people quit the plow, the workshop, the country store, the office and even the pulpit, to rally to the defence of the Union. Then, the reconstruction and the new-construction period, in which Iowa prospered under the leadership of *men*—men who knew their duties as well as their rights, men who recognized, and insisted upon recognition of, that "sovereign law, the state's collected will." And now, an epoch of reviving patriotism coupled with a world-embracing passion for democracy, in which the youths and young men of the state are consecrating their strength, their talents and their lives to a great cause.

---

[1] Editor of the "Midland Monthly" and author of "Life of James Harlan," "Iowa—Its History and Its Foremost Citizens," "An Old Man's Idyl," etc.

[2] Midland Monthly, March, 1894.

[3] Midland Monthly, February, 1894.

[4] Midland Monthly, June-July, 1895.

[5] Country Life in America, October, 1902.

[6] In the Midland Monthly, v. 6, p. 27.

[7] Midland Monthly, March, 1897.

[8] Poetry, Chicago, June, 1913.

[9] Paine—Life of "Mark Twain."

[10] "Memories" from "A Book of Verses," by Nixon Waterman, 1900.